IN THE EVENT OF MY DEATH

When Grace Dalton is found dead, she leaves behind a houseful of suspects, all of whom are mentioned in her will. Is the killer Esther Milroy, who booked an expensive holiday just before the tragedy? Or Esther's brother Matthew, who is facing financial ruin? Or Verity, spurned by her lover, who believes that a bigger income would make the man who got away come back again? The dead woman was a friend so DCI Kelsey has a personal involvement in a case which proves to be one of the most difficult in his career.

IN THE EVENT OF MY DEATH

IN THE EVENT OF MY DEATH

by
Emma Page

Magna Large Print Books
Long Preston, North Yorkshire,
England.

British Library Cataloguing in Publication Data.

Page, Emma
In the event of my death.

A catalogue record for this book is
available from the British Library

ISBN 0-7505-0878-7

First published in Great Britain by HarperCollins Publishers,
1994

Published in Large Print December, 1995 by arrangement with
Harper Collins Publishers Ltd., and the copyright holder.

Magna Large Print is an imprint of
Library Magna Books Ltd.
Printed and bound in Great Britain by
T.J. Press (Padstow) Ltd., Cornwall, PL28 8RW.

For Kath
with love,
remembering the old days

CHAPTER 1

The rain had blown itself out in the night and Tuesday morning was fine, unusually mild for the first week in February.

In the spacious front bedroom of his substantial Edwardian dwelling in Oakfield Gardens, in one of the best residential suburbs of Brentworth, a thriving town of considerable size, James Milroy had slept soundly, as he did every night, from very soon after getting into bed. At six-thirty, as every weekday morning, the radio alarm on his bedside table sprang suddenly to life at the start of a news and current affairs programme.

James came awake, as always, on the instant. He threw back his covers and got out of bed, all his movements performed with his habitual minimum of noise. He gave his customary close attention to the recital of events and opinions, overnight market reports.

He was a tall, lean man of forty-nine, he looked fit and energetic. His hair was still thick and dark, he had kept his trim waistline; he could easily pass for ten years younger. He had a high forehead, a quiet face, shrewd and subtle, a penetrating gaze, a controlled manner. He looked very much what he was: a senior partner in a highly reputable firm of auditors and registrars, with its head office in Brentworth.

James had read law at the university, intending to make a career as a solicitor, but had later changed his mind, deciding instead to qualify as a chartered accountant. He had sprung from a background that was far from privileged and had made his way by dint of single-minded determination and unremitting hard work.

In the equally spacious front bedroom across the landing, the insistent trilling of her alarm clock finally roused James's wife from a heavy, unrefreshing sleep; it was years since Esther had gone to bed without a sleeping pill.

She dragged herself out of bed to make a sketchy toilet before going down to cook breakfast for James. She was five years younger than her husband. She had married at eighteen in a flush of girlish romance; she had borne her first son before the year was out, her second, two years later. She had been very pretty as a girl, with a slender figure, delicate features, curly brown hair and a beautiful skin. Now she was thin and bony, with the look of a trapped bird. The curly brown hair had thinned and was showing threads of grey; the fine skin had developed a pervasive pattern of lines while she was still in her thirties. She appeared now a good ten years older than her husband.

Before she went downstairs, she drew back her curtains and opened wide the casement windows. The birds were astir, the sky was streaked with rose. She leaned out into the gentle air. To be away from it all, on her own, to be done with demands, role-playing, to begin life all over again, in some far off, peaceful place, on her own terms this time—whatever those might prove to be. She drew a long sigh and turned from the window.

As she closed her bedroom door, James came out of his room on his way to the bathroom. She gave him a consciously bright greeting, adding in a rush, 'It's really quite warm this morning.' He responded with detached courtesy. They might have been total strangers making conversation

11

in a station waiting room.

Esther went on down to the kitchen and set about making her husband's breakfast exactly as he liked it, as she had done throughout the twenty-six years of their marriage. She was an excellent cook, a punctilious housekeeper.

Upstairs, a little later, as James stood before the long mirror of his wardrobe, casting a final comprehensive glance over his reflection, he suddenly remembered the damp patch in the chimney breast in his wife's bedroom, recently attended to by the local jobbing builder. He went across the landing to see how the repair had withstood the driving rain of yesterday evening.

It had stood up very well, not a sign of water coming through. As he turned to leave the room, he glanced about. He scarcely ever set foot in the room these days.

A couple of books on the bedside table caught his eye. He picked up the top book, looked at the cover, skimmed through the blurb. It was a best-selling blockbuster novel about a woman who left her cold-blooded, overbearing husband to branch out on her own, ending up, it seemed,

12

with a succession of well-heeled lovers, spectacular business success, a sensational wardrobe and a lifestyle that whirled her continually about the globe.

As he picked up the second book, he saw beneath it a number of brightly-coloured travel brochures. His look sharpened. He set the book down again and picked up the brochures. They extolled the charms of distant islands, exotic lands. He glanced swiftly through them before replacing them exactly as he had found them.

He stood for some moments in thought, then he crossed the room to where framed family photographs were ranged on the chest of drawers. He selected one and stood gazing intently down at it: the formal wedding group of Esther's brother, Matthew Dalton, five years her senior. James had been best man at the wedding, seventeen years ago. His own face looked back at him from the group, composed, faintly smiling, revealing nothing.

His eye travelled on and came to rest on the bride. Nina. Twenty-three years old on her wedding day, nine years younger than her bridegroom. Deliciously pretty, smiling confidently out at the camera.

Esther was there, as matron of honour,

expensively dressed, without elegance, her youthful prettiness already fading, her expression anxious, her shoulders a little hunched.

He put the photograph back in its place and left the room. At seven-thirty on the dot, as every weekday morning, he went downstairs with a springy step. His breakfast was properly laid and served in the breakfast room opening off the kitchen, although there were only the two of them these days, now that both boys were grown up and gone. James would never have countenanced the slipshod eating of a meal at the kitchen table; things must be done with order and propriety. Esther joined him only in a cup of coffee, taken on the wing, as she fussed about between the two rooms.

James ate with a good appetite. He said not a word about the damp patch or his visit to his wife's bedroom. He glanced through his newspaper as he ate. When Esther brought in the post he glanced through that too; there was nothing of any urgency.

Esther's mail arose largely from her voluntary work for various charities, local and national; she concerned herself especially with the welfare of the elderly and the terminally ill.

'Have you anything interesting on today?' James asked casually as he proffered his cup for a refill.

'I'm visiting one or two patients at the hospice,' she told him. The Brentworth hospice was housed in large, rambling premises, soundly built, that had at one time been a private school. The hospice was long established, well supported locally; it had received a number of substantial legacies over the years and was in a strong financial position.

For some years now, Esther had given time to befriending individual patients. When death claimed one of their number she added another to her list. There had been a drive a year or two back to encourage the hospice volunteers to acquire some degree of nursing skills and a course had been arranged. Nina Dalton had been a enthusiastic advocate of the scheme and had persuaded Esther to enrol. Esther had dutifully attended every class and had just about scraped through to gain her certificate. Nina had been the star pupil.

'Then I'll be addressing envelopes later

on for the Cannonbridge appeal,' Esther continued. 'I promised Nina I'd put in a couple of hours.' Nina was a tireless worker for many good causes in the area. She had a good deal of professional expertise, having been a paid employee of a well-known charitable organization before her marriage. Esther greatly admired Nina; she would dearly have liked to achieve her confidence and elegance. She had even tried buying the same designer clothes but they never looked right on her, she couldn't carry them off as her sister-in-law could.

The appeal currently occupying much of Nina's attention was for a proposed new hospice over in Cannonbridge, a town somewhat smaller in size than Brentworth. Cannonbridge had only a small hospice, set up many years ago, at the start of the hospice movement, struggling along now in run-down and inconvenient premises.

A patient who had spent the final months of his life in the hospice last year, a well-to-do businessman with no surviving relatives, had made a new will shortly before he died, leaving his entire fortune to go towards the provision of a new, purpose-built hospice.

His proposal received enthusiastic local support and an appeal was set up to secure the rest of the finance. It wasn't long before the project grew more ambitious. The hospice would now be larger than originally intended; it would, in certain circumstances, admit a proportion of patients from the rest of the country. The scope of the appeal widened and fund-raising events were held in many towns and parishes. One such event was a buffet lunch, organized by a club James belonged to; the lunch would be held this coming Friday in a central hall in Brentworth.

James finished his breakfast and stood up from the table. 'I'll be eating out this evening,' he said, as more often than not these days. Years ago, after the birth of her second child, Esther had begun to suffer from nervous trouble and had struggled against it ever since. James had early taken to entertaining clients and associates at a restaurant or one of his clubs, in order to save his wife trouble; he had never departed from the habit.

He gave her a perfunctory kiss on the cheek as he left; he always got to the office early. The forced lightness of Esther's manner vanished as soon as he was gone, to be replaced by the inward

17

looking expression, resentful and bitter, she now habitually wore when alone; it was beginning to show in her face in company these days more often than she realized.

She cleared the breakfast table, leaving everything tidy against the arrival of her daily help, a competent woman who had been with her for years. She went slowly up to her bedroom. The sky was now a soft blue, the morning sunny. Down in the garden there were drifts of snowdrops under the trees.

As she changed her housecoat for a towelling robe, she paused by the chest of drawers to look down at the photographs of her sons at various ages. She had been overjoyed when her first son was born. How proud and pleased James had been, how delighted her parents. What hopes she had entertained in that euphoric time that the birth of his first grandchild might bring her closer at last to her father. But that hadn't come about. Nor had the birth of the second grandchild wrought the miracle either.

James had worked ever harder, pushing his way unflaggingly up the ladder; she saw less and less of him. She had made her life round her sons; that had got her along in a fashion. But as they grew older they clearly manifested themselves as their father's sons, not hers—in looks, brains, interests, ambitions. They humoured her, patronized her, never sought her views on anything. Now they had grown up and gone. The elder was working for an international finance house and was currently spending twelve months in Tokyo; the younger was taking his master's degree in business administration at Harvard.

She went along to the bathroom and ran her bath. Nina and Matthew had no children. Nina had made no bones about it: she didn't want any. She had made that clear to Matthew from the start. Matthew, it seemed, hadn't minded one way or the other and had cheerfully fallen in with her wishes. Esther had felt vaguely shocked and disapproving when Nina had first casually mentioned this—but look at the difference between her and Nina now. Nina leading a busy, extrovert life, happy and useful, totally absorbed in what she did, admired and welcomed everywhere, with a husband plainly devoted to her. Nina had kept her looks, her figure, had even improved on them since her marriage. And what of herself? What had she to show for twenty-six years of marriage and motherhood? A husband who addressed barely half a dozen sentences to her in the course of twenty-four hours, sons who condescended towards her. A personality, mouse-like enough to start out with but now so dimmed that she often felt invisible as she went through the motions of her routine existence. Much of the time she found her work for charity—the same work that gave Nina stimulus and satisfaction—little more than a tedious chore; on her worst days it served only to depress her still further.

She lay back in the water and raised one arm above her head. With her other hand she began her obsessive daily palpating of her breasts, always fearing to discover some tiny lump. Her mother had died of breast cancer at the age of forty-six, only two years older than herself at this moment. Esther had been fifteen when she first learned that her mother was ill, seventeen when she died. She and Matthew were both away at school or college in those years. Every holiday, when she came home, she would see the steady, remorseless decline. She had greatly loved her quiet, gentle mother; greatly grieved when she was gone.

One ray of hope she had permitted herself in all the heart-rending sorrow: that it might bring her closer to her father. But that hadn't come about.

She had minded a good deal when he had married again, three years later, although she had been married two years herself by then. She had tried hard not to mind his marriage, she didn't want him to be lonely. The rational part of her understood and accepted the remarriage—but not the deeper, instinctive part.

She had never been close to her father. Bernard Dalton had been a reticent, undemonstrative man, a religious man of strong character and strict principles. Energetic and hard-working, devoting much of his time to building up the family business: printing, with a certain amount of specialist publishing. He did a good deal of charitable work, always endeavouring to put his principles into practice as a private citizen and in his business life.

Esther had always feared him, had always striven her utmost to please him. It was in an attempt to win his regard that she had first begun to work for charity.

But she had always been close to her

brother. There had always been love between them, unalloyed and uncritical on her side, tolerant and understanding on Matthew's. She had envied the seemingly easy way Matthew had been able as he grew up to shake himself free from the powerful governance of their father and strike out on his own, something she could never have dreamed of attempting herself.

It was through Matthew she had met James Milroy, a few months after the death of her mother. The two young men had been students together—not that they had ever been close friends, then or now; their temperaments were too different.

Esther had been very ready to fall in love; she saw marriage and motherhood as shining goals. She had been overjoyed when her father gave his blessing to the match. She had married before she was properly grown up, before she had tasted anything of life.

When she took her marriage vows she took them unequivocally, for life, in the certainty that James felt the same. They had both been brought up to shudder at the thought of divorce.

But she no longer shuddered at the thought. She yearned now to be done with her arid marriage. Time might be running out for her, as it had for her mother. If she was ever to gather the courage to make another life for herself she had better not leave it much longer.

What held her back? She could answer that in one word: money. She had none of her own, had never earned a single penny; she had no qualifications, no training. She had been dependent on others from the day she was born, she had always been accustomed to comfort and plenty; she quailed at the thought of having to set about earning her own living for the first time ever.

She had received only a modest legacy on her father's death, all dribbled away in the six years since then. The bulk of his estate had been left in trust for Grace, his second wife, fifteen years his junior; it wouldn't be distributed till after her death.

She pulled out the plug and got to her feet. She reached for a towel and began to dry herself.

She had no legal grounds of any kind for divorcing James; she was certain he would never agree to a divorce by mutual consent. It suited him to have his home well run by a compliant wife, to present a façade of conventional domestic harmony to the circle in which he moved. If she simply took herself off she would be forced to wait five years to secure a divorce. She was equally certain James would contribute nothing to her support in those five years. He had a sharp legal brain, he would get the better of her in any contest she might try to set up.

There was nothing for it; she would have to look out for herself.

CHAPTER 2

As club treasurer, James had helped organize the charity buffet lunch, as he had helped to organize—always with considerable success—other charitable events over the years for his various clubs.

Friday was always a good day for such an event; the approach of the weekend lent a relaxed, holiday air to the proceedings. Folk were more willing to give up a little time to attend, loosen their purse strings, heed the voice of compassion.

The food was excellent, the coffee first class. James circulated diligently, drumming up donations and promises of donations. By one-forty-five he had achieved a very respectable figure—with more to come; people were still arriving. Among them he caught sight of the tall figure of his brother-in-law, Matthew Dalton. Matthew was chatting expansively to another late-comer, glancing cheerfully about, with his ready smile. Never short on the charm, James said to himself.

A minute or two later, James made his way across the hall to where Matthew stood surveying the array of buffet dishes. Nowadays, it wasn't only Matthew's manner that was expansive; years of affluent living had done little to hold his waistline in check. His good looks were also losing the battle. His hairline was receding, he had the slightly flushed face of the man who drinks a little too much. Like James, he was a chartered accountant, but, unlike his brother-in-law, he had set up on his own twenty years ago. His offices were situated in an upmarket block close to the centre of Brentworth.

Matthew watched James cross the floor towards him; James exuded his customary air of power, positive success. 'A pretty good turn out,' James commented as he came up. 'Better than I'd hoped for.' He directed Matthew's attention to dishes he considered especially good. 'I'll give Nina a ring when I've got the final figures,' he added. 'She'll be delighted.'

James drank a sociable cup of coffee as they stood chatting. He passed on to Matthew a rumour he had heard earlier in the day: a firm of asset managers in a neighbouring town was being investigated by the Fraud Squad. Matthew expressed surprise at the rumour; he would have thought the firm soundly based; they were certainly long established.

'You can't always go by that these days,' James said with a knowing movement of his head. More than one good firm had gone down in the recession through spiralling difficulties, and the sorry saga was not yet over, even though better times were on the way. 'A bit of speculating, soon it's robbing Peter to pay Paul, next thing it's outright gambling. Over-extended all round, no margin anywhere, teetering along on the edge of the precipice. Only takes the smallest extra shove—some international ruckus, a blip on the currency markets—and over they go, for good.' He eyed Matthew. 'How are you finding things these days?'

Matthew helped himself to a particularly appetizing dish. 'Pretty good, all things considered,' he responded heartily.

As James set off once more in pursuit of donations, Matthew stood gazing after him. Oh, boy, he said wryly to himself, if you only knew the half of it. There wasn't much anyone could tell Matthew about the perils of recession and the unorthodox easements always so temptingly close to hand. He gave a little shudder and closed his eyes for a moment.

He had a brief flash of vision: his father's face, his shrewd eyes contemplating him. What would that principled man of business have to say if he could see him now, could know the dire straits he had got himself into? He shuddered again at the thought. His father would dearly have liked him to go into the family business but Matthew had little interest in printing and publishing, and shrank moreover from the idea of working for the father he had always found intimidating.

All he had received outright on his

father's death had been a modest legacy of precisely the same amount as that left to his sister, Esther.

He began to eat, scarcely tasting the food. If he could just manage to keep going, struggle through into the boom that must surely come, without ruin or disgrace—or, paralysing thought, a gaol sentence. If he could scrape through without Nina ever having to know. That would be the part of any catastrophe he would relish least of all, letting down his beloved Nina, having to break the news to her that the glory days were over, the gravy train had finally smashed into the buffers. Pray God it never came to that, but if, God forbid, it ever did, then thank God for a wife with backbone and loyalty. Whatever happened, Nina would never whine or indulge in self pity. However low the depths to which he sank, there was always the cast iron certainty that she would stand by him in the end.

A business acquaintance came up, calling out a friendly greeting. Matthew at once switched on his cheerful smile, his look of lively interest, his genial, on-top-of-the-world manner.

CHAPTER 3

It was easy to imagine Nina Dalton as a fashion model, with her tall, willowy figure, fine-boned face, honey-coloured skin and large, expressive eyes of a clear golden amber. Her wealth of pale blonde hair, full of natural waves and curls, was taken up on top of her head, displaying the graceful line of her neck.

She had worked for charity in one capacity or another, paid or voluntary, since the day she had left secretarial college. She wasn't a native of Brentworth but came from a small town some distance away. It was when she was on the payroll of a national charitable organization that she had first met Matthew Dalton; she had called on him in the course of a fund-raising campaign directed largely at businessmen.

She had walked in through the door of his office at a crucial moment in Matthew's life. He had just managed to break away from a long entanglement with an older woman, a divorcée, good-looking and sophisticated, with more than one string to her bow. Matthew had finally realized the relationship was leading nowhere, it was time his bachelor days were done; what he needed now was a conventional marriage, settled and supportive. He married Nina three months after she walked into his office.

She had spent the latter part of Friday morning dealing swiftly and competently with the affairs of a small local charity set up a hundred and fifty years ago for the benefit of retired governesses by a wealthy widow who had herself been a governess before her marriage. The endowment, so munificent seeming in its day, was now greatly eroded and governesses were a dying breed. These days, the charity's business required only an hour or two of Nina's time on alternate Friday mornings. For this purpose she was allowed a corner in the Brentworth office of a national charity for the welfare of the elderly: Friends of the Third Age. Any mail that arrived for her was always put aside unopened against her next visit.

On Friday afternoon, Nina gave her time to the Cannonbridge hospice appeal, taking her seat at a desk in one of the rooms behind a thrift shop in a side street; the shop had offered free use of the room for the duration of the appeal.

The bulk of essential money had now been raised and building work was due to start on the hospice site at the end of February. A well-known television entertainer, a dedicated supporter of the hospice movement, had promised to lay the foundation stone a month later. But there could be no slackening in the fund-raising. Money would be needed for the upkeep and running of the hospice, for the many extras, improvements and refinements that would be looked for along the way.

Nina spent the first part of her stint sketching out yet another publicity campaign; publicity was one of her fortes. She was still busy with minor matters at the end of the afternoon when the other voluntary workers had gone. The phone rang on her desk: James Milroy, acquainting her with the outcome of the buffet lunch. As he had predicted, she was delighted with the figures.

'Wonderful weather we're having just now,' James went on to remark. 'I imagine you'll be thinking about opening up the cottage any day now.'

'I imagine I will,' she agreed. The cottage stood in beautiful countryside, the best part of two miles from the nearest village, in a spot roughly equidistant from Brentworth and Cannonbridge. It had belonged to the Dalton family for a great many years and currently formed part of the trust property. James and Esther had spent weekends there in the early days of their marriage and Esther had made regular use of it later, when the boys were small; she still retained a key. The cottage was now used chiefly by Matthew and Nina. Nina had devoted considerable time and effort to having it extended and modernized, the furnishings and decorations renewed, the garden set to rights. Esther made little use of her key these days. She would sometimes drive over there when she felt particularly low, wandering round the garden in a fruitless nostalgic attempt to recapture the happiness of the first years of her marriage when her days were full and satisfying, without the need to go searching for activities to fill them.

'I might take a run over there myself, one day next week, if the weather holds,' James continued, his voice light and easy.

'Might you, indeed?' Nina returned, equally lightly. In theory, James and Esther were as free to use the cottage as Matthew and Nina, but in practice Matthew and Nina would seem to have taken over the property completely.

'Maybe I'll see you there,' James added.

'I rather doubt it.' Her tone was friendly, touched with amusement, but with a hint of underlying granite; she kept from her voice any lingering echo of old sentiment. She had known James before she met Matthew, she had encountered him in the same way, through her fund-raising activities. If James had not been a married man with two young sons, a man still moving up the ladder, careful not to blot his copybook in any way, Nina would in all probability at this moment have been Mrs James Milroy instead of Mrs Matthew Dalton.

Nina glanced round at the sound of the door opening. A woman came into the room, a voluntary worker with a problem to be solved. Nina brought the conversation with James to a rapid conclusion.

Shortly after the woman left, Nina had another caller: a publican with a handsome cheque from various fund-raising activities organized among his customers. Nina thanked him warmly and wrote him out an official receipt. His eyes rested on the elegant gold pen she used, an engraved inscription discernible along the barrel; he made an admiring comment. Nina smiled and held out the pen for him to read the inscription. The pen had been presented to her a few years ago after she had worked night and day to raise money for a local day centre, threatened with closure, for handicapped and disabled youngsters. The pen hadn't been bought out of the money raised for the centre but by a private whip-round the youngsters' parents had made among themselves, in appreciation of Nina's prodigious—and wholly successful—efforts.

After the publican had departed, Nina rang Matthew, as she always did, to ask what his plans were for the evening, what he wanted her to do about a meal. He told her he'd be staying on at his office again, he'd be home around eight.

'That'll be fine,' she assured him. She didn't stay chatting, she knew how busy he was these days. She could now work on at her desk a little longer, there were still matters to attend to. She made a number of phone calls, checking and finalizing arrangements for a sponsored half marathon to be run shortly by older pupils from local schools. Then she sat considering the merits of making another round of all the business premises in town, deciding at length in favour of it. It could be carried out this time by a team of pretty girls; that would surely bring in a worthwhile sum. She could get Verity Thorburn to round up a decorative bunch from among her fellow students.

Verity was a connection of Nina's by marriage, a great niece of Nina's father-in-law, Bernard Dalton. Over the years, Bernard had gathered more than one stray chick under his wing. As an orphan and a relative, Verity had had a double claim to his protection. She was at present taking a course at the Brentworth College of Further Education. She was always ready to assist Nina, always willing to do what she could for the hospice appeal.

Nina looked at her watch. Too early to ring Verity now, she would still be at the college; she had a late class on Fridays. She would ring her at her flat later this evening.

The college was a large building, put up after the Second World War. Verity was taking a two-year course, begun shortly after her seventeenth birthday, eighteen months ago. She had chosen a somewhat unusual combination of subjects: secretarial skills, cordon bleu cookery and art. She enjoyed them all and was doing well.

At a few minutes after seven she came out of the college, bound for the little basement flat where she lived alone. She had moved there six months ago from the larger flat she had shared with two other girls, both students at the college.

She was slightly built, not very tall, with an elfin face, big brown eyes, a vulnerable look. Her long dark hair hung straight and heavy. Her temperament was highly mercurial; she harboured deep feelings of insecurity, due in no small measure to the abrupt and brutal fashion in which she had been orphaned at the age of nine.

Her parents and maternal grandparents had all beeen medical missionaries in Africa; the grandmother was a sister of Bernard Dalton. When the grandparents were retiring, they decided to spend a month at the mission station run by Verity's parents before returning to England for good.

In the middle of their visit, Verity attended a birthday party given for the daughter of friends living some distance away; she was to stay overnight. In the early hours of the morning the mission station was attacked by a roving band of marauders who had slipped over the border from a neighbouring territory under cover of darkness. The buildings were looted and burned, every man, woman and child—black or white—savagely butchered.

A week later, Verity was sent home to England, into the care of her great uncle, Bernard Dalton, and his second wife, Grace.

Now, on this fine February evening, as she set off for her flat, she caught sight of someone standing by the entrance gates, looking across at her. Her heart gave a wild leap of joy. It was Ned Hooper; it was more than a week since she'd set eyes on him.

Then her heart sank. He didn't come forward to meet her but remained unsmiling by the gates, waiting for her to reach him. It didn't augur well.

Ned was eighteen years older than Verity.

37

Tall and strongly built, good-looking in a very English way, with fair hair and blue eyes, an open expression. He had studied art at the college and now did occasional supply teaching in the art department, to eke out the exceedingly slender living he contrived to make as an artist.

'Are you coming along to the flat?' Verity wanted to know, the moment she had greeted him. Her manner was intense and eager. Her main reason for moving to a flat of her own was so that the pair of them could be together without the knowledge of her flatmates—or her relatives and guardians.

Ned shook his head with resolution. He knew once they were indoors she'd try every trick in the book to get round him. Or else she'd set about creating the kind of scene he couldn't stomach. He gestured in the direction of a small public garden near by. 'We can talk over there.'

They walked side by side, in silence, not touching, till they reached the garden. At this time of evening there were few strollers along the gravel paths. They found a seat beside the beds of winter heather; in silence they sat down, a little apart. She sat stiffly upright, gazing straight ahead, waiting for him to begin.

'We've had some good times,' he said at last. 'I don't forget them. But they're over now, it's definitely finished.' Her head came sharply round, she darted a beseeching look at him from her great dark eyes. It was those eyes he had first noticed, fixed on him in class, with that intense, searching gaze, the gaze he had once found so intriguing.

'It doesn't have to be finished,' she declared vehemently.

He didn't waver. 'I'm afraid it does. It really is over. You'll meet someone else, someone your own age. You'll forget about me in no time at all.'

She clenched her fists. 'I don't want anyone else. I want you.'

'I'm afraid you can't have me,' he threw back at her with asperity. 'I'm bowing out for good.' With an effort he softened his tone again. 'You must accept it's over. It does no good trying to argue about it.'

'It's Mrs Bradshaw,' she said with sudden ferocity. 'You're moving in with her, aren't you?'

'Yes, I am moving in with her,' he replied brusquely. 'I'm a free agent.'

Her voice rose. 'You don't love her! You can't! She's old and fat.'

'She's neither old nor fat,' he retorted. Mrs Freda Bradshaw was in fact forty-two years old. She might carry a little more flesh than was currently fashionable, but it was certainly no hardship to look at her. She had been a good-looking girl and was still an attractive woman. She was the widow of a man more than thirty years her senior, the owner of a chain of cut-price clothing stores up north. She had started out at sixteen as a sales assistant in one of his stores and had early taken his eye. When his wife died, Freda lost no time in stepping into her shoes.

She had played fair throughout the years that followed. She had been genuinely fond of her husband, had looked after him devotedly in his old age, nursed him in his last illness. She had inherited everything. There had been no children from his first marriage, no relatives to argue the toss.

Freda had then set wholeheartedly about enjoying the rewards of her devotion. She sold the business and salted away the proceeds, then she set off for fresh pastures. Some wind blew her before long to Brentworth. She came across Ned

Hooper at an art exhibition.

'I can't bear to think of you with that woman.' Verity laid an urgent hand on his arm. 'If it's just her money, you know I've got money coming to me one day. Quite a lot of money. You can have it all.'

He shook off her hand. 'I don't want your money,' he said roughly. 'What do you take me for?'

She wasn't done yet. 'I'm sure I could get hold of some of the money now. You can have every penny.'

He made a contemptuous gesture of dismissal and got to his feet. She remained seated, looking pleadingly up at him. 'You'd better get it into your head,' he said with profound irritation. 'This really is goodbye.' He went rapidly off along the path.

She sat biting her lip, staring after him as he plunged out of the garden, disappearing from view along the busy evening pavement.

Shortly before seven-thirty, Esther came out of the Brentworth hospice where she had been putting in a little extra visiting, as she not infrequently did on evenings

41

when James wouldn't be home before bedtime. She didn't use her car if the weather was fine, as it was tonight; the walk both ways helped to fill the long stretch of time.

She set off without haste in the direction of Oakfield Gardens and her solitary supper, choosing her usual route that took her through the town centre with its cheerful bustle and brightly-lit shop windows, postponing as long as possible the moment when she must let herself in to the silent house.

As she approached the block where Matthew had his offices, she glanced up to see if any of his lights showed, as they had so often done of late. Yes, light was showing. She slowed her pace to a halt and stood pondering, then she made up her mind and went quickly in through the swing doors, into the deserted entrance hall.

She could hear someone rattling about, along a corridor; the caretaker, no doubt. She wasn't anxious to encounter him; he was a dour character with a chronically gloomy view of the world. She slipped quietly up the stairs to the floor where Matthew had his offices.

CHAPTER 4

The weather continued mild. On Sunday afternoon, Verity Thorburn sat with Barry Fielding, another of her great uncle's protegés, in the tea room attached to the Brentworth Art Gallery. They had just made the rounds of an exhibition of late-Victorian watercolours. Barry had cycled over from his boarding school, a mile or two outside Brentworth, to join her for the afternoon; they often went to concerts and exhibitions together.

Barry Fielding was the last of Bernard Dalton's stray chicks; he was a year younger than Verity. Bernard had died twelve months after making himself responsible for Barry's welfare. Barry was a tall, spindly lad, serious and studious. He was in the sixth form, working hard to gain a place at university, where he hoped to read medicine.

He and Verity were very close, they had been closer than a good many siblings since they were first introduced

43

to each other seven years ago. They were now both wards of the same brace of guardians: Bernard Dalton's widow, Grace—whom Verity always addressed as Aunt Grace—and Grace's solicitor, son of the man, dead now for three years, who had been Bernard's solicitor. Barry had begun by addressing his benefactors as Mr and Mrs Dalton but had gradually fallen into using the same terms as Verity; no one had ever offered any objection.

Barry no longer had any relatives of his own. His mother had died when he was six years old. His father had been one of Bernard Dalton's employees, an ambitious and hard-working young man from a Cannonbridge council estate; he had looked after Barry with the help of neighbours. When Bernard Dalton retired, he sold the business and Fielding was one of a number of men who decided not to continue with the new employer but to make use of the generous severance money on offer, to set up in business on their own.

Things went well enough with Fielding for a year or two, until boom gave way to recession. He struggled along with mounting difficulty. He was a man who

44

bottled things up, kept his worries to himself; he grew increasingly depressed.

One Saturday morning in the summer holidays when Barry was away at a school camp, Fielding drove down to the little resort on the north coast of Cornwall where he had spent his honeymoon. He booked in at a small bed and breakfast establishment. On Sunday morning he rose early and went out for a swim. He never came back.

He had left his clothes and towel neatly folded on the beach; there was no note. His body was washed up a few days later. There was only a small insurance policy on his life, written in trust for his son's benefit, taken out at the time Fielding set up in business on his own. The inquest returned a verdict of death from drowning, with insufficient evidence to show the state of the mind of the deceased.

At the time Bernard Dalton took over responsibility for Barry, Verity Thorburn had already been in his care for two years; he had sent her to the boarding school his daughter Esther had attended. Verity had been spending her school holidays with Esther and James, whose schoolboy sons were also home from boarding school.

Verity was far from happy at the Milroys', though she did her best not to show it. Esther strove to be kind but the age gap between Verity and the boys was too great to be easily bridged. And Verity had remained for a considerable time in a withdrawn state, able to bear little in the way of teasing or boisterous games, liable to rush off to her room to give way to fits of silent weeping when a chance word or snatch of music touched some chord of memory. The only person to perceive the depth of her unhappiness was Nina Dalton. She couldn't take Verity in the holidays herself as she was often out all day, endlessly busy.

But when Barry arrived on the scene, Nina put forward the idea that both youngsters might spend their holidays at Elmhurst, the Dalton family home, near Cannonbridge. Bernard and Grace readily agreed and the plan proved very successful. A strong friendship developed between the two orphans, working wonders for them both. They had the freedom of the grounds. The gardener, Gosling, an amiable man, made friends with them and his wife was endlessly kind.

Now, as they sat in the tea room, Barry

talked of how his training was coming along for the sponsored half marathon. He was an ardent fund-raiser for the new hospice, heading the sixth form committee at his school, masterminding the boys' efforts.

Verity asked if he had done anything yet about Aunt Grace's birthday present. It would be Grace Dalton's seventieth birthday on Saturday, 7th March. Grace was set on holding a family gathering at Elmhurst that weekend; she had always greatly enjoyed such occasions. She had been in poor health for the past two years but her doctor believed the little celebration would do her good, provided care and moderation were exercised.

'I've found a book I think she'll like,' Barry said. He'd come across it in an antiquarian bookseller's: a photographic history of Cannonbridge, from the turn of the century to the late 'thirties; it was handsomely bound, in excellent condition. 'There are several photographs of the grammar school,' he added. 'Her father's in one of them.' Grace was Cannonbridge born and bred; her father had been senior history master at the grammar school.

'She'll love that,' Verity responded with

conviction. She was giving a watercolour of Elmhurst she had painted herself. 'I'll give you a lift over there that weekend,' she added as they stood up from the tea table. She had her own little car, bought six months ago from money she'd come into on her eighteenth birthday, a legacy of no great size, from her great uncle.

They walked across to where Barry had left his bicycle; he had to get back to school. 'The birthday weekend could easily be cancelled,' Barry pointed out. 'If Aunt Grace isn't well enough.'

'She'll be well enough,' Verity retorted. 'She'll live to be a hundred, heart or no heart, she's as tough as old boots.' Her face took on a brooding look. 'There she is, sitting on all that money,' she suddenly burst out. 'Why should an old woman, no blood relation of mine, someone who just happened to marry my great uncle, have control over what I do?'

Barry mounted his bicycle. 'She's only doing her duty, doing what Uncle Bernard wanted.' He gave her a straight look. 'She's been very good to both of us,' he reminded her. 'She's always treated us fairly and kindly. And she doesn't take decisions about us on her own, everything has to

48

be agreed between her and Mr Purvis.'

Ah yes, Mr Purvis, Verity thought. Her expression lightened as she waved Barry off. She'd been forgetting Mr Purvis, the Dalton solicitor. She set off briskly for her little flat, in a surge of renewed optimism.

CHAPTER 5

Elmhurst, home of the Dalton family for over a century, stood in extensive grounds, sixty acres and more, on the outskirts of a village close to Cannonbridge. Over the last thirty years, developers had turned hungry eyes on the Elmhurst land, rapidly becoming a prime site as the town advanced steadily nearer. More than one entrepreneur, with plans for a high-class development in mind, had approached the local authority to discover its views. Planning permission would undoubtedly be granted and would be welcome locally.

Bernard Dalton had received a number of offers. The figures mentioned rose as time went by, occasionally making spectacular leaps. But Bernard had never for one moment contemplated selling, and his widow was of precisely the same mind.

Grace Dalton had been a spinster of forty-six when she married Bernard. She had worked for the firm since leaving secretarial college; she had been Bernard's personal assistant for several years. She had never had a boyfriend but kept house for her widowed schoolmaster father until his death, two years before her marriage.

Bernard had consulted neither his son nor his daughter when he contemplated remarrying; he would have been astonished at such a suggestion. Nor would his children have dared to voice any contrary opinion they might have felt.

The second marriage had been highly successful. Grace had continued to play a significant part in the affairs of the firm until Bernard's retirement. She had also served as a magistrate and parish councillor and had taken an increasing interest in charitable work. But she had been forced to give up these activities after being laid low two years ago by a serious heart condition complicated by other health factors. She had made a fairly good recovery but had suffered a setback the previous autumn. She had been strongly advised to take things very easily indeed in future, and was conscientiously obeying orders. 'With care, she could live another two or three years,' her doctor had recently told Matthew Dalton. 'But, there again, she could go at any time.'

With the very quiet life Grace led nowadays, the Elmhurst staff, indoor and outdoor, was greatly reduced from what it had been in the days before Bernard's retirement. The gardens, though far from neglected, were no longer kept up to the same high standards, everything now being geared to simplicity and ease of maintenance. The head gardener, Gosling, managed these days with the help of a couple of stalwart village lads; he even acted, when required, as Grace's chauffeur, though that was rarely necessary now, when she went out so little.

Gosling's father-in-law had looked after the Elmhurst gardens before him. He was an old man now, widowed, living with the Goslings in their cottage in the grounds. Mrs Gosling had been born in the cottage. She had worked in the

51

house from leaving school, continuing after her marriage, whenever her family duties permitted. Now that her children had grown up and left home, she put in a few hours most days, as she was needed.

When it became clear to Grace two years ago what her future would be, she moved out of her first-floor bedroom and took over instead a downstairs room with glazed doors leading on to a patio, sheltered and secluded, where she could sit out in warm weather. A small adjoining room was converted into a bathroom. On this fine Monday morning, the February sun, though cheering to the spirits, was nowhere near strong enough to permit the pleasure of sitting out.

Shortly before noon, Dr Surridge called to see her. It was a measure of her sustained progress that he called now only once a week, putting her name by no means first on his list. Grace had a good deal of faith in Dr Surridge, a genial man in his middle fifties, with a calmly reassuring manner. He had been her doctor since taking over the practice three years ago, on the retirement of old Dr Wheatley.

Today Dr Surridge was well pleased

with his patient. As they sat talking after his examination, Grace lay on her sofa, comfortably propped against a pile of cushions, the position she always adopted now when resting or sleeping. She still retained her air of command. Her steel-grey hair, long and thick as ever, was carefully dressed, high on her head; her blue eyes still sparkled, her pink and white skin was still soft and smooth.

'I rang Dr Wheatley yesterday evening,' Dr Surridge told her. 'He's all set to take over in ten days' time.' Dr Surridge and his wife were shortly flying off to Australia for three months. Their schoolteacher son had gone out there some time back on a year's exchange. He had met an Australian girl, married her, decided to settle out there. Their first child had been born a few months ago.

Dr Wheatley had been happy to act as locum for Dr Surridge during shorter holidays in each of the three years since his retirement and was greatly looking forward to his longer spell. He was a childless widower whose work had been his whole life and he often found the long hours of unaccustomed leisure hung heavily.

And Grace was looking forward to seeing

him again. He had been not only her doctor but her good friend, as he had been also to Bernard and Bernard's first wife.

When Dr Surridge left Grace's room at the end of his visit, he found the housekeeper, Dorothy Nevett, waiting for him in the hall, to ask how he had found Mrs Dalton. Dorothy was a native of Cannonbridge, a stockily-built spinster a few years from sixty. She was highly competent at her job, a woman to be reckoned with, as might be seen in her determined countenance, the stubborn set to her jaw. Her greying brown hair, short and straight, was cut without concession to fashion. She had worked at Elmhurst since leaving school, starting out as a kitchen maid in the time of Bernard's first wife.

Dr Surridge gave her his report. He had a high regard for Miss Nevett's nursing ability. She had helped to nurse the first Mrs Dalton, and later, Bernard, in his last illness. The doctor believed she could have taken up nursing professionally and been very successful at it.

'Would it be all right if I went off for a day or two this coming weekend?' Dorothy asked as she walked with him to the door. 'I haven't spoken about it yet to Mrs Dalton, I thought I'd check with you first. I feel I could do with a break. I thought of leaving on Friday morning and coming back Monday afternoon, I'd get back before supper. Mrs Gosling would be in charge—and of course, Jean would lend a hand.' Jean Redfern was a girl of twenty who acted as a general help to Grace, carrying out a variety of duties. The tone in which Miss Nevett referred to her displayed a certain coolness.

No, Dr Surridge had no objection to Dorothy going off for a few days. 'You'll be going to the caravan?' he asked chattily.

She nodded. 'My friend will be there for the weekend.' Dorothy owned a little caravan by the coast in Dorset, in conjunction with her lifelong friend, Alice Upjohn, a spinster like herself. The caravan was kept on a small farm. 'It's in a sheltered spot,' she added. 'It should be very pleasant down there just now, if the weather holds.'

As soon as the sound of the doctor's departing car reached Grace Dalton's ears, she touched a button on the console she had had installed when she moved into the room; it enabled her to summon assistance, day or night. One press for the housekeeper, two for Jean Redfern. She pressed it twice.

In a very short time, Jean came along with her customary swift, noiseless tread, from the garden room where she had been doing the flowers. A quiet girl with an unassuming manner, pretty enough in an everyday fashion, nothing in any way striking about her appearance. She was the illegitimate child of a woman named Redfern who had worked as a maid at Elmhurst from leaving school until five years ago when she had married an American widower she had met on holiday and had gone to live with him in the States.

Jean had come into the world as the result of a brief association between her mother and a travelling salesman with a roving eye and a persuasive tongue. When Jean's mother—barely eighteen at the time—realized her predicament she tried to kill herself, but the attempt was frustrated by Dorothy Nevett who got the truth out of her and then went straight to her employers. The Daltons were very kind to the girl, who had no family to turn to. They kept her on and looked after her. She was at first determined on an abortion but they managed to talk her out of it. When the baby was born she wanted it put up for adoption but they persuaded her to keep it.

Jean was a well-behaved child, quiet and secretive. She lived in the servants' quarters and was never in any way a nuisance in the household. She learned very early the useful skills of compliance and self-effacement; the Daltons were scarcely aware of her presence. As she got older, both her mother and Dorothy Nevett saw to it that she learned to perform little tasks about the place.

Bernard Dalton had been dead twelve months when Jean's mother met her American and jumped at the chance to marry him. She asked Grace if she would allow Jean—then fifteen years old—to remain at Elmhurst until she finished her schooling; in return Jean would continue to do whatever she could in the way of household tasks. If Grace wished to employ her on a formal basis after she left school, well and good; if not, Jean could leave and look for employment elsewhere.

Grace readily agreed and Jean's mother went blithely off to America. Grace saw

57

to it that Jean kept in touch with her mother, but in spite of her efforts the correspondence soon diminished to an exchange of letters at Christmas. The marriage produced children Jean had seen only in very occasional photographs.

Grace did her best to persuade Jean to stay on at school, take some kind of training, but Jean wasn't interested. Nor did she show any inclination to leave Elmhurst and go out into the world on her own. Before long, she had established herself as a very useful extra pair of hands about the house; she was always pleasant and willing.

Her position in the household began by degrees to alter. Grace started to make use of her in a more personal way, take greater interest in her; her footing became more like that of a companion help. This alteration found little favour in Dorothy Nevett's eyes. Dorothy was a firm believer in knowing one's place in life and sticking to it. She was deeply opposed to any attempt to turn sows' ears into silk purses. And she was more than a little resentful, though she attempted not to show it, of what she saw as the girl's favoured position in the household—a girl who had, after all, been born on the wrong side of the blanket.

In her last year at school, Jean had taken classes in shorthand and typing. When she left school she began to assist Grace with her correspondence, proving herself meticulously careful, reliable and conscientious. Grace wanted her to take a proper secretarial course to qualify for a good post in the business world but Jean quietly and stubbornly resisted.

She had helped with nursing Grace over the last two years and here she had been a good deal less resistant when it was suggested she might take a course. She had been one of those Nina Dalton's enthusiasm had swept into enrolling. Nina had found a place for her in a course held in Cannonbridge and she had acquitted herself very creditably.

There had been one brief period three years ago when Jean had caused Grace some real concern. She had met a boy two years older than herself, a good-looking drifter. She had fallen in love with him, wanted to marry him, there and then. Grace had put her foot down very firmly and the boy had drifted off elsewhere. There had never been another boyfriend.

Today, when Jean went along to Grace's bedroom in answer to her summons, Grace gave her directions about various tasks, then she asked how Jean was getting on with her reading. Grace had drawn up an improving reading list and was encouraging Jean to plough her way through it.

As Jean was leaving the room again, Grace asked if Mrs Gosling was in the house and was told she was. Would Jean send her along?

Mrs Gosling came hurrying into the room a few minutes later, a cheerful, motherly woman with a ready smile. Grace asked how her quilting was progressing—Mrs Gosling was an expert quilter and at Grace's suggestion had embarked on a set of cushion covers to be given as one of the prizes in a raffle in aid of the new hospice. She told Grace she was now working on the final cover and hoped to finish it in a couple of days. Grace was delighted; the draw was to take place next week. Grace had long been a supporter of the present Cannonbridge hospice and had helped from the start to raise funds for the new building, even in her invalid state, encouraging everyone connected with her to join in.

When Mrs Gosling had gone off again, Grace lay back and closed her eyes. She was feeling somewhat fatigued; time for a little rest before lunch. Inside a very few moments she had slipped into a pleasantly somnolent state in which the chirruping of the garden birds, the distant sounds of the household, mingled together in a lulling murmur.

By two-thirty lunch was over, the kitchen restored to order and Mrs Dalton settled down for her nap. Dorothy Nevett was up in her room on the top floor, enjoying an hour or two of leisure. She liked having her room up here, so beautifully private; she had had the whole floor to herself since the staff had been reduced. She paced about the room, her head full of the phone call she had received yesterday evening from her friend, Alice Upjohn.

Alice had lived next door to Dorothy when they were children; they had sat next to each other in school. When Alice was thirteen her father was transferred on promotion by his firm to a branch down south and the family was uprooted. But the two friends kept in regular touch, by

61

letter in the early years but later spending holidays together.

When Alice left school, she began work as a clerk in a local government office; she continued living at home. The years slipped by. When she was forty-five her father died and her mother's health soon afterwards began to deteriorate; she spent her final years in care. The house was sold to pay the nursing home fees and Alice moved into a small rented flat near the home; her mother lingered on for several years.

Alice had recently been offered early retirement in a cost-cutting exercise and had immediately accepted. She would be finishing work at the end of March; she would have a pension and a lump sum.

Dorothy and Alice had long shared a dream of buying a little cottage to retire to, in their favourite resort on the Dorset coast. As soon as Alice accepted the offer of early retirement, before saying a word to Dorothy, she contacted estate agents in the resort but quickly discovered that prices were out of reach. Then she had an inspiration. She got on to every solicitor in the area and came at last upon what she was hoping for: a small cottage still to be disposed of at the tail-end of an estate, the executors ready to let the property go for a very reasonable sum if the transaction could be speedily put through. Alice's lump sum, together with her savings and what she had inherited from her mother, could provide her half of the purchase price, as she had joyfully informed Dorothy over the phone yesterday evening. What about Dorothy? Could she provide her half?

Dorothy had her savings, she'd always been thrifty, but they were nowhere near enough. Then perhaps she could raise a mortgage for the balance, Alice suggested. 'We'll have to decide very quickly,' Alice had gone on to say. 'We'll never get another chance like this.' She had liked what she'd been told about the cottage but hadn't yet had a chance to view it. 'Try to get away for the weekend,' she urged Dorothy over the phone. 'If we find it's what we want, you'll have a few days after you get back to try to raise the money.'

Dorothy had approached Grace at lunchtime to ask if she could take a weekend break but she had said nothing about the cottage. Grace had readily assented.

Dorothy halted in her pacing to pick up

from the top of her bureau a long frame holding three photographs of Alice: as a schoolgirl of thirteen, with dark curly hair and a shy smile; as a young woman, on their first holiday together; and the mature Alice, a few years ago, on another of their long succession of shared holidays, her figure almost as slender, her smile little changed.

She replaced the photograph, took down a jacket and left the room. She went quietly down the back stairs, out by a side door into the garden. No sign of Gosling. She spotted a garden lad at work in a greenhouse; he gave her a wave as she went by. She walked rapidly through the cultivated gardens, striking out for the fields and woods where she could stride about undisturbed, to think out her thoughts.

How would her bank or building society be likely to look upon an application for a mortgage from a woman of her age, in her financial situation? Two years ago, when Grace Dalton was sufficiently recovered to be able to look calmly at her future, she had sent for Dorothy and told her she was making a new will. It had long been understood between them that Dorothy would retire at sixty with a pension, in recognition of her long and faithful service. Grace had asked if Dorothy would now forget about leaving at sixty and would agree instead to remain with Grace until the end, whenever that might be. In return she would receive a larger pension, together with an additional benefit—a lump sum based on the total number of years she had worked at Elmhurst. If she agreed, she would receive these new entitlements, even if Grace were to die within a very short time.

Grace hadn't been coy about mentioning actual figures and Dorothy's eyes had opened wide when she heard them. She had needed no time to think the offer over and had at once accepted.

But that was two years ago now. Dorothy had believed then that Grace wouldn't last out the twelvemonth. But the doctor spoke now of the possibility that she might with care live a few more years. Suppose she did manage to raise a mortgage and they did buy the cottage: how would Alice relish living there on her own for that length of time? She frowned in thought as she wheeled about in the dappled sunshine of the woodland.

How long, realistically, was Grace likely to live? That was undoubtedly the question.

Dusk was falling on Monday evening, a week later, as Dorothy reached the crossroads marking the final stage of her journey back from Dorset to Elmhurst. She usually enjoyed driving but today she had found the journey wearisome. It had been altogether a tiring weekend, with so much to weigh up and ponder.

The cottage had turned out to be even better than she had hoped; it would do them beautifully. Not too small, a decent stretch of garden, neglected now, but they could soon put that to rights. They had found a surveyor to go over the cottage and he had been able to assure them the property was structurally very sound. A few repairs would be needed but nothing too expensive. He foresaw no difficulty in raising a mortgage.

She frowned out through the windscreen as she drove through the light-splashed twilight. It was her own share of the purchase money that now presented the only remaining stumbling block. The solicitor had agreed to give them a week to reach a decision. Next Monday evening she was to ring Alice at 7.45, to tell her if she would or would not be able to raise the money. She had fixed on that precise time in order to be certain of making the call without being overhead. Mrs Dalton would be settled down after her supper, watching TV or reading, maybe listening to music or to the radio. Jean would either have gone out or be glued to the TV in the staff sitting room, absorbed in the latest instalment of her favourite soap opera.

First thing the following morning, Tuesday, Alice was to phone the solicitor, to give him a straight yes or no.

CHAPTER 6

At half past four on Wednesday afternoon, Matthew Dalton came out of the Brentworth office of the Inland Revenue, carrying a briefcase stuffed with papers. He set off back to his office with a light step and an air of profound relief. He'd managed to stave off disaster, for the present, at least. He well knew the euphoria would have drained away by morning but he intended to enjoy it while it lasted—take the evening off for once from his ceaseless juggling, spend it at home with Nina, a rare treat these days.

Shortly after six he bounded up the front steps of his house, a fine late-Georgian dwelling. Nina had always admired the property and Matthew had bought it a few years back, very near the peak of the market, as it later turned out; he had cheerfully taken out a massive mortgage. It hadn't appeared an act of lunatic folly in those palmy days when it seemed the gravy train would thunder along full tilt for ever. And Nina had been overjoyed. She loved the house, loved living in it, often said as much. He intended to hang on to it for her if humanly possible.

Esther Milroy spent the late afternoon visiting one of her special patients at the Brentworth hospice, an elderly man with an overpowering need to recount the events of his long life. He asked little in the way of response, merely a willing listener. He occupied an out-of-the-way single room and she was able to stay with him for a good stretch of time without being disturbed. When at last he drifted into a peaceful sleep, she gathered up her things and went noiselessly from his bedside.

Six-forty-five. Too late to embark on a visit with another patient and she had in any case almost come to the end of her patience and cheerfulness. But ahead of her lay only the long empty evening at home. She cast about for some escape from the dreary prospect. She made her way quietly from the building, encountering no one in the maze of passages.

Twenty minutes later found her walking up the front steps of her brother's house. Matthew and Nina were sitting at ease in the drawing room, enjoying a glass of sherry in anticipation of the delectable supper, almost ready. At the sound of the doorbell Matthew uttered a groan. 'Who can that be?' he exclaimed as he set down his glass. 'I'll get rid of them, whoever it is.'

But when he drew back the front door and saw Esther standing before him, gazing up at him like a lost dog, he could do no less than smile and invite her in. He gave Nina a glance of amused resignation as they entered the drawing room. Nina stood up at once, greeting her sister-in-law with warm friendliness. She sat Esther down, took her things and laid them on a nearby table. Matthew poured another glass of sherry.

A few minutes later, Esther reached for a carrier bag bearing the name of a high-class department store in the town. 'I bought Grace's birthday present this afternoon,' she told Nina. 'I don't know if I've made the right choice. I'd be glad of your opinion.'

She took out a nightwear set of nightdress and matching negligée, unfolded them, held out each garment in turn for Nina's inspection. 'It's a very good make.' She indicated the label. 'The material's a wool and cotton mixture, nothing synthetic.' White, printed with an all-over background pattern of rose-pink dots the size of a pinhead, scattered with delicate sprigs of rosebuds. A lavish use of frilled trimming, lace edging, satin ribbons. 'You don't think it's too fussy?' she asked with an anxious frown. 'It was Verity chose this set. I happened to meet her in the street as I was going into the store. She had a couple of free periods from the college so she came along to help me choose. If you don't think Grace would like it, I could take it back and get something else.'

'It's not at all too fussy,' Nina assured her. 'Grace will love it.'

'I like the little rosebud sprays,' Matthew said benignly. 'It's a very pretty pattern.'

Esther looked pleased and relieved. 'I'll keep it then,' she decided, as she folded the garments away again. 'I feel settled about it now.'

Early on Thursday morning, Dr Wheatley set out from his home in south-west Wales where he had chosen to retire. He was a tall, stoop-shouldered man with a mild countenance, white wings of hair. He was very much looking forward to another stint as locum to his successor—and a good long stint, this time. He would greatly enjoy seeing his old patients, driving round his old stamping ground. He was particularly looking forward to seeing Grace Dalton again, his old, dear friend.

CHAPTER 7

On Thursday evening Detective Chief Inspector Kelsey came down the steps of the main Cannonbridge police station and walked across the forecourt. He was a big, solidly built man with massive shoulders, a fine head of thickly springing carroty hair, shrewd green eyes, craggy features dominated by a large, squashy nose.

He smiled to himself as he reached his car. It would be Monday morning before he was due to walk back up those steps again. He had recently come to the end of a long and gruelling case and was about to savour the luxury of a few days off.

But there could be no lying in bed tomorrow morning, he must get to the supermarket before the aisles got too crowded. There was never any way of knowing when he would find himself involved in another marathon stint, so his first thought in these breaks always was to restock his larder, invariably depleted at the close of a protracted assignment.

And he was up betimes next morning. In the supermarket he loaded his trolley with his old reliable standbys: cans of soup, spaghetti, baked beans, corned beef, ravioli, meatballs, stews. Anything that could be ready to eat in five minutes flat from the moment of putting his key into the front door, or even, in extreme fatigue, consumed cold, with a spoon, straight from the can. He had given up laying in a fancy assortment of frozen dishes. In hunger and exhaustion it was only too easy to make mistakes with a microwave, but, half dead or not, he always knew where he was with a can-opener.

Last of all, he added to his trolley a vast supply of that most essential of commodities: indigestion tablets.

He went through the check-out, stowed his purchases in the boot of his car and returned his trolley to its rightful place. As he was walking back to his car again, he spotted the Elmhurst station wagon turning into the car park, with Gosling at the wheel. Beside him, Dorothy Nevett sat staring out with a look of anxiety, as if lost in her own thoughts. Kelsey had known them both since the day he had first walked in through the Elmhurst gates

73

as a boy of eight, a cadet in a church lads' brigade, looking for any odd job within his powers, to earn a few shillings to swell the brigade funds.

He walked across to where Gosling was pulling up. They both caught sight of him as he approached, they looked pleased to see him. After some initial chat, he inquired after Mrs Dalton. Busy as he was these days, he called to see Grace at least once or twice a year. If anything to do with Elmhurst cropped up in the line of duty, he made a point of dealing with it himself. In Grace's more active days, he had regularly come across her when she had served as a magistrate.

Dorothy told him about the birthday celebrations in two weeks' time. 'I'd like to call in to offer my good wishes,' Kelsey said. 'I'll look in a day or two before. I'll give you a ring first, to check it's OK.'

'And be sure to call in to see my father-in-law, while you're about it,' Gosling chipped in. 'Nothing the old man would like better than a chat with you.' Kelsey told him he wouldn't forget.

'How's Jean Redfern these days?' he went on to ask. He had been a young constable when Jean was born; he had seen her grow up. 'I take it she's still at Elmhurst?'

Dorothy gave a vigorous nod. 'She certainly is.' She slanted at the Chief a glance full of meaning. 'That good for nothing boyfriend of hers is back. Shaun Chapman. I've seen him round the town. You remember the fuss there was a few years back, when Jean wanted to marry him.'

Indeed, the Chief did remember. Mrs Dalton had asked him to look into the lad's background. He hadn't come up with anything very terrible—or particularly reassuring. The Chapmans lived on a Cannonbridge council estate; Shaun was the eldest of several children. The father had never been in trouble with the law but neither could be be described as a pillar of society. He was fond of a drink, never held a job down for long. His wife did occasional cleaning.

'I'm positive Jean's seeing him again,' Dorothy averred with conviction, 'though she swears she isn't. She's going out more in the evenings, all dolled up. She says it's with girlfriends, but I'll lay good money it's not.'

'Does Mrs Dalton know she's seeing

75

Shaun?' Kelsey asked.

She shook her head. 'I haven't said anything yet, I don't want to worry her. But I may have to say something if it goes on, she's got a right to know.'

Kelsey changed the subject. 'How's your friend Alice?' he asked with a smile. Once, in his early days at Elmhurst, when Dorothy was a young woman, he'd been sent up to her room with a message and he'd noticed Alice's photograph, prominently displayed. 'That's my friend, Alice Upjohn,' Dorothy had informed him in a tone of possessive affection. She had shown him other photographs, she had told him about her friendship with Alice, going right back to infancy. From time to time after that he would inquire after Alice and Dorothy would reply with a fond smile, giving him the latest tit-bit of information, showing him the latest snapshots.

Today, however, Dorothy gave him no answering smile, supplied no tit-bit of news but merely replied: 'She's very well, thank you,' and left it at that.

Not content with his supermarket foray, Chief Inspector Kelsey spent part of Saturday afternoon shopping for more personal items in a department store in the centre of Cannonbridge. He left the store just before five-thirty, bound for the car park.

As he made his way along the crowded pavement, a bus pulled up a little way ahead. He saw Jean Redfern jump off the bus into the arms of a young man waiting at the stop. The Chief was briefly halted by the press of folk. The pair turned his way and came past him, arms round each other's waists, laughing, chatting; they didn't see him.

Jean looked flushed and pretty. The young man was tall and loose-limbed, undeniably good-looking. Three years older than when the Chief had last set eyes on him, but there could be no mistaking his identity: Shaun Chapman.

On Monday evening, as time drew near for her phone call to Alice, Dorothy Nevett kept a watchful eye on the clock. She didn't want to use the phone in the front hall, which was far from private, so at 7.40, with Mrs Dalton nicely settled after supper and Jean Redfern absorbed in her TV soap opera, she went silently up the back stairs to the room Jean used as an office, next door to her bedroom. She was careful to close the door properly behind her—she had said nothing to Jean about using the office.

The instant her watch showed 7.45, she tapped out Alice's number. The receiver at the other end was snatched up at the first ring.

'Dorothy?' Alice's voice was brittle with tension.

'It's all right,' Dorothy swiftly reassured her. 'You can tell the solicitor the answer's yes. We're definitely buying the cottage.'

When Chief Inspector Kelsey had been back at work a week, he managed to arrange himself a few hours off on the Tuesday morning. The weather was spring-like as he turned his car in through the tall wrought iron gates of Elmhurst. The grassy banks bordering the drive were thickly clustered with daffodils, starred with primroses.

He had taken time and care to select a suitable birthday card and gifts, deciding at last in favour of a decorative basket of fruit and a box of Grace's favourite Elvas plums.

As he pulled up by the house, he

saw Gosling walking along a path with his father-in-law; they waved a greeting. The old man was leaning on a stick but he looked hale enough, with a bright eye and a fresh complexion. Kelsey went across to speak to them, promising to call in at the cottage after his visit to Mrs Dalton.

He was admitted to the house by Mrs Gosling. Kelsey had always liked her. When he first walked in through the Elmhurst gates she had been a young girl, working in the house. She had always been kind and friendly, had often slipped him some little treat from the kitchen. He stood chatting to her now for a minute or two before she took him along to Mrs Dalton's room.

Grace was pleased to see him. She had been working on a piece of embroidery but put it aside as he came in. She lay on the sofa, propped up against cushions. She looked handsome and elegant in the ruby-coloured velvet housecoat Nina and Matthew had given her for Christmas.

She received the Chief's congratulations and good wishes, his card and gifts with expressions of pleasure. 'It's lovely to see old friends,' she said with a warm smile.

'We've known each other a good many years now.' She looked back for a moment at the old days, when the Chief was a bare-kneed lad weeding beds and borders for his shilling, picking up windfalls in the orchard. Bernard Dalton's first wife had still been alive in those days, still mistress of Elmhurst. Grace had been Bernard's personal assistant, she was often at the house. The two women had been the same age, they had always been on good terms.

'Not many old friends left now,' Grace added with a tiny sigh. Over the last few years the old vicar had retired and gone elsewhere to live. There was no vicar now in the parish which had been amalgamated with others, currently in the care of a very much younger man, a very different kind of cleric from his predecessor. 'I fear I don't see eye to eye with him on many aspects of the church,' Grace said with a regretful shake of her head. What with that and her poor state of health, she no longer attended services.

She still missed the old solicitor who had died three years ago but she was getting used to his son. She had been delighted to see Dr Wheatley again. 'Not that I've anything against Dr Surridge,' she was quick to add. 'I have a lot of faith in him.' She looked up at Kelsey. 'It's a hard lesson to learn, but you have to accept change, you can't be continually harking back.' She smiled slightly. 'You can't afford sadness as you get older, it's a debilitating emotion.'

She rang through to the kitchen for coffee and Jean Redfern brought it along without delay. She looked as quiet and self-effacing as the Chief had always known her at Elmhurst—not at all the lively, smiling girl he had seen ten days ago, jumping off the bus into Shaun Chapman's arms. He exchanged a few words with her; she replied in her usual demure fashion.

When she had gone and they sat drinking their coffee—decaffeinated for Grace—the Chief asked if Barry and Verity were expected at the birthday celebrations. Yes, they were, Grace was happy to tell him. They would be coming a little ahead of the others, the arrivals were being spaced as far as was practical, to avoid undue excitement for the invalid.

'They're both doing well at their studies,'

Grace commented. 'Verity's in a little flat of her own now, she seems happy there.' When Verity had first decided to take a course at the college, it was Esther Milroy—at Grace's request—who had arranged for Verity to share a flat with two older girls, also students at the college—sensible girls, known to Esther; both came from families active in the church Esther attended. They could be relied on to keep an eye on Verity. 'But she's got to the stage when she wants to be more independent,' Grace observed. 'I have to be pleased at that, when I remember what she was like when she first came here, so nervy and withdrawn.'

She glanced at the array of family photographs on a nearby side table. Among them was the face of her schoolmaster father who had been in his last years a senior history master when Kelsey attended the Cannonbridge Grammar School. The Chief remembered him with respect and affection; a scholarly man, dedicated to his subject, his profession. On the mantelshelf stood a handsome clock presented to him on his retirement; Kelsey had been among those who had subscribed to it. Some years later he had been among the former pupils who had attended his funeral.

On either side of the hearth hung a pair of watercolours Kelsey had always admired. The one on the left had belonged to Grace's father; it showed the old part of Cannonbridge, including the grammar school. The other was a view of Elmhurst, painted shortly after the house was built.

Grace nodded at a photograph of two young men, very alike, with sharply intelligent good looks. 'Esther's sons can't be here for my birthday, of course,' she said on a note of regret. 'They both came to see me when they were last at home. They're doing exceptionally well. They're ambitious and hard-working, like their father.' She grimaced. 'Just as well they didn't take after their mother or they'd probably both be sitting around, waiting for someone to organize their lives.' She half smiled. 'If I'd had a daughter I'd have wanted her to be like Nina.' She looked up at Kelsey. 'She came from a very ordinary background, you know, though you'd never think it. Everything was done very quickly when Matthew decided to marry her. We never met her parents, she never produced them. She gave us to understand her father had retired early from business because of ill health, and her mother was a shy woman; they went about very little.' She moved her hand. 'Bernard had discreet inquiries made. It turned out they were small shopkeepers, not retired at all, both of them working long hours for a modest living. Very respectable, decent, honest folk.'

She smiled slightly. 'I never let on to Nina that we'd been so nosey. I could well understand why she'd said what she said. I liked her from the start, I always knew she was right for Matthew.' She gave a decisive little nod. 'Best thing he ever did, marrying Nina.' She was silent for a moment. 'I've often felt sorry for James, married to a nervy wife.' She expelled a little breath. 'Poor Esther, she does try so hard to please. She comes to see me regularly but I find her visits rather depressing, she will fuss over me.'

She went on to talk about the new hospice, how devotedly everyone was striving to raise money. The Chief told her he had every intention of seeing the foundation stone laid. 'It will have to be something pretty cataclysmic to keep me away,' he assured her.

'It would be lovely if I could be there myself,' she said. 'But if not, I can listen to it on the local radio. And I can see it on regional TV in the evening.'

'I'll hope to see you at the ceremony then.' The Chief glanced at the clock, mindful that he mustn't tire her. They went on chatting for a little longer, then he rose to leave. He stooped to kiss her cheek.

'If either one of us doesn't make it to the ceremony,' Grace said, 'do come and see me again when you can.' She smiled up at him. 'Better not leave it too long.'

On Tuesday evening, when Grace had been settled down for the night, Dorothy Nevett was crossing the hall when the phone rang. She answered it and heard Alice's voice. She stood listening intently, putting in a question or two. 'You're not to worry about it,' she said at last. 'Leave it to me, I'll think of something.' When she replaced the receiver she stood looking down at the floor, frowning, thinking, thrusting out her lips. Then she moved slowly off through the hall and up the stairs to her room.

CHAPTER 8

On Wednesday morning, Dorothy Nevett, with Mrs Gosling in tow, busied herself with the preparation of bedrooms, in readiness for the weekend visitors. Esther and James would have the large, twin-bedded room at the front of the house, across the landing from the best bed-room—the one occupied by Mrs Dalton until her illness, and now no longer used. Nina would require only a single room as Matthew wouldn't be staying the night. He would arrive towards the end of Saturday afternoon and would leave again after the birthday dinner, to drive back home. He was one of the organizers of a charity golf tournament to be held on the Sunday morning, in aid of the new hospice and would be playing in the tournament himself. James was also taking part in the tournament but as he wasn't involved in the organizing and wouldn't be playing in any of the early matches, he had no need to hurry back to Brentworth and would be staying the night at Elmhurst.

Verity could occupy a single room near Jean Redfern's bedroom. There was never any need to ponder about where to put Barry: around the corner from Jean's room, along a passage, in the snug little room he had always had, from the very first night he had ever slept at Elmhurst. He was fond of the room and looked on it by now as his own. He would have been astonished and dismayed to find some interloper installed in his place and himself banished to other quarters. Not that Dorothy would dream of playing any such trick on him. She had always had a soft spot for Barry who had been unfailingly considerate and well-mannered towards her, even as a young boy, stunned by his father's death.

Verity was another matter entirely. She had certainly been subdued enough when she first came to Elmhurst but Dorothy had felt from the start there was a volcano simmering away deep down inside, waiting to erupt. She had always struck Dorothy as someone who might, under the thrust of events and emotions, be capable of almost anything.

At eleven-thirty on Thursday morning, Dr

Wheatley called to check that all was well with Grace, in readiness for the birthday celebrations. He brought with him his card and birthday gift, a handsome Welsh knee-rug, gorgeously coloured.

During the afternoon, Jean washed and set Grace's hair. She had grown used to the task over the last two years and took pride in achieving an ever more pleasing result. She had early on got Grace to agree to the purchase of a salon-type hairdryer and now went about the operation with almost professional expertise.

The first guests to arrive were Verity and Barry, on Friday afternoon. They went along separately to see Grace and have a chat, leaving an interval between their visits, mindful of the need not to tire her.

The early evening brought Esther on her own; James would be arriving on Saturday afternoon. She had a chat with Grace before supper. Later, when Verity and Barry were sitting together, absorbed in their own conversation, Esther wandered off to the old playroom, where so many hours of her childhood had been spent. The room was large, furnished with cupboard, shelves and drawers. It looked out over the garden, at the rear of the house.

The last children to use it had been Verity and Barry. The only use made of it in more recent years was as a green room at Christmas and other domestic festivals when it had always been an Elmhurst tradition to play charades, get up playlets or revue-type shows. Everyone, servants and all, had been pressed into these productions.

There had been none of these entertainments since Grace's illness, but the big dressing-up chest was still there, with garments belonging to Daltons dead and gone. A roomy cupboard still housed an assortment of items useful as props.

Esther opened the cupboard and glanced over the shelves. She lifted the lid of the chest, fingered the contents. She crossed to the rows of bookshelves. One shelf held old bound copies of magazines. She took down a volume and went over to a window seat. She sat slowly turning the pages, sunk in thought.

Saturday morning was bright and calm, crisply invigorating. After an early breakfast, Matthew Dalton went off to his office. Nina put her bag in her car for the overnight stay at Elmhurst and drove over to the Dalton cottage. She wore old casual clothing; her hair was tied up in a scarf, in readiness for whatever jobs might present themselves, indoors or out.

The Dalton cottage stood some twenty yards along a twisting lane. Nina didn't immediately halt there but drove on, as she always did, for another quarter of a mile along the lane, to the nearest dwelling, the Ayliffes' cottage, in order to have a word with Mrs Ayliffe. She was a competent, good-natured woman whose children were now grown up, out in the world. She was happy to keep an eye on the Dalton cottage, putting in an hour or two at cleaning or other household tasks that might be required; her husband had helped with the garden restoration and he also carried out repairs and maintenance.

A few minutes later, Nina drove back down the lane to the Dalton cottage. She must remember to watch the time. She was expected for lunch at Elmhurst, she must allow herself time beforehand to wash and change, look in on Grace.

Over at Elmhurst, Grace's birthday celebrations had begun. The mail had been delivered, the florist's van had called.

After a late breakfast, Grace reclined on her sofa to receive the good wishes of her household. She was delighted with all their offerings and had them set out by Jean on side tables where they might be seen to advantage, admired at leisure. Esther had brought with her the cards and presents chosen by her sons when last they were home.

Then it was time for Grace's rest and she was left in peace and quiet to enjoy a little nap.

Near the centre of Cannonbridge, Saturday morning shopping was severely disrupted as workmen dealt with a burst watermain. In the offices of Purvis, the solicitor, the windows were closed tight against the sound of the drills, but still the vibrating racket penetrated every crevice of the building. In the middle of the morning a phone rang in the outer office. Purvis's secretary picked up the receiver and held it close to her ear, clapping a hand over the other ear in an attempt to shut out the insistent din. She was able after a few moments to make out that it was Mrs Dalton calling from Elmhurst. She apologized for the noisy background and asked Mrs Dalton if she would be kind enough to speak more loudly.

Amid fresh bursts of drilling she managed to discover that Mrs Dalton would like Mr Purvis to call on her. There was no immediate hurry; the middle or later part of next week would do. During a brief and blessed pause in the reverberating tattoo, an appointment was finally made for eleven-thirty on Wednesday morning.

Nina arrived at Elmhurst in good time to smarten up for her visit to Grace. She had brought with her only a token gift, a box of handmade chocolates from the best confectioner in the country. Matthew would be bringing their joint present in his larger car: a fine Victorian canterbury, to stand by Grace's sofa.

Grace didn't join the rest of them for lunch but ate alone in the quiet of her room. Nina conducted a lively conversation with Verity and Barry over the meal. Esther's hesitant, low-voiced contributions were as often as not lost in the light-hearted interchanges of the others, the happy wash of their laughter.

Grace woke refreshed from her nap before

James arrived. He went along to see her but was careful not to stay too long. It was almost five by the time Matthew reached Elmhurst. Esther was wandering about in the darkening garden when she saw his car coming along the drive; she went across to intercept him. She stood talking as he carefully lifted out the canterbury. She ran a hand over the silky wood. 'It's beautiful,' she said. 'Grace will love it.'

Mrs Gosling had heard the car and appeared now at the front door, looking out at the two of them standing with their heads together. Maybe they did take after different sides of the family, she thought, and maybe they were very different in temperament. But for all that and in spite of the five-year gap between them, they had always been deeply attached. And of all the folk assembled at Elmhurst at this moment, she reflected, they were the only two closely related by blood. And blood's a good deal thicker than water, Mrs Gosling added to herself with a little jerk of her head. Always has been and always will be.

There would be no sitting up late for Grace, birthday or no birthday; dinner would be served at seven. She took an extra nap by way of precaution before Jean came along to help her get ready for the evening.

She felt happy and tranquil as Jean assisted her into her long-sleeved dress of lightweight wool in a becoming shade of slate-blue; it had a long back zip for ease in changing. At the corners of the square-cut neckline she wore the diamond clips Bernard had given her on their tenth wedding anniversary.

Jean gave her a light make-up and dressed her hair with special care, adding the diamond-studded tortoishell combs that had been Bernard's last Christmas present. Grace put on the diamond bracelet Bernard had given her, diamond earrings, another gift from him; on her fingers she wore her wedding and engagement rings, with other rings he had chosen to mark other anniversaries.

When she was ready, Matthew came along to escort her to the drawing room where drinks were to be served. Grace looked splendidly regal as she entered on his arm. Almost like the old, spacious days, when Bernard was alive, James Milroy thought, looking round at the scene. He glanced up at the large portrait of Bernard that hung to the left of the fireplace. To the right, Bernard's father gazed out from another ornate gilt frame; Bernard's grandfather had pride of place above the mantelpiece. It was the same face in all three portraits, James reflected: shrewd, unsmiling, disciplined, all three pairs of eyes meeting his own with the same expression, resolute and uncompromising.

James turned his head and glanced across at his brother-in-law who was talking to Grace with animation and a look of smiling affection. Matthew's countenance was clearly cast in the same mould as the three Dalton men who had gone before him, but the lines were less sharp, blurred by good living, nor did he wear the same air of steely purpose.

How dearly James would have loved to have been born into such a family, such a home. And how casually Matthew had always seemed to regard the fortunate position fate had allotted him at birth, how much he had always taken it for granted. James had done what he could to redress the balance, but he had known all along that the solid and enduring advantages of birth and background cannot be duplicated in any other way.

On the stroke of seven, they all moved into the dining room. The table looked superb, glittering with silver and crystal. Gosling had surpassed himself with the flowers, beautifully arranged by his wife and Jean. The food was delicious but in no way rich, to avoid any possibility of upset for Grace. At the end of the meal Matthew made a graceful little speech, in loving tribute to Grace, proposing a toast. Grace remained seated as she spoke a few words in reply, thanking them all, her eyes bright with tears.

They adjourned to the drawing room for coffee, liqueurs and brandy, an assortment of confections, but Grace didn't stay long. When she said good night, Matthew gave her an affectionate farewell kiss on the cheek. He would be leaving almost at once for his drive back to Brentworth. Nina and Jean took Grace off to her bedroom. A few minutes later, when Matthew left the house, Esther walked out with him to his car.

In Grace's bedrooom Nina and Jean helped her prepare for bed. She put on the new nightdress and negligée, admiring them yet again. Jean removed the combs from her hair, took down the tresses and brushed them, plaiting them neatly for the night.

Nina assisted her across to the bed. Jean removed the negligée and laid it over a chair. They helped Grace into bed and propped her comfortably up, arranging the pillows behind her with care. Nina fetched Grace's sleeping pill from the bathroom cabinet, then she checked that the patio doors were locked and bolted. Jean carried the vases and bowls of flowers out of the room for the night.

As Nina stooped to bestow a good night kiss she saw that Grace was almost asleep. Nina turned in the doorway to put out the lights, leaving on Grace's customary night-light, a low-wattage electric lamp standing on a bedside table. Grace's eyes were closed, she was breathing deeply. Nina drew the door to. It was never now completely closed at night but left slightly ajar by means of a small wooden wedge, so that Dorothy Nevett might glance in on her way to bed, to make sure all was well, without disturbing Grace.

At eight-thirty on Sunday morning, Dorothy

made a start on breakfast preparations and Jean began her round of the bedrooms. Tea for everyone except Verity and Barry. Freshly-squeezed orange juice for Verity. That was what had always greeted her day in Africa, what she still liked, a frail link with that long-ago past. Barry never took anything at all. He had never been accustomed to it at home and it was certainly not the practice at his boarding school to waken pupils with bedside beverages.

Jean delivered first Verity's orange juice, to get that out of the way. Then back to the kitchen for Nina's tea; back again for the cups for Esther and James. At every call she gave a single light tap on the door, entering at once without waiting for an answer. She would then cross to the window, draw the curtains back a little, set down her offering on a bedside table with a murmured good morning and leave the room again.

She returned to the kitchen once more, for Mrs Dalton's tea, specially made by Dorothy, who always timed it so that it was just right when she poured it out. Jean placed the cup and saucer on a tray with a small plate holding the single digestive biscuit Grace always liked.

With Mrs Dalton, Jean's drill varied somewhat. She didn't leave the bedroom when she had set down her offering but made a little more noise, speaking Mrs Dalton's name. When Grace was roused, Jean would help her into a more upright position, inquire how she was, what kind of a night she had had. She would then hand her her tea. Before leaving the room she always asked if there was anything else Grace needed.

When Jean had left the kitchen, carrying Mrs Dalton's tray, Dorothy remained standing by the table, her head tilted back, her eyes closed. It was so quiet everywhere. A little birdsong from the garden, faint sounds of movement inside the house.

A sudden burst of running feet, from the direction of Mrs Dalton's room, broke the calm. Jean ran back into the kitchen, empty handed, sobbing, her face ashen. 'Mrs Dalton!' she gasped as she collapsed into a chair and buried her face in her hands, her shoulders heaving.

Dorothy didn't stay to ask questions but went at once with all speed along to Mrs Dalton's room. The door stood wide open.

The night-light was still on, the curtains half drawn back. The tray had been set down on a bedside table; nothing on it had been disturbed.

Grace reclined in her customary position. She looked peaceful, sound asleep.

'Mrs Dalton,' Dorothy said. There was no response. 'Mrs Dalton!' she said again, more urgently. And a third time, louder still. No response. She laid her fingers on Grace's forehead. She could feel no warmth. She raised Grace's eyelid. The eye stared fixedly out. She turned back the bedclothes and picked up Grace's hand. She could find no pulse.

She placed a hand on Grace's chest but could detect no heartbeat.

CHAPTER 9

As Dr Wheatley came out of Grace's bedroom, he moved the wooden wedge aside with his foot and closed the door behind him.

Esther waited nearby. She had phoned Matthew to break the news and he was now on his way back to Elmhurst. Nina and James stood together, a little farther along the corridor, and beyond them, Verity and Barry, side by side. Out of sight from the corridor, Dorothy Nevett, flanked by Mrs Gosling and Jean, stood by the kitchen doorway, straining their ears to interpret what was happening, from distant sounds.

'I don't believe Grace in any way overdid things yesterday,' Dr Wheatley told Esther reassuringly. 'I'm sure you all took every care. I've seen this happen more than once. A patient keeps going for some special event, then lets go when it's over, just slips away. I'm sure Grace had a peaceful end. She would have gone to sleep very happy, she would have known nothing about it. Her heart simply stopped beating.'

Smethurst's was the largest firm of undertakers in Cannonbridge, long established. They had handled the funeral of Bernard Dalton as they had handled that of his first wife, his father and grandfather; now they were to handle Grace's funeral. She had made her wishes known; her funeral was to bc as quiet and modest as possible. She would lie beside her husband in the village churchyard.

It was Esther who was making all the decisions. She had taken command of the situation from the moment Dorothy Nevett had interrupted her cup of tea in bed with the news of Grace's death. Gone now was her habitual nerviness and hesitation. She appeared stimulated and emboldened, behaving as if she were now the mistress of Elmhurst. Dorothy had expected Nina, as wife of the son of the house, to take charge until Matthew returned, but Nina had made no such attempt. She showed neither resentment nor opposition at the way Esther had assumed command, but went along with all Esther's proposals with no more than an occasional glance of surprise at her sister-in-law's changed demeanour. Nor did Matthew, when he got back, try to take over from Esther or alter anything she had decided.

Esther looks a different woman, Mrs Gosling thought in some amazement; she looks miles better, she's quite perked up. Mrs Gosling had always had a pretty shrewd notion of the way Ester had felt about her father's second marriage, but she would never have credited such a rapid transformation.

And the way she was behaving towards Nina, not inviting her opinion on anything, treating her quite brusquely, with a sort of triumphant air, as if there had been a great deal of resentment of her sister-in-law's looks, and talents smouldering away for years, and now all at once she felt herself top dog, no need to take second place any more. Even her manner towards her husband had altered, Mrs Gosling reflected. Esther had always deferred to James, always played the dutiful, obedient wife. But now she was organizing and arranging without any reference to James; her only consultations were with her brother.

Esther had announced her intention of staying on at Elmhurst for the present, at least until after the funeral. She would see to everything; there was no need for any of the others to remain, they all had obligations elsewhere. They would, of course, all be returning for the funeral. The date hadn't yet been decided but Esther wanted it to be as soon as possible. Grace had made it clear to Esther and James some time ago that if she were to die while their sons were abroad, she wouldn't wish them to be summoned home for the funeral.

Knowing Grace's opinion of the new vicar, Dr Wheatley had suggested inviting the old vicar to officiate at the burial service, and Esther had at once agreed. She would get in touch with him right away, she was certain he would come.

Something else had surprised Mrs Gosling: the speed with which Esther had dispatched Grace's body from the house. She had got on to the undertaker even before Matthew returned. Her brother had scarcely had time to go along to Grace's bedroom to spend a few minutes alone with her in farewell before Smethurst's men were at the door.

Mrs Brodribb was a widow, a retired district nurse, one of a small team of women employed on a casual basis by Smethurt's for laying-out work. She lived alone, not far from the funeral parlour; she never had any objection to working outside usual hours. A spell of duty helped to relieve the monotony and loneliness, and the money was always welcome.

She had a phone call from Smethurst's in the middle of Sunday morning. 'I'm sorry to hear that!' she exclaimed with a genuine rush of emotion when she was told it was Mrs Dalton who had died. Mrs Brodribb was Cannonbridge born and bred. Her father had spent his whole working life at Dalton's. Her husband had been a pupil at the grammar school when Mrs Dalton's father was a master there. She supported several charities Mrs Dalton had worked for and had come into contact with her on many occasions over the years.

When she reached the funeral parlour she approached her task with particular diligence and solicitude, conscious of performing a last service for a lady she had greatly admired. She set about removing the nightdress Mrs Dalton was wearing. Such beautiful quality, so pretty, with its pattern of rosebuds; it looked brand new. She unbuttoned the long front opening with its lavish, jabot-like trimming. She eased the garment carefully off, turning it inside out in the process. She began to turn it right side out again, intending to fold it and lay it aside to be returned to the family.

She froze suddenly. She frowned, gazed intently down. The inside of the nightdress was plain white, unpatterned. What she was staring at was a bead of dried blood, at the base of the front opening.

She turned back to the body, reached down and delicately raised the left breast. She stooped and peered closely down.

No doubt whatever. A puncture mark, plainly visible, with a tiny rim of dried blood.

CHAPTER 10

The postmortem examination of Grace Veronica Dalton took place on Monday morning, at the Cannonbridge General Hospital. Dr Wheatley finished his round of calls in time to be at the hospital before the postmortem ended. He stationed himself in the corridor nearby. When at last the door opened and the pathologist emerged, followed by Chief Inspector Kelsey, Dr Wheatley went forward to meet them. He looked anxious and harassed, every day of his age, and more.

'No question about it,' the pathologist told him. 'It was definitely murder.' Neatly and carefully done, the instrument in all probability a hatpin. He saw the look on Dr Wheatley's face. 'You mustn't blame yourself for not spotting it,' he said with compassion. 'Knowing the patient's history, you had no reason to suspect anything.'

Before leaving for Elmhurst, the Chief rang Grace Dalton's solicitor, with whom he had some slight acquaintance. Purvis made a swift reappraisal of his appointments for the rest of the day. Yes, he could see the Chief in forty minutes, he could spare him half an hour.

The Chief set off at once for Elmhurst, with Detective Sergeant Lambert driving. No one had left the house; they were all awaiting the autopsy results.

The Chief spoke to Matthew and Esther together, giving them the findings. He had encountered the brother and sister only very rarely since they had left home, but he had come across them now and then over the years in photographs Grace had shown him, taken at family gatherings. It was no surprise, therefore, to see that Matthew had put on weight and that Esther had lost her looks—though she seemed not at all the nervy creature he had expected, from the way Grace had talked of her; she seemed calm and self-possessed.

They both received the Chief's report in silence, with no appearance of surprise—it was, after all, what they could only have been expecting, after the Chief's visit yesterday. During that visit the Chief had made a tour of the house but could find no sign of any break-in. Nothing had been stolen. Grace's birthday presents lay undisturbed on the side tables in her bedroom. He had taken the precaution of sealing the room.

He explained now that he must leave again at once, for an appointment, but he would return immediately afterwards; he didn't tell them the appointment was with Grace's solicitor.

He found Purvis still in a state of shock—not over Mrs Dalton's death, as he had been prepared for that for some time, but over the undeniable fact of her murder. And the equally undeniable fact that the only reason he could think of for her murder was that the killer would receive financial benefit by her death. From the release of trust funds, perhaps. Or a legacy under Mrs Dalton's will. Or, of course, from both.

'I don't know if you're aware,' Purvis said as the two policemen took their seats, facing him across his desk, 'that Mrs Dalton had made an appointment to see me. I was to go out to Elmhurst for eleven-thirty on Wednesday morning.'

'No, I wasn't aware of that,' the Chief replied sharply. 'Do you know why she wanted to see you?'

'It seems she intended to make some alteration to her will. I didn't speak to her myself. My secretary took the call.'

'Did Mrs Dalton often make alterations to her will?'

Purvis shook his head. 'She made this last will two years ago, she made no alteration to it since.' Purvis had been appointed sole executor.

He summoned his secretary and the Chief took her through her telephone conversation with Mrs Dalton. The secretary explained about the road drilling, the difficulty in hearing what was said. But she was certain Mrs Dalton hadn't said which part of her will she wished to alter, nor had she mentioned any names.

Was it one or more than one alteration Mrs Dalton had contemplated? The secretary wrinkled her brow in an effort to

109

remember. She rather thought Mrs Dalton had referred to 'an alteration' but she couldn't now be certain. No, Mrs Dalton hadn't sounded in any way agitated or distressed.

I wonder why Grace didn't get Jean Redfern to ring up to make the appointment, Kelsey thought as the secretary left the room again. Could it have been because the alteration concerned Jean herself and she didn't wish the girl to know of it?

He asked what the situation was now, in relation not only to Mrs Dalton's will, but also to the trust fund set up by her husband.

'The capital sum set aside under the trust to provide Mrs Dalton with an income is now released,' Purvis told him. So also was the house and its surrounding acres, together with the weekend cottage, the Elmhurst furnishings and equipment of all kinds, all paintings and *objets d'art*. The main property would now undoubtedly be sold for development. The proceeds of the sale, together with the released capital sum, would go to Matthew, Esther and Verity, the lion's share being split equally between Matthew and Esther; the remainder—considerably smaller but still certain to prove a very substantial sum—going to Verity, though she wouldn't receive her full share for some time. She would initially receive only a modest amount. The rest would be paid over in two unequal instalments, the smaller when she reached the age of twenty-one and the larger at twenty-five. The trust would continue to pay all her fees and living expenses until her education was finished.

Barry Fielding's position under the trust would in no way be altered by Mrs Dalton's death. The trust would continue to support him until his education was completed. He would then receive a modest capital sum to start him out and that would be that. When the trust had discharged its obligations to both youngsters it would be wound up, any remaining monies going to a named charity.

There had never been any provision under the trust for Jean Redfern. At the time of Bernard Dalton's death, Jean had merely been the fourteen-year-old daughter of a household servant. Bernard considered he had done well enough by the girl in providing her with free board and lodging since her birth. And Jean's mother had not yet taken herself off to America.

Purvis then turned to the matter of Mrs Dalton's will. Her estate wouldn't bear comparison with the size of the trust fund but it was nevertheless very substantial, looked at from a more everyday viewpoint. As well as the income she had received from the trust, Grace had been left a sizeable capital sum outright by Bernard. She had also inherited her father's house and savings, a year or two before her marriage. By shrewd investment she had considerably increased these inheritances.

She had left a generous sum for the new Cannonbridge hospice and she had made a number of minor bequests: to various churches and charities, to old friends and distant relatives, to Gosling and his wife. There were token legacies for Esther's two sons and for Barry Fielding; even the two garden lads had not been forgotten. Money had been set aside to provide the pension and lump sum for Dorothy Nevett, as agreed with the housekeeper two years ago.

Nor had Mrs Dalton forgotten Jean Redfern. She had left the girl enough to buy herself a small flat, provide her with some training and start her out in life.

Grace had owned a quantity of valuable

jewellery, given to her by her husband. She had looked on it as family property belonging to the Daltons, and had left it to be divided between Esther, Nina and Verity, specifying which pieces should be allotted to each, in an effort to make as equal a division as possible. Verity's share of the jewellery would not be handed over to her until she reached the age of twenty-one.

The rest of Grace's personal effects went to Nina. The remainder of her estate, amounting roughly to two-fifths of the whole, she left to Verity, to be paid over in three equal instalments: the first right away, the second at twenty-one, the third at twenty-five.

The Chief asked if the contents of Mrs Dalton's will had been known to her chief beneficiaries. Certainly Dorothy Nevett had known, Purvis told him. He was equally certain that neither Verity nor Jean Redfern had known. Mrs Dalton had specifically told him she didn't wish either girl to know; she had felt the knowledge might weaken their resolve to work towards their own independence.

The Chief asked the same question with regard to the Dalton trust. How far were all its terms known to those affected by the trust? He was told the trust terms were known to all those affected by the trust, including Verity and Barry.

Had Purvis any clue as to what kind of alteration to her will Mrs Dalton might have been contemplating?

'One or two thoughts come to mind,' Purvis said. 'I very much doubt it would have been an alteration to any of the minor bequests—I can't see Mrs Dalton troubling herself with that in the middle of a family gathering. And I don't see her changing her mind about the disposition of the jewellery, nor about leaving her personal effects to Nina. I can't see how she could alter what she was leaving to Dorothy Nevett, that had been agreed between them.'

He put the tips of his fingers together. 'That leaves the bequests to Jean Redfern and Verity. It could have been either—or both—of those girls she was thinking about. She would be at perfect liberty to reduce or cancel the bequest to Verity. She was under no kind of legal or moral obligation to provide for her, and Verity is in any case amply provided for under the trust. It could be, of course, that Mrs Dalton had been thinking things over and decided it might be wiser to delay the paying out of the first instalment of the bequest till Verity was twenty-one, or even delay paying out any part of the bequest till Verity was twenty-five.

'The situation with regard to Jean Redfern is somewhat different,' Purvis went on. 'During the last few years Mrs Dalton had more or less made herself responsible for Jean, and the girl is not provided for from any other source. If Mrs Dalton simply struck out the bequest and the matter later went to court, I feel sure the court would take the view that the girl had some entitlement as a dependant and would probably reinstate the original bequest—the figure is not an unreasonable one. But I could never see the matter getting to court. The family wouldn't want it and I think all of them would agree Mrs Dalton had some responsibility for the girl. Certainly my advice would be to settle.'

He levelled a glance at the Chief. 'Mrs Dalton would be aware of all these points, so I'm pretty sure she wouldn't be thinking of cancelling the bequest to Jean. But she may have been thinking of revising the actual amount. Possibly downward, but I think far more likely to be upward; I know she felt Jean had given her devoted service since her illness.'

Had Mrs Dalton been aware that Shaun Chapman was back in the area and that Jean had been seeing him?

Purvis looked surprised. 'I've no idea if she knew or not,' he replied. 'She made no mention of it to me. I knew nothing of it myself.' He paused. 'But if she did know about it, she might very well have wanted to ask me to suggest some way of letting Jean benefit without giving her full control over the money, to prevent anyone else laying hands on it—in so far as such a thing is ever possible.' He grimaced. 'Not very easily done, in my experience.'

'Then, as matters stand now,' Kelsey said, 'Jean is free to do exactly as she likes with her legacy? She doesn't have to spend any of it on buying a flat or taking some training? She can hand the whole lot over to Shaun Chapman if she takes it into her head?'

'Yes, that's about the size of it,' Purvis agreed.

There was a brief silence, then Kelsey asked: 'And Verity? Do you know of any reason why Mrs Dalton might have wished to alter her bequest to Verity?'

No, Purvis didn't know of anything specific. 'But there is something I'm pretty sure Mrs Dalton wasn't aware of,' he added. 'I think it might interest you. Verity came to see me a few weeks back. She wanted to know if it would be possible for her to get some of the trust money advanced to her ahead of time.'

Kelsey sat up. 'Did she say why she wanted it?'

Purvis shook his head. 'I pressed her hard on that but she wouldn't say. I thought she might have got herself into some sort of scrape but she assured me she hadn't, she just wanted to get her hands on a good slice of capital right away. I told her it was out of the question. I read her a lecture about living within her means. If she had any genuine need for extra money, then she must approach the trustees—Mrs Dalton and myself—in the proper way, giving proper reasons. We would consider the matter and see what could be done, maybe increasing her personal spending allowance. But that was as far as we were empowered to go. We certainly wouldn't be handing over any lump sums of capital.'

And he had said nothing about all this to Mrs Dalton?

No, he had not. Verity had particularly asked him not to, but he would have said nothing in any case, he wouldn't have wanted to worry Mrs Dalton. 'Verity tried to pump me about the contents of Mrs Dalton's will,' he went on. 'Of course, I refused to tell her. I said she could try asking Mrs Dalton herself if she really wanted to know.'

'What did she say to that?'

'She pulled a face and said, "You know I can't do that. Aunt Grace would have a fit." '

But Verity's a sharp enough girl, Kelsey thought. And, it would seem, a determined one. She might very well have managed to ferret out, one way or another, what was in Grace's will. Or she might simply have guessed that she was likely to inherit substantially from Grace. She might also have convinced herself that the whole of any such legacy would come to her outright on Grace's death, and not merely some portion of it.

'Matthew and Esther,' Kelsey said. 'They stand to get a great deal of money under the trust, now that Mrs Dalton is dead. Do you know if either of them is in any urgent need for money?'

118

'Not to my knowledge,' Purvis answered. 'Matthew lives very comfortably, he always seems well-heeled. And I can't see why Esther should need money. James has done pretty well for himself. I'm sure he doesn't keep her short.'

'There's nothing wrong with Esther's marriage?'

Purvis moved his shoulders. 'Not as far as I know.' He glanced at the clock. Kelsey followed his gaze and saw that his half hour was up. He pushed back his chair.

'You might like to know,' Purvis said as he walked with the Chief to the door, 'that Mrs Dalton left you three items in her will.' The pair of watercolours Kelsey had always admired. And the clock that had belonged to Mrs Dalton's father.

CHAPTER 11

As soon as the Chief got back to Elmhurst he sought out Dorothy Nevett and Jean Redfern, to ask if Mrs Dalton had owned any hatpins. The significance of his question was not lost on either of them and they both regarded him in shocked silence for some moments. Then Jean explained shakily that most of Mrs Dalton's hats were furnished with a length of millinery elastic designed to be slipped under the hair at the back, to keep the hat in place. 'There is just one hat,' she added, 'that has a pin of its own, it's a dark blue velour.' She took the Chief upstairs to where the hats were kept, in a dressing room opening off the bedroom Mrs Dalton had formerly occupied. She opened a deep drawer and indicated the blue velour; the hatpin had a fancy, beaded end. The Chief lifted out the hat, careful not to touch the pin; he carried it downstairs by the brim.

In the meantime, Dorothy Nevett had had time to think. 'There are quite a few hatpins in the playroom, with the dressing-up clothes,' she told the Chief. She led the way along to the playroom and threw open a cupboard. The shelves were stacked with head gear of every kind: scarves, gloves, fans, handbags. A large velvet pin-cushion was stuck with hatpins of varying lengths, many with ornamental knobbed ends. The Chief lifted out the cushion without touching any of the pins; it would join the velour hat on its way to the forensic laboratory. He asked if Dorothy or Jean knew of any other hatpins anywhere else in the house, but they both shook their heads.

Shortly afterwards, general fingerprinting was carried out. When it was James Milroy's turn, he told the Chief he would like to get back to work as soon as possible; he had appointments he was anxious not to cancel. He would be happy to answer any questions but would be grateful if he could be dealt with early—right away, if possible. The Chief had no objection and they went off to the drawing room, to talk in private.

It was some time since the Chief had encountered James but he found him altered scarcely at all. The same sharply intelligent face, the same subtle look. He had kept his hair, his lean figure. The Chief took him through his movements on Saturday evening. They were very straightforward, James told him. No one had stayed up late, they were all in bed by eleven. He had gone up shortly before Esther, who had stayed talking to Nina; she had come up just as he was dropping off to sleep. The room had twin beds; he had occupied the bed by the window. He had slept soundly all night, as he always did. If anything, he had slept more heavily than usual, he had allowed himself an extra dram of the excellent Scotch whisky always kept at Elmhurst, as he didn't have to drive home. He had noticed no unusual behaviour or occurrence during the weekend.

As James stood up to go, he observed with an air of regret: 'We won't know this place by the time the developers have finished with it.' He glanced about the spacious room. 'I well remember the first time I came to Elmhurst, the first time I entered this room.' He smiled slightly. 'Very different from the home I grew up in.' He was silent for a moment. 'I'll miss coming here.' He tilted back his head and surveyed the portrait of Bernard Dalton. Bernard gazed down at him with a shrewd, uncompromising look. 'I always liked the old boy,' James said. 'I wonder what he'd make of all this.' He sighed and shook his head. 'I suppose the house will be turned into flats, it's the usual fate.' He turned to the door.

'You see the place being sold pretty quickly?' Kelsey said.

James nodded. 'As soon as maybe.' He jerked his head. 'However soon the money comes in, I doubt it'll be too soon for Matthew.' He broke off, flashing a glance at the Chief.

'Implying what?' Kelsey demanded.

'Implying nothing,' James responded lightly. 'We all like to get our hands on serious money. Matthew as well as the next man.'

'What about your wife?' Kelsey asked. 'Is she in pressing need of money?'

'Esther?' James said on an incredulous note. 'Of course she's not in pressing need of money. She has all the money she wants, always has had.'

Matthew Dalton had no appointment that couldn't be postponed but he would still like to get back to his office as soon as he could be spared. He had rung Grace's solicitor to ask for a few minutes of his time today, if it could possibly be managed. Purvis had promised to squeeze out a few minutes for him between clients. 'I want to get the gist of Grace's will,' Matthew explained to the Chief. 'Mainly to find out what the position is about Jean Redfern, she'll be anxious to know how she stands.' No, Jean hadn't raised the matter with him.

I wonder if Jean's quite as ignorant of the contents of the will as Matthew appears to believe, Kelsey thought. Jean would undoubtedly have had access to some of Grace's papers and might have made it her business to gain access to others. He remembered her, even as a small child, slipping about the house and garden like a shadow, noticing, listening, watching.

Kelsey cut short these ponderings and told Matthew he would deal with him right away, he would keep him no longer than was necessary.

He got down to brass tacks at once. He asked Matthew if he was short of money.

Matthew didn't appear taken aback or in any way put out. He gave the Chief a wry look. 'Short is hardly the word for it. It's been rough going this last twelve months and more; I've been just about hanging on by the skin of my teeth.' He paused. 'I'm sorry Grace is gone. And I'm horrified at the way she went. I've always been fond of her, always admired her. She was a wonderful wife to my father.' He moved his head. 'But there's no denying her death has just about saved my bacon.'

The Chief took him through his movements from the time he said goodbye to Grace after the birthday dinner. Matthew told him he had walked out to his car with Esther, chatting about the way the evening had gone. He had driven straight home to Brentworth and had immediately gone to his study to check over the arrangements for the golf tournament. He had watched the television news, had a bath and gone to bed. He had made no phone calls and had received none. He was about to leave for the clubhouse next morning when Esther rang to tell him Grace had died.

'How would you be getting out of your difficulties now, if Mrs Dalton was still alive?' the Chief wanted to know.

'God only knows,' Matthew replied fervently. 'I might not have been able to get out of them, I might have come a cropper in the end.' He gave the Chief a direct look. 'But I didn't kill her, for all that. I had nothing to do with her death, however convenient it is for me. I would never have wished her the slightest harm. I certainly never wished her dead.'

'Would you wish her back again now—if you had the power to bring her back?'

125

There was a brief silence. 'That's a tricky one,' Matthew said at last. 'I wouldn't know how to answer it truthfully.'

'Do you expect your share of the inheritance to put you straight?' Kelsey asked.

Matthew waved a hand. 'It'll do a good deal more than that. It should turn out a pretty hefty sum.' He half smiled. 'I promise you, I've learned my lesson, it's going to be caution and safety first all the way, from now on.' He broke off, throwing the Chief a frowning glance. 'I haven't been advertising my difficulties. Nina knows nothing about them, nor do any of the others. I certainly don't want anyone knowing now, not after I've been slaving my guts out day and night, making sure it didn't get out.'

CHAPTER 12

Kelsey stood in the middle of Grace Dalton's bedroom, looking round. The room was still as it was when Jean Redfern had fled from it to collapse sobbing on

126

to a kitchen chair, except for traces of the attentions of the forensic team—and the fact that Grace's body was no longer there. And that at some stage someone had removed the tray of tea Jean had set down on the bedside table.

The Chief didn't expect anything useful from prints taken from this room or the adjoining bathroom. He still could see no motive for the murder other than the need or desire for money, and everyone benefiting to a substantial degree by Grace's death had recently been in the bedroom, with every right to be there.

According to the pathologist, Grace had been deep in a sedated sleep when the pin was run up into her heart; she would have known nothing. She had died between one and four in the morning, at the hands of someone who knew exactly what he—or she—was about. Not that the degree of medical knowledge needed was very great; it was no more than could have been acquired by any intelligent person in any public library. But it was a tricky operation, all the same, requiring a cool head and a steady nerve.

There was no real alibi for anyone. All, according to their own accounts, had been asleep in bed. Any one of them could have stolen along to Grace's room in the night, using a torch to light the way. Back into bed again in no time at all, not a soul the wiser.

The patio doors leading into Grace's bedroom were locked and bolted. There was only one key to the doors and Dorothy Nevett had charge of that. It was kept in the kitchen, with the rest of the household keys. Nina clearly recalled checking that the patio doors were properly secured on Saturday night, and Jean Redfern could remember Nina walking over to check the doors.

The task of going round the house at night, locking up, was normally carried out by either Dorothy or Jean. On Saturday night it had been carried out by Jean. Both Matthew and Esther still had keys to the front door, from when they had lived in the house; they had never relinquished them. Both said they had had no occasion in recent years to make use of the keys. Both Dorothy and Jean had keys to a side door, for their own personal use. The Chief had checked all the keys. There had been no difficulty in producing any of them: all were where they should have been.

According to Matthew, he was asleep in his bed in Brentworth at the time of Grace's death. But he had no proof of that, any more than the rest of them. He could have driven back to Elmhurst in the early hours of the morning, left his car discreetly parked, out of sight and earshot, walked silently along the drive. All it required was for someone inside the house to have stolen downstairs to draw back the bolts of the front door, after the household had retired for the night. And for that same someone to steal down again later, after Matthew had left the house for the second time, to make sure the front door would be found properly bolted when the household awoke in the morning. In the confusion of yesterday morning, Dorothy Nevett had not got around to unbolting and unlocking the outside doors until some time after Grace's body had been discovered. She had found everything as usual. She was positive she would have registered the fact if she had found the front door unbolted, even in the midst of all that shock, all the grief and flurry of that moment.

Grace's negligée still lay folded over the back of a chair. Could it have been the sight of the negligée set, with its all-over pattern of rosebuds and pinhead dots, its froth of frilling and trimming veiling the area around the front opening of the nightdress, that had suddenly flung up into the mind of someone already harbouring thoughts of murder, the notion of exactly how that murder might be safely committed? Someone in no way involved in the actual choosing of the negligée set? Or had the set been especially chosen with the murder already in mind?

He passed a hand across his jaw. The set had been on display in the bedroom, along with all the other gifts. Everyone had seen it, had been called on to admire it. Who had actually chosen it? According to Verity, Esther had asked her to go into the store with her, to help her choose a present. A negligée set had been Esther's idea, that particular set had been Esther's choice.

Esther remembered things differently. It was Verity who had offered to go into the store with her, Verity who had suggested a negligée set, Verity who had decided on that particular set.

Verity, Kelsey pondered. Verity, who had tried to get trust money advanced to her; Verity, who had tried to ferret out from Purvis the terms of Grace's will.

He went off in search of that young lady, with Sergeant Lambert following. 'Verity's out in the garden,' Dorothy Nevett told them. 'Barry's with her.' She added on a note of distaste. 'She's been in quite a state, crying and carrying on.' She slanted a look at the Chief. 'It's news to me that she was all that fond of Mrs Dalton when the poor lady was alive.' She jerked her head. 'But there you are, she may have been. You never can tell with Madame Verity. I never have known what goes on in that young woman's mind.'

The two policemen went out through a side door. The garden lay serene and peaceful in the gentle sunlight. The Chief caught sight of Nina, some distance away, walking alone along a path. She didn't see them, she was looking down, she seemed lost in thought. The path curved round, bringing her back towards the house. She became aware of their approach and glanced up from her absorption.

Kelsey asked if she had seen Verity and Barry. Yes, she had seen them, they were in a summerhouse; she gestured over at it before continuing on her way. The Chief stood looking after her for a moment.

There was little sparkle about Nina today. She had a detached air, flattened and subdued, as if standing at a remove from what was happening.

They found Verity in the summerhouse. She was still sniffing, dabbing at her eyes, her head lowered, her heavy fall of long, dark hair hiding her face. Barry was seated at her side. He looked deeply distressed and grieving himself but he was doing his best to comfort her, talking to her in low, soothing tones.

The Chief explained that he would like to talk to her alone. Barry at once made to leave but Verity grasped at his sleeve. 'I want Barry to stay,' she declared, with a mutinous set to her jaw. The Chief didn't argue and Barry sank down again into his seat.

The Chief plunged in without further ado. Why had Verity wanted money advanced to her from the trust fund?

She looked defiantly back at him, her dark eyes red and swollen with weeping. 'I'm over eighteen,' she retorted. 'I don't see why I should be treated as a child, made to wait for the money.'

'I understand,' the Chief went on, 'that you also tried to find out from Mr Purvis the contents of Mrs Dalton's will. I take it you now know how you stand under the will.' Matthew Dalton had driven back to Elmhurst after his visit to the solicitor; he had given the gist of Grace's will to those affected by it.

'Why did you move out of the flat you were sharing?' Kelsey wanted to know.

'I wanted to be on my own, able to live my own life, not be under the eyes of a couple of Esther's goody-goody girls all the time, reporting back to her everything I did.' She glowered at Kelsey. 'Just because I stayed with Esther at one time, years ago, she thinks it gives her some sort of right over me.'

The Chief executed a swift change of tack. 'Did you know Mrs Dalton had made an appointment with her solicitor for this Wednesday morning?'

She flashed him a challenging look. 'No, I did not know. Aunt Grace wasn't in the habit of discussing her appointments with me.'

'You could have overheard her on the phone, making the appointment.'

'I don't go round listening at doors,' she threw back at him.

'Or Barry may have overheard the phone

call and mentioned it to you.'

Barry's head jerked round. 'I did nothing of the sort,' he said energetically. 'I never overheard any phone call.' He laid a protective hand on Verity's arm. They certainly present a united front, Sergeant Lambert thought.

'You had a chat with Mrs Dalton soon after you arrived on Friday afternoon,' Kelsey reminded Verity. 'Did she say anything then about changing her will?'

Verity shook her head with force. 'She never mentioned her will to me. Then, or at any other time.'

'Did she tackle you about anything at all on Friday afternoon? About some aspect of your life, perhaps, that she didn't approve of?'

She gave another forceful shake of her head.

Kelsey sat regarding her. Certainly no one had mentioned observing any sign of displeasure from Grace towards Verity—or indeed towards anyone else under her roof—during the weekend.

She gave him back look for look. He let it go at that, for the time being, at least, and went back to the house.

He ran Jean Redfern to earth in a

134

utility room. She was keeping herself busy sprucing up the various flower arrangements in the house, changing the water, removing dead blooms, trimming greenery, adding fresh flowers and foliage. 'It calms me down,' she told the Chief. 'Helps to take my mind off things.' She looked tense and nervous.

'I gather you've been told how you stand under Mrs Dalton's will,' the Chief began.

Yes, Matthew had told her. She had had no idea beforehand of what was in the will. She had been immensely relieved to learn of the provision, much more generous than she had ever dared hope for. Mrs Dalton had never mentioned the matter to her, had never led her to believe she intended making any provision at all for her. Jean had schooled herself to accept that she might receive nothing. No, she hadn't resented the thought. She had never considered herself any responsibility of Mrs Dalton's; she counted herself lucky to have been able to live for so long in such pleasant circumstances. She had grown progressively more attached to Mrs Dalton during the last few years. She felt tremendous gratitude towards her, for her kindness over the years and for her generosity in the will.

'Did Mrs Dalton know Shaun Chapman was back in Cannonbridge?' Kelsey asked. 'Did she know you were seeing him again? Did she say anything about him to you?'

Jean was filling a vase with water. She uttered an exclamation as the water ran over the top. She set down the vase and began to mop up the spillage. 'She said nothing about it to me,' she replied as she went to the sink to squeeze out her cloth; Kelsey couldn't see her face.

'You didn't tell her you were seeing Shaun again?' he persisted.

She shook her head. 'I wasn't seeing him in the way you mean. I only met him a couple of times. I ran into him in the town, purely by chance. He said he wouldn't be staying long in Cannonbridge. It wouldn't have occurred to me to mention it to Mrs Dalton, there was nothing in it.' She went back to her flower arranging.

'Did you mention it to Dorothy Nevett?'

She grimaced. 'She's the last person I'd have told. She's always been jealous of me, she's always been ready to stir up trouble for me when she could.'

'Where is Shaun now?'

She snipped at flower stalks. 'I don't know. He could still be in Cannonbridge. Or he may have gone off somewhere.'

'Where was he staying in Cannonbridge?'

She trimmed a spray of greenery. 'He was staying with his parents.' She didn't ask if the Chief wanted the address and the Chief didn't ask her for it. He remembered it well enough from three years back.

'Do you expect Shaun to be in touch with you again?' he continued.

She shook her head in silence.

'Would you like to take up with him again?'

'No, I would not,' she replied with energy. 'I still like him, he's good company.' She smiled a little. 'I still think he's good-looking. But that's all. I'm not a silly teenager any more.'

'What about Shaun? Would he like to take up with you again?'

'He said nothing about it to me. He never tried to get in touch with me over these last three years. If I hadn't run into him in the street I'd never have known he was back. I daresay he's had other girls in those years, I expect there'll be others in the next few years. I shouldn't think he takes any of them very seriously.'

'He was pretty serious about you three years ago.'

She moved her shoulders. 'We've both grown up a bit since then.'

'If he does turn up again, will you see him?'

'Yes, of course I will, if he wants to see me.' She sounded surprised. 'Why shouldn't I see him?' She stepped back to survey the results of her work. 'That looks a bit better, don't you think? Neater, anyway.'

Esther was in the kitchen, talking to Mrs Gosling. When the Chief asked if he might speak to her she glanced at Mrs Gosling who at once left the room.

Esther asked the two men to sit down. 'How can I help you?' she asked briskly as they took their seats. The Chief gave her an assessing look. Where now was the hesitant tone, the apologetic manner?

He asked if Esther knew of anything concerning Verity, something Grace might recently have learned, something that might have caused Grace to reconsider her mention of Verity in her will.

Esther answered without hesitation: yes, she did know of something. 'I was talking

138

to the two girls Verity used to share a flat with,' she told the Chief. 'It was a week ago, after church on Sunday. I hadn't had the chance to speak to them for some time. I asked them how Verity was getting on at the college. The older girl, Jan Otway, said there was something she thought I ought to know. Verity was making a fool of herself over one of the part-time lecturers, there was gossip among the students. Jan had tried to talk to Verity about it but Verity wouldn't listen, she told Jan to mind her own business. She was over eighteen, she could do as she pleased.

'Did you tell Grace about this?' Kelsey asked.

Esther nodded. 'Yes, I did, in the end. I couldn't make up my mind whether to tell Grace or not. I did think about tackling Verity myself but I decided I'd probably get the same sort of response Jan Otway had got. When I was chatting to Grace on Friday evening, she asked if I knew how Verity was managing on her own in her flat. I said something non-committal but Grace saw at once there was something I wasn't saying. She asked me what it was. She reminded me she was one of Verity's guardians, she had a duty to keep an eye on her. She said, "If you're worried about upsetting me, you can forget that, I'm not easily upset." ' Esther moved her shoulders. 'So I passed on what Jan had told me.'

'What did Mrs Dalton have to say to that?'

'Not much. She said, "Just as well you told me." '

'Did she say she intended speaking to Verity about it?'

She shook her head. 'She didn't say anything more about it at all, she started talking about something else.'

'Did you mention this conversation to Verity?'

'No, I certainly did not.'

She didn't know the name of the lecturer Verity was mixed up with, Jan hadn't told her. But she was able to give the Chief Jan Otway's address.

Kelsey stood in the hall, pondering. The weekend visitors were now free to leave Elmhurst. All of them, including Esther, were at this moment in the process of leaving.

He had wanted another word with Dorothy Nevett, but she had taken a couple of aspirins and retired to her room to lie down, temporarily overcome by the stresses of the day.

He glanced at the clock. Better get a move on. He was anxious to catch Jan Otway but he had first to call in at the police station.

But they were delayed at the station and when they reached the flat Jan Otway shared they found no one at home. 'We'll look in at the college tomorrow,' the Chief said as they got back into the car. 'We'll catch her there.'

CHAPTER 13

Tuesday morning brought a conference, followed by a news briefing. In the ordinary way, Grace Dalton's death would have rated a couple of columns on an inside page of the local paper, plus a photograph from the files. But the circumstances of her passing had propelled the event into a totally different category. It had aroused the keenest interest in the town, coupled with considerable shock and disbelief.

The first question asked by a journalist was the one they all had in mind: were the police looking for an outsider in connection with the murder? The Chief returned a non-committal answer: the police were at present keeping a completely open mind on the matter.

In the early afternoon, Sergeant Lambert drove the Chief over to the boarding school where Barry Fielding was a pupil. The school was housed in a former mansion, with extensive grounds and playing fields. It wasn't the school Bernard Dalton had chosen for his own son, but it had an excellent reputation. Bernard and Grace had decided on it because it wasn't too large, it had a pleasant, homely atmosphere, and the headmaster and his wife had struck them as kind and understanding.

The headmaster was expecting the Chief; he took the two policemen along to his study. He was acquainted with the history of both Barry and Verity and never put any obstacle in the way of their continuing friendship.

Kelsey didn't wish to speak to Barry, who was attending classes as usual. He wanted to know the headmaster's opinion of the boy. He was told Barry was a quiet lad, sensitive, but with plenty of sound common sense. A responsible boy, hard-working and ambitious. He had made some good friends at the school and was well thought of by both staff and fellow pupils. He had been deeply affected by Mrs Dalton's death.

'He was very fond of her,' the headmaster said. 'He feels he's lost a very good friend—and he's also losing the place he looks on as home. I understand Elmhurst is to be sold.' Matthew Dalton had called at the school yesterday afternoon, on his way home from Elmhurst. He had explained that Grace's death in no way affected Barry's position under the trust; his school fees and other expenses would continue to be paid, exactly as before.

'Barry's certain to get a university place in the autumn,' the headmaster added. 'It should be the start of a whole new life for him.'

They went straight from the school to the Brentworth College of Further Education. At the Chief's request, Jan Otway was summoned from class to a side office, where Kelsey was waiting to speak to her. She was an earnest-looking young woman, with a composed manner. She knew of Mrs Dalton's death and at once accepted the need for the police to make inquiries about those connected with her; she answered every question readily.

She told the Chief Verity had never given any cause for concern during the twelve months she had shared the flat. She had never been very communicative but she had always been pleasant enough; well-behaved, tidy about the flat, ready to do her fair share of the chores; she had never expressed any dissatisfaction with the flat-sharing arrangement. She had worked hard at her studies. Her flatmates knew, via Esther Milroy, of Verity's long friendship with Barry Fielding, but Barry never came to the flat. There didn't appear to be any romantic interest in Verity's life.

Shortly before her eighteenth birthday, Verity asked them to look out for another girl to take her place as she would soon be leaving the flat; she had got permission from her guardians to rent a small flat on her own. They saw little of her after she left; until recently they had heard nothing about her to cause any anxiety. Then college gossip about Verity's behaviour reached Jan's ears. She had never had occasion to come across the lecturer concerned but she had made it her business to take a look at him, find out what she could, as she still felt some measure of responsibility for Verity.

His name was Ned Hooper. He was unmarried, tall and good-looking, in his mid thirties. He lived in a bedsit in a run-down area of Brentworth and rented a studio of sorts in an even seedier quarter nearby. She had tried to raise the matter with Verity, without success. She had later mentioned her concern to Esther Milroy. No, she hadn't told Verity she had spoken to Esther.

When Jan had returned to her class, the Chief went along to the main office to ask if Ned Hooper was in the building. He was told Mr Hooper no longer taught at the college. He had informed them some four weeks ago that he would no longer be available for supply work. Yes, the clerk could supply Mr Hooper's address.

It took them to a dilapidated Victorian dwelling let off in bedsits. The landlady emerged from her own quarters to tell them Mr Hooper no longer lived there. He had left a month ago, to move into a friend's flat near the centre of Brentworth.

145

She didn't know if the friend was male or female; Mr Hooper hadn't said and she hadn't asked. She removed her cigarette from the corner of her mouth and tapped off the long cylinder of ash. 'Must be a well-heeled friend, whoever it is. Those flats are furnished, pretty pricey.'

The entrance to the block of flats was guarded by a uniformed doorman. He told the Chief Mr Hooper had moved into a first-floor flat a month ago. The flat was let to a Mrs Bradshaw who had taken it last autumn. There was no one in the flat just now as the pair of them had gone off to Paris for a week. They had left on Friday morning and were expected back around Friday tea-time.

A thought struck the Chief as he turned to go. 'Has there been a girl round here, looking for Mr Hooper?' he asked.

'There has, indeed,' the doorman responded with energy. She had given her name as Thorburn, Miss Verity Thorburn. She must have called half a dozen times in all. He had let her go up to the flat the first time, but after that Mr Hooper had told him to keep her out. 'She's a persistent young woman,' the doorman added. 'She

146

keeps on turning up.' The last time was this last Friday; she had called around one o'clock. 'I told her they'd gone off to Paris for the week. She was wasting her time coming round, she wasn't going to get to see Mr Hooper again.'

'How did she take that?' Kelsey asked.

'She didn't say anything, she just stood there, looking at me, then she went off again.' He shook his head. 'We haven't seen the last of her. She's a pretty determined character.'

CHAPTER 14

An hour later found Sergeant Lambert turning the car into the Cannonbridge council estate where the Chapman family lived; he pulled up outside the Chapman's semi.

A baby's pram stood on a patch of grass at the side of the house. As Sergeant Lambert approached the front door to lay a thumb on the bell, the Chief glanced in at the pram's occupant. A chubby-faced infant a few months old lay on its side, peacefully sleeping. He had scarcely time to join Sergeant Lambert before the front door opened. 'Oh, it's you,' Mrs Chapman said flatly by way of greeting. She was a short, plump woman, not yet forty. She had clearly once been pretty. A toddler sucking a dummy held on to her skirts.

Kelsey asked courteously if they might come in; he would welcome a chat. Before she could reply, her husband called from the kitchen. 'Who is it?' He emerged into the hall, clutching the evening paper, a cigarette between his fingers. He frowned at the sight of the two policemen. He was a year or two older than his wife, with a slack figure, the remains of good looks.

The Chief politely repeated his request. The pair exchanged glances. 'All right, then,' Mrs Chapman agreed. 'But you can't stay long. I don't want you here when the kids get in from school.'

'We'll be as quick as we can,' the Chief promised, as they all trooped into the kitchen. A girl, fifteen or sixteen, obviously pregnant, stooped awkwardly by the cooker, taking a tray of little cakes from the oven. She flashed the visitors a searching look as she straightened up and put the tray on the table. Undeniably her mother's daughter, undeniably pretty. Without a word she filled the kettle and plugged it in. She took beakers from a shelf, milk from the fridge. Lambert saw that the numbers of beakers included one for the Chief and himself. He also saw that the girl's fingers were bare of rings. He spent a moment or two trying to decide if the baby outside belonged to the mother or daughter, but could reach no conclusion.

Mrs Chapman pushed forward chairs for the callers and dropped into another herself, taking the toddler on to her ample lap. Chapman stayed by the door, leaning against the wall.

'It's really your son, Shaun, we've come to see,' the Chief began.

'He's not here,' Mrs Chapman broke in swiftly. 'What do you want him for?'

The Chief didn't answer that but asked: 'Has he been here lately?'

'Yes, he was here for a few weeks,' she replied. 'But he's gone again.'

'Where is he now?'

She mentioned a town some distance away. 'That's where he said he was off to. He has a mate over there.' The kettle came to the boil and the girl made the tea.

149

'When did Shaun leave here?' Kelsey asked.

'Saturday morning,' Mrs Chapman answered instantly.

'You're sure it was Saturday?'

'Of course I'm sure,' she retorted.

'Had he told you he intended leaving on Saturday morning?'

She shook her head. 'We knew he wouldn't be staying much longer. He just got up on Saturday morning and said he was off.'

'How did he go? Train? Bus?'

'He went in his car.'

'He bought an old car soon after he got here,' Chapman chipped in. 'He worked on it while he was here, made a good job of it, too. He's good with anything on wheels, always has been. He keeps his eyes open for a bargain, does it up, sells it for a nice profit. Then he starts all over again.'

'How long has he gone for?' Kelsey asked.

'He didn't say,' Mrs Chapman replied.

'But you do expect him back this way before too long?'

She thrust out her lips. 'We never expect Shaun. He'll be back when he feels like it.

150

He's hardly been here at all over the last three years. He never came once during the first twelve months after he and Jean Redfern split up.'

'Did he see much of Jean while he was here this time?'

'He did see something of her. She came here quite a few times.'

'And they went out together?'

'Yes, of course they did. Why shouldn't they? He was very fond of her at one time. Still is, come to that.'

The girl poured the tea. Chapman produced a packet of cigarettes and offered them round. The two policemen declined; all three Chapmans lit up. The girl passed round the plate of cakes. The Chief shook his head but Sergeant Lambert, ever hungry, made swift work of one; it was delicious. The girl gave him a pleased grin and slid the plate towards him again. He dispatched another couple without delay.

Mrs Chapman levelled a frowning glance at the Chief. 'What are you asking all these questions for, anyway? Shaun's never been in any trouble with the police. Is he supposed to have done something?'

'Not as far as we know,' the Chief

responded blandly. 'Do *you* think he's done something?'

She shook her head vigorously. 'No, of course I don't. He's a good lad. A good worker, too, he can turn his hand to anything. He just doesn't like stopping in one place too long, he gets bored, he has to move on. He'll grow out of that, he'll settle down one day.'

'Do you expect him to settle down with Jean Redfern?'

She jerked her head. 'He could do a lot worse. We like Jean. And she likes us. She always mucks in when she comes here, no fancy airs and graces. She'll wash up or bath the baby, doesn't make a big favour of it, either.'

I could see how this slap-happy set-up might appeal to Jean, Sergeant Lambert thought. With her origins, a mother who hadn't even wanted her born, it might give her an illusion of being part of a family.

'I don't know why Mrs Dalton had to go and break things up between Shaun and Jean three years ago,' Mrs Chapman went on. 'She should never have interfered, it wasn't right.' She stopped suddenly. 'We were very sorry to hear about Mrs Dalton,' she said after a moment. She gave the

Chief an inquiring glance. 'It'll be one of the family did it, I daresay, wanting her out of the way, to get their hands on the money.'

Kelsey made no response to that. He pushed back his chair and stood up. He glanced over to where Chapman still lounged against the wall, cigarette in hand. 'We're off, then,' the Chief said. As he reached the door, he said casually to Chapman, 'Shaun left here on Sunday morning?'

'That's right,' Chapman confirmed.

'Not Sunday, Saturday,' his wife broke in sharply.

Chapman drew on his cigarette. 'Yes, of course. Saturday morning.' Sergeant Lambert's eyes were on the daughter. She looked from one parent to the other but she said nothing.

'This mate of Shaun's, where you say he's gone,' Kelsey said. 'Could we have his name and address?' Mrs Chapman supplied the name but no one knew the address. It seemed the mate's father was a ganger on construction work. Shaun thought there might be a chance of something there, he'd done casual work for the ganger before.

153

It was turned five by the time they were able to set off for the town Shaun was said to have made for. When they got there, their first call was at the main police station. Shaun Chapman's name wasn't known but they did know the name of the ganger; he was well known and respected locally.

They found him at home; a quiet, well-spoken man. He answered the Chief's questions readily, asking none of his own.

Yes, he knew Shaun Chapman, Shaun was a friend of his son. He had worked under him a number of times over the last few years. He had always found him a good worker, reliable and easy to get on with. Shaun had never stayed longer than two or three months, not because of any disagreement but because he wanted to move on.

Yes, he had seen Shaun recently, as recently as last Saturday evening. Shaun had called at the house to ask if there was any work going. The ganger told him he had nothing for him at the moment but there could be something in another ten days. There was a contract due to start work on 18th March. He'd keep a place for Shaun, provided he showed up by 17th

154

March. Shaun thanked him and said he'd definitely be back.

'You're sure it was Saturday evening he called here?' Kelsey queried. 'Might it not have been Sunday evening?'

The ganger was positive it was Saturday; it couldn't have been Sunday. Shaun had called at around seven o'clock and at seven o'clock last Sunday evening, as every Sunday evening, the ganger and his wife were in the local church, attending evening service.

Did the ganger know where Shaun was now? He was sorry, he couldn't say. But his son might know. His son was a draughtsman, sharing a flat with other young men in a suburb a few minutes' drive away.

They found the son in the flat, changing to go out. A pleasant, well-mannered young man. Yes, Shaun had turned up at the weekend, as he did from time to time, always without warning. He had rung the doorbell on Saturday evening, at around seven-thirty. He was certain it was Saturday and not Sunday. He hadn't been at home on Sunday evening. He had spent the day with friends living several miles away; he hadn't got back till after eleven.

155

Shaun said he'd just called to see his father, to ask if there was any work going. He'd been told to come back in ten days. He spent the night on the sofa and left around eight next morning. He said he was making for the West Country. He'd worked on farms in that part of the country before, he thought he might be able to pick up a bit of casual work to tide him over until 17th March.

CHAPTER 15

Gosling was walking across to the green-houses on Wednesday morning when he saw Chief Inspector Kelsey's car coming along the drive. He changed direction and went across to where Sergeant Lambert was pulling up by the front door.

He's taking it hard, the Chief thought, as he got out of the car. Gosling looked years older, deeply saddened. His manner was subdued as he greeted the Chief.

It seemed that Matthew Dalton had called on the Goslings yesterday morning, to explain their present position. They would both be kept on at Elmhurst until the property was sold. He informed them of their financial entitlements and assured them these rights would be generously interpreted. There was no question of the cottage they occupied being demolished by developers if the Goslings wished to remain in it. He gave his word that any sale agreement would uphold their right to occupy the cottage for the rest of their days.

Gosling was still two years from sixty, his wife a few years younger. If either or both of them wanted to go on working after the sale of Elmhurst, it was highly probable there would be suitable work for Gosling in the grounds or gardens of the development, and a niche for his wife in one or other of the new households.

'But I don't know that we'd want to go on living in the cottage, or working for the new folk here,' Gosling told the Chief with a despondent shake of his head. 'Not when it would all be so different.' If they chose to leave the cottage after the sale of Elmhurst, suitable housing would be purchased for them elsewhere, with the right to occupy it for the remainder of their lives.

'We might decide to go and live in the village,' Gosling added. 'We could both find work there easily enough, if we wanted it. There are plenty of well-to-do retired folk living round here these days. They don't mind paying for help in the house and garden. Paying well, too, from what I hear.'

The Goslings had always known that Elmhurst was likely to be sold on the death of Mrs Dalton. They had also been aware that she hadn't been expected to live much longer, though they had cherished hopes that she might soldier on for some years yet. 'It's the dreadful way she went that's shattered the pair of us,' Gosling said heavily. 'For someone to do that to her. Work the whole thing out and then go and do it, bold as brass. Just for the money—it must have been that, there's no other reason you can think of why anyone should want to do it.' His voice shook. 'It's knocked the missus sideways. She was that fond of Mrs Dalton. She liked the first wife well enough, she got on fine with her, but she really loved his one.' Tears shone in his eyes. 'Who could have done such a terrible thing to a wonderful lady like that? It's got to be someone we all know, someone who was here for the birthday. That's the worst part of it, that's what we can't get to grips with. Not knowing which one of them it was.' His tone was anguished. 'Not knowing which of them you can trust any more.'

Dorothy Nevett admitted the Chief to the house a few minutes later. She looked her old brisk self again this morning and the Chief had a fleeting notion as she opened the door that she was about to tell him to wipe his boots, as she had so often done in years gone by when he was a scrubbed-faced lad in short trousers.

If the same thought crossed Dorothy's mind, she didn't give voice to it. She took them along to the kitchen, sat them down and plied them with coffee and biscuits. Yes, she was feeling a good deal steadier.

The Chief asked the question he had wanted to ask her on Monday evening: had she told Mrs Dalton that Shaun Chapman was back in Cannonbridge and Jean Redfern had been seeing him?

'I'm afraid I did let it slip,' Dorothy admitted in tones of apology. 'I hadn't intended saying anything, I wouldn't have wanted to upset Mrs Dalton. But she happened to say something about Jean not being able to get out to see her girlfriends for a day or two, because of the birthday; we'd have to make sure she got extra time off afterwards, to make up. I didn't say anything much to that but she must have seen something in my manner. She gave me a sharp look. She said: "It isn't girlfriends she's been seeing, is it?" I still didn't say anything. She said: "It's some boy, isn't it? It's not Shaun Chapman, is it? Is he back again?"

'I thought it would be even more upsetting for her if I didn't answer so I told her yes, Shaun was back. I was sure Jean was seeing him, though she swore she wasn't. I asked her not to let Jean know I'd told her, I didn't want Jean thinking I was telling tales about her. Mrs Dalton promised not to say anything.'

She grimaced. 'In the end I let it out myself. We were in the kitchen on Saturday evening, clearing up after the party, just Jean and me. It was bothering me that I'd told Mrs Dalton about Jean and Shaun. I thought for sure Jean would be fibbing to Mrs Dalton again, next time she went out to meet Shaun, she'd be saying she was meeting some girlfriend.

160

So I told her Mrs Dalton knew Shaun was back and that she was seeing him again, I'd let it slip out without meaning to.'

'How did Jean take that?' Kelsey asked.

'She didn't look angry or upset. She just stood there, looking at me. She asked me when I'd told Mrs Dalton, exactly what time. That surprised me but I told her it would be about nine-thirty that morning, when I was talking to Mrs Dalton after breakfast, going over the arrangements for the day.'

'Did Jean say anything else?'

She shook her head. 'She stood there a bit longer, as if she was thinking hard, then she got on with what she was doing. She never said another word about it, then or later. I was relieved she'd taken it so well.'

CHAPTER 16

Jean was upstairs, in her bedroom. She came to the door at the Chief's knock. 'We'd like a word with you,' he told her. She didn't ask them inside but stepped out

161

without a word into the corridor, closing the door behind her. She led them, still in silence, down to a small sitting room where she took a seat opposite them and sat waiting with folded hands for the Chief's questions.

'We've talked to Mr and Mrs Chapman,' Kelsey began. 'It's clear you saw more of Shaun recently than you gave us to understand.'

She said nothing, merely moving her head slightly in acknowledgement.

'Had Shaun been in touch with you at all since he left Cannonbridge three years ago?' Kelsey asked.

She shook her head.

'I daresay you thought about him sometimes during those three years?'

She moved her shoulders. 'Hardly at all. I'd put all that behind me.'

'Did it never cross your mind that you might have been married to him if Mrs Dalton hadn't interfered?'

By way of reply she merely moved her shoulders again.

'Did you resent that interference?' Kelsey went on.

She shook her head at once, with decision. 'I never thought about it at all.

It was over and done with.'

'You were happy, all the same, to start going out with Shaun again, as soon as you bumped into each other.'

She gave him a challenging look. 'Why shouldn't I go out with him? I still like him. I still think he's very attractive. But I wasn't tempted to take up with him seriously again. I wouldn't want to be serious about anyone for the next few years. I want to make something of my life first.'

'When were you last in touch with Shaun?' Kelsey asked.

'Last Thursday evening,' she answered, after a moment's thought.

'Do you know where he is now?'

'I imagine he's at his parents' house,' she replied.

'No, he's not,' Kelsey informed her. 'He's left Cannonbridge.'

She appeared neither surprised nor upset, merely responding: 'I knew he'd be off again soon, but he didn't say exactly when.'

'Do you expect to hear from him again?'

'I've no idea,' she answered with composure.

'Would you be pleased to hear from him again?'

'Yes, of course I would. We haven't fallen out.'

'Have you any idea where he thought of going?'

'He said he might try for work on a construction gang he'd worked on before.' She mentioned the town the Chief had visited. 'Or he might try his luck on a farm in the West Country.'

The Chief regarded her for some moments, then he said abruptly: 'Are you aware that Dorothy Nevett told Mrs Dalton Shaun was back and you were seeing him again?'

She nodded. 'Dorothy told me that on Saturday night, when we were in the kitchen clearing up. She suddenly came out with it. She wasn't too nice about it, either. She said, "By the way, I shouldn't bother telling Mrs Dalton any more of your little fibs about meeting girlfriends when you go out all dolled up in the evenings. She knows Shaun Chapman's back, she knows you're seeing him again, she knows because I told her myself, I considered it my duty to tell her." ' Jean looked calmly across at Kelsey. 'Dorothy really enjoyed saying all that. She sounded so spiteful, so pleased with herself.'

'She didn't make out she'd let it slip by accident?'

She gave a vigorous shake of her head. 'She certainly did not. She made it plain she'd told Mrs Dalton deliberately.' She gave the Chief a resentful glance. 'She had no right to go running to Mrs Dalton with tales about me, especially not with Mrs Dalton being in a poor state of health—and at a time when she was supposed to be happy, enjoying her birthday.' She moved in her chair. 'I'm not a child, I have a right to see anyone I please, I don't have to account to anyone for how I spend my free time. Dorothy thought Mrs Dalton made too much of me over the last few years, favoured me over her.' She turned her head and stared out of the window. 'Dorothy never wanted me to be born. Or if I had to be born, then I should have been put up for adoption. I know that because my mother told me.'

She turned her head again and gave the Chief a direct look. 'Dorothy wasn't so keen on telling Mrs Dalton every last little thing about her own affairs. I'm pretty sure she never said a word to her about buying a cottage.' She stopped abruptly.

'Buying a cottage?' the Chief echoed.

'What cottage is this?'

She was silent for a moment. When she answered, it was in an altered tone, quieter and less confident. 'She's buying a cottage in Dorset with her friend, Alice Upjohn.'

'Did Dorothy tell you that?'

Jean made no reply and Kelsey repeated his question. She still said nothing. 'I can find Dorothy now and ask her myself, if you choose not to answer,' he pointed out.

That opened her mouth. 'Dorothy never told any of us about the cottage.'

'Then how do you know about it?'

A tide of red began to rise in her face. 'How did you find out about the cottage?' Kelsey pressed her.

Her cheeks flamed crimson. 'I happened to overhear a phone call Dorothy made to Alice,' she replied at last.

'You happened to overhear a phone call?' the Chief repeated. 'You mean you stood outside a door and listened to what was being said over the phone.'

She clenched her fists but made no reply.

'Tell me about this phone call,' he commanded. 'Exactly when did it take place? Exactly what was said?'

166

The flush drained away, leaving her pale and weary-looking. With a visible effort she kept her voice steady. 'It was on the Monday evening, a couple of weeks ago, a week after Dorothy got back from Dorset. I was watching TV. I went upstairs for a handkerchief during the break. I saw the light under the door of my office, I knew it must be Dorothy, I guessed she was using the phone.' She didn't meet his eyes. 'I wondered why she wasn't using the phone down in the hall. And she hadn't said anything to me about wanting to use the phone in the office. I'd never known her use it before. I went along and stood outside the door. I could hear what she was saying.'

'What did you hear?'

'She was talking to Alice about a cottage they wanted to buy together. Dorothy said it would be all right about a mortgage. Alice should go ahead and tell the solicitor in the morning, they were definitely buying the cottage.'

'Does Dorothy know you overheard the call?'

'No, she doesn't,' she replied in some alarm. 'And I don't want her to find out.

I could tell she was going to ring off, from what she was saying, so I slipped next door, into my bedroom. I didn't put the light on. I waited till she'd gone. I heard her go up to her bedroom, then I went back downstairs, to the television.'

The Chief asked if she had said anything to Mrs Dalton about Dorothy buying a cottage.

She shook her head with energy. 'I never said a word. If Dorothy wanted to make a secret of it, that was her affair. It wasn't for me to pass on.' She's certainly protesting strongly enough about that, Sergeant Lambert thought. Possibly a shade too strongly? But then again, if she'd gone ahead and opened her mouth, Mrs Dalton would surely have asked her how she'd learned about the cottage. Jean would scarcely wish to advertise to Mrs Dalton her habit of listening at doors.

Dorothy was still in the kitchen, engaged now in assembling ingredients for a casserole. She glanced up as the two policemen entered. 'You off, then?' she asked, three-quarters of her attention on her task.

'Not quite,' the Chief told her. 'We'd

appreciate another word with you first. It won't take long.'

'It had better not,' she retorted good-naturedly. 'I've got to get this in the oven. You won't mind me carrying on?'

The Chief made no objection. When she had sat them down she picked up a knife and began to cube a slab of beef with speed and skill. 'Right, then,' she commanded. 'What is it you want to know?'

'You remember your old dream of a cottage?' Kelsey said. 'You always used to say you wanted to retire to the seaside one day, with Alice.' She made no response but went on dexterously cubing. 'Did you ever do anything about it?' Kelsey asked.

She flicked him a razor-sharp glance. 'You've no need to play games with me,' she said crisply. 'I can see you know full well I did do something about it. We've bought a cottage between the two of us, Alice and me. The sale's going through now. We should get possession around the beginning of next month.'

'When did you decide to buy the cottage?' Kelsey asked.

She supplied the date without any pause for reflection. 'February the twenty-fourth. I rang Alice that evening to tell her.

She went along next morning to the solicitor, that would be February the twenty-fifth—not a date I'm ever likely to forget, the first property I've ever owned.' She turned her attention to a bowl of vegetables, already peeled and washed. She began to slice and chop. 'Lovely little cottage,' she observed with deep pleasure. 'Just right for the two of us. Stroke of luck, the way we came by it. It was Alice's doing, she found out it was going cheap, a real bargain at today's prices.'

'At the time you decided to buy it, when did you intend going to live in it?' Kelsey wanted to know.

She didn't look up from her slicing. 'Alice was going to move into the cottage as soon as we got possession. She's taking early retirement, she finishes at the end of the month. I was going to join her after Mrs Dalton's death, whenever that might be. Of course, I'd be going there for holidays in the meantime, odd weekends, whenever I could get away. Alice didn't mind living there on her own, she's been used to that ever since her mother went into the nursing home.'

'And now I take it you'll be moving into

the cottage yourself, as soon as it's legally yours?'

'That's right,' she confirmed with relish. 'I've spoken to Matthew Dalton about it. He says I can leave whenever I want. Mrs Gosling can take over here, and she'll have Jean to help her. The pair of them will manage fine till the place is sold.'

'Did you tell Mrs Dalton you were buying a cottage?' Kelsey asked.

She shook her head. 'I intended telling her after the sale had gone through and the cottage was actually ours. I wasn't going to tell anyone before then. I'm superstitious that way.' She half smiled. 'Silly, I know, but I always have the feeling it's tempting fate to say too much beforehand about something you've set your heart on.' She took a casserole from a cupboard and put it down on the table.

'Are you splitting the purchase price of the cottage fifty-fifty with Alice?' Kelsey asked.

'Yes, that's right.' She began to layer the meat and vegetables swiftly and neatly in the casserole.

'How were you intending to provide your share of the money at the time you decided to buy?'

'I was going to take out a mortgage for part of my share with a building society I've had an account with for years. I have enough savings to cover the rest. The mortgage would have been interest-only, I intended repaying it in full from the lump sum coming to me after Mrs Dalton's death, I knew exactly how much that would be.' She placed the casserole in the oven.

'And now, of course, you won't need the mortgage,' Kelsey observed.

She looked steadily across at him. 'That's right,' she confirmed.

'How far did you get with the business of taking out the mortgage?' he asked.

She wiped the table and washed her hands. 'I hadn't actually signed anything, so I was able to give backword on the mortgage without any trouble.'

'When had you intended signing the papers?'

She took down a mixing bowl from a shelf and set about making a pudding. 'I was due to sign tomorrow.'

'How did you give backword?'

'I rang the manager of the building society. He was very understanding.'

'When did you ring him?'

'On Monday.'

'What time on Monday?'

'Monday morning.'

'What time on Monday morning?'

She didn't answer but occupied herself rubbing fat into flour with the tips of her fingers. 'I daresay the manager will remember the time,' Kelsey said.

That produced an answer. 'I rang him at nine o'clock.'

'You were pretty quick off the mark,' Kelsey observed.

She didn't look up from her task. 'It was Alice who thought about giving backword, it hadn't crossed my mind with all that was going on here. I phoned Alice on Sunday evening, to tell her Mrs Dalton had died. When I was ringing off, she suddenly said, "I've just thought: you won't need the mortgage now, you'd better ring the building society first thing in the morning and tell them." So that's what I did.'

'When you rang the manager, which phone did you use?'

She glanced up in surprise. 'I used the phone in Jean's office,' she said after a moment. 'I didn't want everyone knowing my business. The downstairs phone isn't all that private.'

'Did you tell Jean you wanted to use that phone?'

She broke eggs into a basin. 'No, I didn't. She was busy downstairs. I just popped into the office.'

'Do you often use that phone?'

'No, not often. Only if it's something I don't want everyone knowing.'

'And you never mention it to Jean when you use it?'

She whisked the eggs furiously. 'I can't see that it's any concern of Jean's. She doesn't own the phone. Or the office. She isn't one of the family, however she likes to fancy herself. She's only a servant here, like the rest of us.'

The weather was turning cold. Grey clouds scudded before a chill wind as the two policemen set off for the forensic laboratory in the late afternoon.

They weren't kept long at the laboratory. Tests had clearly identified one of the hatpins from the playroom as the murder weapon: a long pin, with an ornamental head of carved jet. It had been carefully wiped to rid it of blood and finger-prints—probably with a tissue, Kelsey thought, to be flushed down the lavatory

174

before restoring the pin to the velvet cushion on the cupboard shelf.

But when the head was removed from the pin, traces of dried blood were revealed. Recently dried blood, belonging to the least common group, a group shared by only six per cent of the population, the group to which Grace Dalton had belonged.

As they came down the laboratory steps, Sergeant Lambert remarked: 'Using a hatpin might suggest a female killer.'

Kelsey grunted. 'Or a male wanting to give the impression of a female killer.'

During the journey back to Cannonbridge, Kelsey sat in silence, his thoughts revolving round Dorothy Nevett. In so far as she had ever been devoted to anyone at Elmhurst, it had been to the first Mrs Dalton, a gentle and unassuming woman. During her last illness and the three years following her death, Dorothy had ruled Elmhurst as its virtual mistress, a position she had plainly relished. She could scarcely have welcomed Bernard Dalton's decision to marry again—and to marry a woman of stronger character, of energy and intelligence, who could be counted on to put a speedy end to her rule. Dorothy must surely have felt her nose thrust sharply out of joint, even though Grace, who had known the household for years, had understood and sympathized with Dorothy's position, invariably going out of her way to treat Dorothy with due consideration for her dignity. And, to give Dorothy her due, she had, for her part, served Grace faithfully and well.

As they neared the police station, Kelsey roused himself to say: 'We'll see if we can get away tomorrow afternoon. It wouldn't hurt to have a word with Alice Upjohn.'

CHAPTER 17

The town where Alice Upjohn lived was a large industrial sprawl of little beauty. Her rented flat occupied the ground floor of a tall Victorian dwelling in a quiet suburb.

Shortly after five-thirty, Sergeant Lambert pulled up outside the house. Alice hadn't long got in from work. She had just changed into old clothes, intending to spend the evening sorting through various possessions, deciding which to take with her when she moved. When Sergeant Lambert set his thumb on the doorbell, she was standing before the mirror in her bedroom, running a comb through her dark curly hair, touched now with grey.

The Chief awaited the opening of the door with keen interest. He had never met Alice but he felt he had known her since his boyhood. The door swung back and there she stood, the flesh and blood reality, after all these years, of the image long graven on his brain. A slight, graceful woman, still with something girlish about her, looking out at them with mild inquiry; the face he remembered from countless snapshots. He would have been able to pick her out at a crowded bus stop.

Before he even introduced himself she knew who he was; her face broke into a smile. Dorothy had often spoken of him, had sometimes enclosed a photograph of him, cut from the local newspaper, in one of her letters.

Yes, she knew of the dreadful crime that had taken place at Elmhurst. Yes, she well understood the routine necessary to check the smallest detail. She cordially invited them inside. She was sure they'd like to join her in a cup of tea.

She took them into the sitting room and

sat them down, then she whisked off to the kitchen. The Chief glanced about with curiosity while she was gone. The room was comfortably furnished, without fuss or ostentation. A number of photographs were ranged on a side table. Dorothy Nevett appeared in several, alone or with Alice. One snapshot showed the pair at the age of five or six, dressed for a summer day in cotton dresses, white socks and ankle-strap shoes. They stood hand in hand in a Cannonbridge street, outside the adjoining terrace houses they had lived in as children. Alice with her shy smile, Dorothy broad-shouldered and stocky, even then, her hair cropped, with a square-cut fringe, gazing stolidly out with an unsmiling look.

Footsteps sounded in the passage and Lambert sprang to his feet to open the door and take the tray. As well as tea it held a plate of substantial sandwiches. 'Go ahead and ask me whatever it is you want to know,' Alice invited as she poured the tea. 'I know how terribly upset Dorothy has been over what happened. I know she'd want me to help in any way I can.'

'It's about the purchase of the cottage that we'd like to check,' the Chief told her.

She showed no surprise, no hesitation in answering. He took her through the whole venture, from the time the purchase had first been mooted, probing into the exact sequence of decisions, paying particular attention to the matter of how it had been proposed to finance the purchase.

She gave him a precisely detailed account, confirming in all respects what Dorothy had told them. On one point the Chief especially pressed her: the giving of backword on Dorothy's proposed mortgage. Yes, Alice had a clear recollection of what had happened. It was she who had raised the matter; it had flashed into her head during Dorothy's phone call on Sunday evening, when she had rung to tell her of Mrs Dalton's death. She had mentioned it at the end of the call. 'Dorothy was very upset,' she remembered. 'I knew she wouldn't be thinking straight for a day or two. It was different for me, I'd never met Mrs Dalton, I wasn't personally affected. I pointed out that she wouldn't need the mortgage, now she'd be getting her legacy. I advised her to ring the building society first thing in the morning. She promised she would.'

The Chief had no more questions for

her. When they stood up to leave she walked with them into the hall. 'It makes a long day for you,' she remarked with ready sympathy. 'Having to drive back to Cannonbridge.'

'The traffic shouldn't be too bad,' the Chief said, 'now the rush hour's over.'

'I'm a good deal more nervous driving now,' she told him, 'than I was when I started, years ago. The traffic's so much heavier.' She gave a reminiscent shudder. 'I had a narrow squeak a week or two back. It was on the Monday morning, when I was driving to work. A van came out of a side road without looking or stopping—late for work, I suppose. I only just managed not to run smack into it, I had to pull right over. By great good luck there was nothing coming the other way, or I wouldn't be here now.'

She looked earnestly up at him. 'It gave me a terrible fright, it made me realize how easy it is to be snuffed out, all in a moment, however careful you think you're being about every part of your life. Your fate isn't always in your own hands.' She shook her head musingly. 'I had a horrible dream that night. I dreamed about a bad car crash, only it wasn't me in the crash, it was Dorothy. When I woke up next morning, I thought: suppose Dorothy was in an accident, suppose she was killed. This was before Mrs Dalton died. We'd always taken it for granted Dorothy would outlive Mrs Dalton, with Mrs Dalton being years older and in poor health. I thought: suppose things don't work out that way? Suppose Dorothy were to die before Mrs Dalton? After she'd taken out the mortgage and we'd bought the cottage. How would that leave me?'

She frowned, clasping her hands together. 'I lay in bed, trying to work it out. There wouldn't be any legacy from Mrs Dalton to pay off Dorothy's mortgage. The building society would want their money back. I wouldn't have much capital left after paying for my half of the cottage, so I wouldn't be able to pay off the mortgage. And I wouldn't be able to take over the mortgage, pay the interest every month—the pension I'll be getting will be a good deal reduced, for early retirement. The building society would insist on the cottage being put on the market, to get back their money, and I'd be left without a home.'

'A worrying situation,' Kelsey agreed.

'Did you do anything about it?'

She gave a vigorous nod. 'Indeed I did. I rang Dorothy that evening, the Tuesday, that would be, and put it to her.'

'What did she have to say?'

'Not very much. She heard me out, then she said: "You're quite right, I hadn't thought of that. But don't worry about it. I'll think of something." '

'And did she think of something?'

She moved her shoulders. 'I wasn't in touch with her again just then, I didn't expect to be, I knew she'd be extra busy, with the birthday, people coming to stay. But I didn't worry about it any more, I did as she said and left it to her. The next thing I heard was on the Sunday evening when Dorothy rang me to say Mrs Dalton had died. So that particular question never came up again, you might say the difficulty solved itself. Dorothy will have her legacy, she doesn't need a mortgage. Whichever one of us dies first, the cottage will go to the other one, absolutely.'

The inquest on Grace Veronica Dalton was set down for eleven on Friday morning. At half past eight Sergeant Lambert drove the Chief out to Elmhurst. Dorothy was in the kitchen, clearing up after breakfast. The Chief wasted no time but got down to brass tacks right away. He told her he'd been to see Alice Upjohn. He mentioned the phone call Alice had made to Dorothy on the Tuesday evening before the birthday weekend. 'This matter that was worrying Alice,' he said. 'How she would find herself situated if you chanced to die before Mrs Dalton. I understand you told her not to worry about it, you'd think of something.'

Dorothy regarded him imperturbably. 'Alice worries too much,' she said. 'She always has done. But she does sometimes have the knack of hitting the nail on the head. It was a very good point she came up with. Such a thought had never crossed my mind but the moment she mentioned it I saw it needed thinking about.'

'And did you think of something?'

She gave an energetic nod. 'Indeed I did. I went straight off to the building society, first thing next morning. I knew I wouldn't have any time later in the week, because of the birthday. I put the position to the manager and asked his advice. He said it wasn't at all an uncommon problem and there was a simple solution. We must be

183

sure to buy the cottage as joint tenants. I must take out a mortgage protection policy, he could arrange that for me. Then, if I died, the policy would pay off the mortgage and my half of the cottage would go to Alice, with not a penny owing.'

'Did you get as far as taking out the protection policy?'

She shook her head. 'I was going to sign up for it at the same time as I signed the mortgage papers. As it turned out, of course, neither of them was necessary.'

On the way back to the police station they called in at the building society where Dorothy had her account. The manager was able to see them right away.

Yes, he knew Miss Nevett well. She had opened an account with the bank way before his time, over forty years ago, in fact; she had been a regular saver ever since. He wished every client was as steady and reliable. When she had approached him in February about the possibility of a mortgage, he had had no hesitation in doing his best to help her.

He confirmed in every particular all that Dorothy had told him, including her phone call on Monday morning, explaining that she wouldn't after all be needing either the mortgage or the policy. She had been most apologetic for all the trouble she had put him to. 'But she wasn't to know the way things would turn out,' the manager said as he walked with them to the door. 'Not unless she was gifted with second sight.'

CHAPTER 18

James Milroy saw no reason to interrupt his busy schedule to attend the inquest on Grace Dalton. His wife and her brother would be there and that would surely be enough to represent the family.

Nor did Nina Dalton have any desire to attend. As she told her husband, she couldn't see that she would have anything to contribute and she certainly didn't wish to sit through what could only be a harrowing procedure. For his part, Matthew would have been only too glad to avoid the occasion, let Esther deal with everything. He was up to his ears at the office and Esther was currently displaying a keen appetite for organizing anything and everything arising from her stepmother's death. But there could be no escaping it; it was clearly his duty to attend the inquest as head of the family; everyone would expect it.

Gosling would be driving his wife, together with Dorothy Nevett and Jean Redfern to the Cannonbridge court house. No one had suggested—least of all themselves—that Verity or Barry should attend.

Esther had been in touch with Chief Inspector Kelsey and had learned that the proceedings were likely to be brief and formal. The inquest would undoubtedly be adjourned without any date set for resumption. The body would in all probability be released for burial.

Esther therefore drove over to the court house prepared to go on afterwards to Elmhurst, where she intended to spend the next few days arranging the funeral, with Jean Redfern's assistance. She had phoned Elmhurst to make her plans known to Dorothy Nevett, who heard them with no great enthusiasm, resigning herself to the irruption with such grace as she could muster.

Nor did Jean Redfern entirely relish

the prospect of being at Esther's disposal throughout the weekend. She had a shrewd notion that with Grace no longer in the picture, Madame Esther might prove a very different customer to reckon with, a good deal more demanding and pernickety.

Before proceedings began, the Chief took up his stand at the top of the court house steps, where he could cast his eye over arrivals. The Elmhurst contingent wore a sombre, subdued air in their dark outfits; Dorothy unfamiliar in a severe hat crammed squarely on her greying locks. Jean Redfern gave the Chief a cool little nod in passing. She appeared composed and watchful, though something in her manner and the way she held herself suggested a high degree of nervous tension under the surface calm.

Dr Wheatley walked slowly up the steps, sad and a little shrunken. Beside him came Esther, in a discreetly modish suit. The years seemed to be rolling away from her, some of her good looks were coming back. Her hair no longer showed threads of grey but was now a new and becoming shade of golden brown. She was doing most of the talking, gesticulating in an animated fashion.

Matthew Dalton arrived only after everyone had gone in. He looked well and buoyant. He glanced across the room at the Chief and raised a hand in greeting before he took his seat beside his sister. The pair sat with their heads together, conversing in whispers, for the few minutes that remained before the inquest began.

There were no surprises, everything went as expected. Afterwards, as they all emerged into the crisp air, there was a brief mingling, a little conversation. The Chief observed the way Matthew made a point of speaking to everyone, his manner, as always, easy and amiable. He saw how the Goslings warmed to him, how Jean relaxed in his presence, the smiling way Dorothy responded.

He was roused from his musings when Esther approached him with a determined step. She spoke briefly about the court proceedings, her intentions about the funeral. What she had in mind struck the Chief as straying some considerable distance from the quiet and simple ceremony her stepmother had wanted. His expression plainly said as much and Esther at once fired off her guns in reply. 'Grace belonged to a great many organizations over the years,' she declared in a tone of strong challenge. 'They'll all want to say goodbye to her, they'll all expect to send a representative. We can't simply ignore them, they'd be very hurt. Grace must have a proper send off. I'm positive she would realize that herself, if she could be here now. We can't let her go as if she'd played no part in any of these associations, as if she'd led a totally different life from the one she did lead.'

The Chief made no reply; there seemed little point. He could see by the resolute gleam in her eye that she was in no way to be moved. He fancied too that he could detect the deep satisfaction it gave her to find herself in a position to sweep aside the express wishes of her stepmother concerning her final appearance on the earthly stage.

CHAPTER 19

Ned Hooper and Mrs Freda Bradshaw were expected back from Paris at tea-time on Friday. In the early evening, Sergeant Lambert drove the Chief over to the apartment block in Brentworth, where the doorman confirmed that the couple had returned.

The door of the flat was opened to them by a tall, strongly-built man in his mid thirties. Good-looking, with fair hair and blue eyes, a frank, open expression.

'Mr Ned Hooper?' the Chief asked.

He gave a nod.

The Chief revealed his identity and asked if they could step inside—Mr Hooper might be able to help them in a case they were investigating.

Hooper made no demur, asked no questions, but readily stood aside to admit them into a spacious hall. As he led them towards a sitting room, a door opened along the hall and a woman appeared on the threshold. In her forties, poised and attractive, well dressed, well groomed. She gave them an inquiring glance. Hooper changed direction and took the two men across to be introduced.

'You'll want to speak to Ned in private,' Mrs Bradshaw said but the Chief told her he'd prefer her to be present. She glanced at Hooper who at once declared he had no secrets from her. Hooper then about turned and took them all across to the sitting room. The flat had the anonymous, expensively furnished appearance of its kind: modern lines, pastel shades, deep-piled carpets.

Mrs Bradshaw and Hooper took their seats together on a sofa. The Chief addressed himself to Hooper. 'I understand there has been a relationship between yourself and a student by the name of Verity Thorburn.'

Hooper gave a great sigh. 'That's right,' he replied with weary resignation. 'I'd been trying to end it for some time, without much success. I finally managed to break it off a few weeks back.'

'How did Verity take that?' Kelsey asked.

Hooper sighed again and shook his head. 'Not too well, I'm afraid.'

'I gather she came round here more than once, to try to speak to you?'

Hooper nodded. 'I spoke to her the first time she came but it didn't get us anywhere, so I told the doorman not to let her in again. I believe she came round another three or four times but she didn't get past him.' He grimaced. 'Until just now.'

'She's been here just now?'

He nodded. 'She left not twenty minutes ago. She must have hung about outside and sneaked in when the doorman wasn't looking.'

'What did she want?'

He grimaced again. 'It was the same old hysterical nonsense, trying to offer me money to take up with her again.'

'Exactly what did she have to say about money?'

'She said she'd have money coming to her very soon now,' Hooper answered in a tone of profound distaste. 'I could have every penny. All I had to do was move out of here and take up with her again.'

'What did you say to that?'

'I tried to reason with her. I told her I didn't want any of her precious money.' He flung out a hand. 'I told her to clear off and stop bothering me, I never wanted to lay eyes on her again. The best thing she could do was to forget me completely, concentrate on her studies, on making a sensible life for herself. And she should make good use of whatever money came to her, stop trying to give it away to whatever man she currently fancied.'

'How did she take that?'

'Pretty badly. She stormed out in the

end.' He looked straight at the Chief. 'I never had any thought of anything long term with Verity. I wish to God I'd never had anything to do with her, but it's a bit late for that now.' He drew a deep breath. 'Can you give me some idea what this is about? The doorman told me the police had been round while we were away, asking about Verity. She may be a damned nuisance but I wouldn't want to get her into any trouble with the law. She's just a silly girl who's lost her head over a break-up. She'll get over it. I can't see why the police need to come into it.'

The Chief didn't answer for some moments, then he said: 'I expect you've heard Verity mention a Mrs Grace Dalton?'

Hooper nodded. 'She often spoke of her. She's one of Verity's guardians, one of her trustees. Verity always called her Aunt Grace, though she wasn't any blood relation.'

'Mrs Dalton is dead,' Kelsey said blandly. 'She was found dead in bed last Sunday morning. There was an inquest this morning. There's no doubt about it, Mrs Dalton was murdered.'

Sergeant Lambert saw Mrs Bradshaw's jaw drop. She sat bolt upright.

'Murdered?' Hooper echoed with incredulity. 'Verity said nothing about that just now. Not one syllable.' He stared at the Chief. 'You're surely not suggesting Verity had anything to do with Mrs Dalton's death?'

'We're suggesting nothing,' the Chief said. 'We have to look into the background of everyone connected with Mrs Dalton, particularly everyone staying at Elmhurst over the weekend, as Verity was. They're purely routine inquiries. Verity isn't being singled out.'

Hooper nodded slowly. He wore an air of profound shock.

Mrs Bradshaw suddenly spoke up. 'May I ask in what way Mrs Dalton was murdered?'

'She was stabbed in the heart,' the Chief told her. 'With a long hatpin. It looked like natural causes at first.'

'A woman!' Mrs Bradshaw declared at once with conviction. 'It was a woman stabbed her with a hatpin. No man ever did that.'

The Chief let that pass. He addressed Hooper again. 'Can you recall exactly when Verity first began promising you money if you stayed with her?'

194

Hooper pondered. 'It would be five or six weeks ago, when I was trying to break off with her. I wasn't seeing much of her at the time, things were developing between Freda and me.'

'What precisely did Verity give you to understand at that time about the money? When she expected to get it? How much it would be?'

Hooper sat for some moments with his eyes closed, trying to recall. 'She said she had trust money coming to her when she was twenty-one,' he said slowly. 'And more, when she was twenty-five. Quite a lot of money, she said, but she didn't mention any figure, she never mentioned figures. She also said she was sure to be left a legacy when her Aunt Grace died, and again she implied it would be quite a lot of money. She said her aunt had heart trouble, so she wouldn't have to wait much longer for her legacy.'

'Did she expect to receive the whole of this legacy on her aunt's death or did she think she'd have to wait for some or all of it until she was twenty-one or twenty-five, like the trust money?'

Again Hooper pondered. 'She always spoke as if she was sure she wouldn't

195

have to wait for the legacy, she'd get the whole of it right away.'

Verity's basement flat was in a pleasant area, not far from the Brentworth college. The flat was in darkness, the curtains closed, when Sergeant Lambert halted the car outside. Repeated rings at the doorbell produced no response. 'It's no good, she's out,' Lambert said at last.

'Or lying down on her bed, behind those curtains,' Kelsey said. 'Sobbing her heart out.' He turned back to the car. 'We'll try again first thing tomorrow.'

And by eight-thirty next morning, Sergeant Lambeth was once more setting his thumb on the bell. This time Verity came to the door, after half a dozen rings. She wore a robe and slippers, she looked only half awake, her eyes puffy, as if she'd slept badly. She opened the door a little way and stared sulkily out at them. 'What do you want?' she demanded.

'If we might come inside,' the Chief said mildly. 'We prefer not to ask personal questions on the doorstep.'

She glowered at him for a moment or two longer, then she grudgingly held back the door for them to enter. She took them into a living room, reasonably tidy. A hotchpotch of landlord's furniture, very workaday, but arranged with an eye for effect. A few striking ornaments, some dramatic decorative touches.

She flung herself into an easy chair without a word. The two policemen sat down uninvited.

'I understand you had a relationship with a Mr Ned Hooper,' the Chief began.

Tears sprang to her eyes. She dashed them away.

'Did Mrs Dalton tackle you about that relationship last weekend?' Kelsey went on.

She dropped her gaze, shook her head forcefully.

'Did she ever mention it in any way at all?'

She shook her head even more forcefully. She frowned, clasping and unclasping her hands. 'I don't believe she ever knew about it.'

The Chief didn't enlighten her. 'I'm told you spoke to Mr Hooper some time ago, about your expectations under the trust and also about what you believed you might inherit under Mrs Dalton's will.'

She gave him a defiant stare. 'What if I did?'

'I'm told you gave him to understand you would inherit a good deal of money from Mrs Dalton. You wouldn't have to wait for the money, you expected to get it as soon as the will was proved.'

She made a sharply dismissive gesture. 'That was pure guesswork on my part. And a lot of wishful thinking.'

A ring sounded on the doorbell. She sprang to her feet and darted off to answer it, closing the living room door firmly behind her. There was a murmur of voices in the hall and then she came back into the room, with Barry Fielding following. He spoke a polite greeting to the two men. Verity took her seat again and gestured Barry towards a nearby chair. But he shook his head and remained standing, close beside her. 'I don't want to interrupt anything,' he said apologetically to the Chief. 'I can't stop long, anyway.' He turned to Verity. 'I tried to ring you yesterday evening, to ask you about the museum.'

'The museum?' Verity repeated. She grimaced. 'Oh, yes, the museum. I'm afraid I'd forgotten about it.'

Disappointment flashed across Barry's face. 'Don't say you're not coming! It's the Egyptian exhibition. You particularly wanted to see it.'

She considered for a moment, then she gave him a radiant smile. 'Yes, of course I'll come. I'd love to see it.'

He looked delighted. 'Right, then. I'll be back at two o'clock sharp. OK?'

'Fine,' she assured him. 'I'll be ready.'

'I'll get off then.'

Verity made to get up but he waved her down. 'I'll see myself out.' He pressed a hand on her shoulder in a warmly reassuring grip.

Verity's mood remained bouncy and cheerful after he had gone. 'I intend having another go at getting my trust money released,' she announced with breezy confidence. 'I'm going to set about it properly this time. I'm going to get Esther to help me; Mr Purvis will listen to her. I don't see why she shouldn't help. She'll be swimming in trust money herself, she shouldn't grudge me getting my hands on my share.' I can't see Esther going along with that, Sergeant Lambert reflected. Even if Esther had the power to influence Purvis, which he very much doubted. It was Esther who had told Mrs Dalton Verity was making a fool of herself, chasing after a college lecturer. But there again, Verity seemed not to be aware of that.

When the two policemen stood up to leave, a few minutes later, Verity went with them into the hall. 'Ned will come back to me,' she declared with smiling certainty. 'And before much longer. It's very far from over between us, whatever it suits Ned to say just now.'

CHAPTER 20

Esther Milroy was due home from Elmhurst on Monday evening. On Tuesday morning, the Chief had Sergeant Lambert drive him over to Oakfield Gardens.

Esther opened the door to them. She showed no surprise; she looked composed and at ease. She took them into a sitting room, furnished with taste, little thought for expense. It was scrupulously neat and tidy, with gleaming surfaces and spring-flower arrangements scenting the air.

It would seem they had disturbed her at her bureau. An upright chair stood before it. The drop-front of the bureau was down. A folded newspaper lay on the writing surface, the edges of other papers discernible beneath it.

The Chief began by asking if the funeral arrangements were going smoothly. She told him they were. She didn't enlarge but sat calmly waiting for him to say what was on his mind. He asked if Verity had been in touch with her in the last day or two, if she had asked Esther to use her influence with the trust solicitor, to persuade him to release some or all of Verity's future entitlement without delay.

Esther set her lips in an implacable line. Yes, that young lady had indeed been in touch with her, and for that very purpose. She had phoned Esther at Elmhurst on Saturday morning. 'I gave her short shrift,' Esther said grimly. 'I told her if she had any money problems she should go to Purvis direct, he's her guardian and trustee. It's nothing whatever to do with me.' She had no influence with Purvis. She had never had very much to do with him, he had never been her own solicitor.

Had she asked Verity why she wanted the money?

She shook her head. 'No, I did not. If it was for some genuine educational purpose, or for reasonable living expenses, she wouldn't need any help from me in persuading Purvis to let her have extra money. And if it was in pursuit of some piece of folly, then I didn't want to know. I've enough on my plate just now without going looking for more responsibility. But I did point out to her she'll be getting the first instalment of Grace's legacy when the will is proved. Surely that ought to be more than enough for a girl of her age, in her position.'

The Chief asked if she could recall at exactly what time on Saturday morning Verity had phoned her.

She thought back. 'It would be around nine-fifteen or nine-thirty.' Sergeant Lambert remembered Verity's buoyant mood as they were leaving her flat. She must have got on the phone to Esther the moment they'd left. 'I can't see Verity getting much joy from Purvis, if she goes ahead and asks him,' Esther said crisply. 'I'm sure the trust is far too tightly sewn up, my father would make sure of that. He'd never leave matters so a girl of eighteen could wheedle money out of a trustee ahead of time. And Purvis has never struck me as a soft touch. I can't see Verity being able to twist him round her little finger.

The phone rang in the hall. Esther excused herself and went along to answer it. The instant the sitting room door closed behind her, the Chief was on his feet, moving silently across to the bureau. He lifted up the newspaper. Underneath lay an assortment of gaily-coloured travel brochures. He flicked rapidly through them. They all showed villa holidays in various Greek islands. Some properties had inked ticks or question marks beside them. He registered the agent's stamp before replacing the newspaper and returning swiftly to his seat. He was gazing placidly about the room when Esther came back.

'I have to go out shortly,' she informed him. 'Is there anything else you want to ask?'

No, there was nothing else.

They made straight for the travel agent's. The manager was able to put the Chief on to the assistant who had handled the bookings for the Milroys over the years.

It had always been Mrs Milroy who had

booked the family holidays. It had always been the same holiday destination, the same high-class hotel at an exclusive east coast resort with a first-class golf course. 'The beach for the two boys, golf for Mr Milroy,' the assistant commented. When the boys got older they took to going off together on activity holidays; the parents still went to the same resort.

But this year it seemed that things might be about to change. Mrs Milroy had called in during the late autumn to pick up brochures advertising a range of holidays, all of them abroad. Villas, treks and safaris, cruises. She had called in three or four times since then, to pick up more brochures. Her most recent visit had been as late as last Thursday. She had struck him then as a good deal more focused and purposeful in her inquiries, which centred now on villa holidays, especially in the Greek islands. She spoke as if she would be in again before long to make a definite booking.

Shaun Chapman had to show his face on Tuesday, 17th March if he wanted a place on the construction gang. At a quarter to six on Wednesday evening, Sergeant

Lambert, with the Chief beside him, pulled out of the station forecourt, bound for the ganger's house.

They found him at home. Yes, Shaun had turned up. He had called at the house yesterday evening, he had started work this morning; nothing was said to him about any police inquiries. The ganger kept a list of landladies willing to take construction workers and after a couple of phone calls he had got Shaun fixed up with lodgings. He was doubtless in his lodgings at this moment, sitting down to a good meal.

And when the two policemen got round there a few minutes later, Shaun had just stood up from the table and was about to go across to the television lounge. His landlady intercepted him to say there were two gentlemen on the doorstep, asking to see him.

Shaun recognized the Chief instantly, for three years back; if he was surprised he didn't show it. The Chief asked if there was somewhere they could talk in private and Shaun took them up to the top-floor bedroom he shared with another construction worker who had already gone out for the evening.

Kelsey began by asking him exactly

when he had left Cannonbridge. Shaun answered without hesitation. 'I left on the Saturday morning, March the seventh, that would be.' He gave the Chief a forthright glance. 'Why do you want to know?'

The Chief didn't answer that but asked if he'd been in touch with Jean Redfern lately.

Shaun frowned. 'I met her a few times over the last few weeks, while I was in Cannonbridge.' Again he asked why the Chief wanted to know and again the Chief sidestepped his question and asked another of his own. 'When was the last time you saw Jean?'

Shaun cast his mind back. 'It was on the Thursday evening before I left. March the fifth that would be.'

'Have you been in touch with her since you left?'

He shook his head.

'Have you been in touch with your family since you left?'

'No, I haven't.' His tone grew urgent. 'Is there something wrong with one of them? Has there been an accident?'

'There's been no accident,' Kelsey assured him. 'All your family are perfectly all right—or they were when I saw them a week ago. And Jean Redfern's perfectly all right.'

Shaun's frown deepened. 'Then what's all this about?'

Again Kelsey responded with another question. 'You remember Mrs Grace Dalton?'

'Yes, of course I do,' Shaun replied with a grimace. 'I'm hardly likely to forget her. She's the woman Jean works for.'

'Used to work for,' Kelsey corrected. 'Mrs Dalton's dead.'

Shaun inclined his head. 'Can't say I'm surprised. She was no chicken. And she had a bad heart.' His voice sharpened. 'What has her death got to do with me?'

'It wasn't a natural death,' the Chief informed him. 'Mrs Dalton was murdered.'

'Murdered?' he echoed in tones of incredulity. 'When did it happen?'

'In the early hours of Sunday morning.'

There was a brief silence. 'It's no good looking at me,' Shaun burst out. 'I had nothing to do with it. I didn't know the old girl. I never clapped eyes on her. I'd nothing against her.'

'She stopped you marrying Jean Redfern,' the Chief reminded him.

He made a sharp dismissive gesture.

'That's ancient history.'

'Jean benefits financially under Mrs Dalton's will.'

'I'm glad to hear it.'

'There's nothing to stop her marrying now if she chooses. She'll have enough to buy a little flat and a tidy sum besides.'

'Is that so?'

'Do you think of marrying her yourself?'

He half smiled. 'If I do, I'll be sure to let you know.'

The Chief changed tack. 'Were you ever inside Elmhurst?'

He looked amused. 'As a matter of fact, I was once, way back. I called for Jean one evening, we were going out. When I say I called for her, I never went up to the house, I used to hang about outside the gates, waiting for her. This time, when she came out, she told me there was no one in the house except Dorothy Nevett and she was upstairs in her bath, she'd be there ages. It was a winter evening, the Goslings were in their cottage with the curtains drawn. Jean knew I'd always wanted to take a look round inside, see how the other half lives. She said she was sure it would be all right if I had a quick nip round. So that's what I did. I had a shufti round the downstairs rooms.' He grinned. 'A bit different from a council semi.'

'Have you been inside the house more recently?'

He shook his head. 'That was the only time.' There was a pause and then he asked: 'Why are you making all this fuss over the death of an old woman with a bad heart?'

'She was murdered,' Kelsey said. 'It's my job to find out who murdered her and bring that person to trial.'

Shaun had more to say. 'She'd had her three score years and ten, she wasn't entitled to any more. She was no plaster saint. She exploited Jean, kept her dancing attendance, stopped her having any proper life of her own.'

'Did Jean complain to you about the way she was treated?'

He moved his shoulders. 'Not exactly.'

'Did you point out to her how badly you thought she was treated? Did you encourage her to think she'd be better off if Mrs Dalton's heart finally gave out? She'd be free to please herself how she lived?'

'I never encouraged her to think like

that,' Shaun replied brusquely.

'Did you ever suggest she might do something about it?'

'I most certainly did not.'

'Did you put it to her that a good time to do something about it might be during the birthday weekend? If the death didn't pass for natural causes, no reason why anyone should look at Jean, plenty of other folk in the house who would benefit a lot more from Mrs Dalton's death.'

'You've got a good imagination,' Shaun said. 'I'll give you that.'

Kelsey executed another change of direction. 'Have you ever had a key to the house? Even for a short time?'

He looked astonished. 'No, of course I haven't. How would I have a key to the house?'

'You might have been lent it.'

'Who by? What for?'

Kelsey didn't answer those questions but fired off another himself. 'Did Jean remind you recently of your visit to the house? Did she refresh your memory of the interior, the layout? Did she bring you up to date about any changes in the way the downstairs rooms were used?'

Shaun set his jaw. 'No, she did not. We

never discussed anything of the sort.'

'Did she draw you a map of the interior? Particularly of the downstairs rooms?'

He clenched his fists. 'She never drew me any map.' He added between gritted teeth: 'This is getting beyond a joke.'

'It's not intended as a joke,' Kelsey returned calmly. 'It's deadly serious, believe you me.'

They sat in silence, regarding each other, then the Chief asked: 'How long do you intend staying in this job you've got now?'

'Till it finishes,' Shaun answered, in command of himself again. 'Could be another six weeks, from what they tell me.'

'And you're definitely staying till it finishes?'

He gave a decisive nod. 'Definitely. If you've anything more to say to me, you'll find me here. I won't be running away. I've no reason to.'

CHAPTER 21

Thursday afternoon was mild and cloudy as the Chief and Lambert set off again for Elmhurst. Mrs Gosling told them Dorothy Nevett had gone into Cannonbridge and would be back shortly. 'It isn't Dorothy we've come to see,' the Chief informed her. 'It's Jean Redfern.'

'Jean's up in her room, having a little rest,' she told him. 'She's only just gone up. She's not very well, she's starting one of her colds. She gets these heavy colds, poor girl, always has done, ever since she was a child. She gets to feeling pretty sorry for herself.'

'We would like to speak to her,' the Chief persisted.

'Oh yes, I'm sure that will be all right,' she conceded. 'I was just going to make her a hot toddy, that always seems to help. Mr Dalton started her off on that, years ago. He always took one himself for a cold, he swore by it. It was one time when Jean was ten or eleven and she had a particularly bad cold, he told her mother to give her some hot milk with a dash of whisky in it—his own good malt whisky that he always had. It seemed to do her good and after that she was always given it. She quite got to like it after a time.'

She smiled at the Chief. 'I'll pop up and tell her you'd like a word. When she comes down I'll bring along the toddy.' She went off, returning shortly to say Jean would be down in a minute. She took them into the sitting room before going off to the kitchen.

When Jean came into the room soon afterwards, she certainly looked far from well, flushed and heavy-eyed. She seemed restless and nervy. Mrs Gosling brought the toddy and Jean sat huddled in her chair, sipping her drink, clasping the beaker in both hands.

'We won't keep you from your rest any longer than necessary,' the Chief promised. 'We've a few questions we'd like to ask.' She gave a nod and he plunged straight in. 'Have you any idea who it was killed Mrs Dalton?'

She showed no surprise, merely shaking her head in reply; she continued sipping her drink.

'No suspicion even beginning to form in your mind as to who it could possibly have been?'

She shook her head again.

'If you did begin to suspect—or even discover—who it was, would you cover up for that person?'

She gave the same slow shake of her head.

'Would you speak out? Would you come to me and tell me what you suspected?'

She was briefly silent, then she said, 'I'm not sure what I'd do.' Her voice was low and hoarse.

'If it was someone you were fond of?' he persisted.

She began to look distressed. 'I'm not sure,' she said again.

He switched to another line. 'Were you never curious to find out if Mrs Dalton had left you anything in her will?'

She shook her head again.

'What did you think would happen to you when Mrs Dalton died?'

'I always thought I'd have to go straight out and look for a job. I thought I'd have to find digs in Cannonbridge.' She went on sipping from the beaker.

'Did Shaun ever ask you how you would

stand if Mrs Dalton died?'

She flushed and shook her head.

'He never once asked you?' Kelsey persisted.

Her colour deepened. 'He may have said something casual once, in passing. I would have told him I didn't know.'

'Did he ever suggest you might try to find out?'

'As a joke, maybe, not in any serious way.'

'Did he tell you Mrs Dalton was exploiting you? Making a dogsbody out of you?'

She looked away. 'He may have said something of the sort but I never paid much attention. He talks a lot of hot air at times, it isn't meant seriously.'

'Did Shaun ever suggest you didn't have to put up with being exploited? You could do something about it?'

She began to shake her head before he had finished speaking. 'No!' she burst out as soon as he had stopped. 'He never suggested anything like that!'

'Did it never cross your mind that if Mrs Dalton didn't last much longer—and if she had made good provision for you in her will—you could be free of her control?

Free to marry Shaun. You could get him to settle down. All he needed was a steadying influence and he'd be a different person, a sensible, reliable young man, with a regular job. He might even start up a little business if he had a bit of capital behind him. Or the two of you might start one up together.'

Throughout all this she was ceaselessly shaking her head. The moment he broke off she burst out again: 'No! No! No! I never thought anything like that!'

He looked at her in silence before continuing. 'On the night of the birthday, it was you who went round locking up?' She nodded. 'Did you leave the back door or one of the side doors unbolted?'

She shook her head at once. 'No, I'm sure I didn't. I've always been very careful over the locking up.'

'I wasn't suggesting you forgot to bolt one of the door. I'm asking if you deliberately left a door unbolted. Or, maybe, later on, after everyone had gone to bed, you slipped downstairs and slid back the bolts of one of the doors. Then, first thing in the morning, before anyone else was up, you nipped down and bolted the door again.'

Her brows came together in a frown. 'No, of course I didn't. Why would I do a stupid thing like that?'

'To allow someone to enter the house with a key after everyone was in bed. Shaun Chapman, for instance.'

Anger flashed across her face. 'I've never been on those sort of terms with Shaun, whatever you may think. I've never been to bed with him. I've never let him into the house at night. I would never do such a thing. And he's never asked me to.'

'I wasn't suggesting you might want to admit him so he could go up to your room.'

'Then what were you suggesting?'

He didn't answer that but fired another question: 'Did you ever lend Shaun your doorkey? Telling him where he could leave it afterwards, so you could pick it up again?'

She had ceased to show surprise. She answered with vigour: 'No! Never! I would never lend my doorkey to anyone.'

'Has Shaun ever been inside Elmhurst?'

'Yes, he was inside once,' she answered without hesitation. 'It was when I knew him before. He came inside one evening for a few minutes when there was no one

217

about. Just to look round.'

'Was he ever inside in more recent times?'

'No, never,' she answered at once.

'Did you draw a map for him in more recent times? To refresh his memory of the layout? To show him any changes in the way rooms are used now?'

'No, I didn't.' She was frowning again. 'I can't see any reason why I should ever do such a thing. Or why you should suggest it.'

'Can't you?' he came back at her. She made no reply.

'Was Shaun in touch with you at all over the birthday weekend?' he went on.

'No, he wasn't.' She sank back into her chair and closed her eyes briefly.

'Has he been in touch with you since that weekend?' There was an appreciable silence. 'I can ask Dorothy Nevett as soon as she gets back,' the Chief said. 'She may be able to tell us if there have been any letters or phone calls for you.'

There was another, shorter, silence, then she said: 'Shaun rang me yesterday evening.'

'What did he have to say?'

'He said you'd been over to see him,

you'd told him Mrs Dalton had died, that was the first he'd heard of it. He was very sorry to hear of it and the way it had happened. He knew I'd be very upset, he wanted to make sure I was all right.'

'What else did he have to say? I want to hear all of it.'

'He knew about the money Mrs Dalton had left me,' she continued after a moment. 'He said you'd told him. He said he hoped I'd be given time to make proper plans before I had to move out of Elmhurst. Then he told me about himself, what he was doing, where he was working. He wasn't on the phone long, he was ringing from a call box and he didn't have many coins with him. He said I must try not to let the funeral upset me too much and I must take care of my cold. He'd ring me again in a day or two to see how I was.'

The Chief sat contemplating her, then he asked: 'Did you know Mrs Dalton rang her solicitor's office on the morning of her birthday, to make an appointment for yesterday, to make some alteration to her will?'

She shook her head.

'You didn't overhear that phone call?'

This time her headshake was brisker.

'You're not going to tell me you'd never dream of eavesdropping on a phone call?' She bit her lip and lowered her head.

'Wouldn't it normally be you, in recent times, who phoned to make appointments for Mrs Dalton?'

'Yes, usually,' she agreed.

'Then why do you suppose she didn't ask you to make that particular call? With all that was going on, because of the birthday, and with her wanting to conserve her energy as much as possible, why not get you to make the call?'

She drained her beaker and set it down. 'I don't know,' she answered.

'Could it have been because the alteration in her will concerned yourself?'

'I've no idea.' A tear trickled down her cheek. She dabbed it away.

'When Dorothy Nevett told you on the Saturday night that Mrs Dalton knew you were seeing Shaun again, did you at once realize what Mrs Dalton's phone call had probably meant? Did it flash through your mind that she intended making a change in her will, concerning you, maybe cutting you out altogether?'

She was shaking her head ceaselessly again.

'You knew what was in her will, you'd made it your business to know. Did you think: "I've got to stop her altering her will"? You helped her get ready for bed, helped her on with the new nightdress, the nightdress with the pattern of dots and rosebuds. Did you see in an instant what might be done without anyone suspecting? After you'd gone upstairs, did you lie awake in bed, thinking it over, working it out? Until a moment came in the early morning when you made up your mind and you got out of bed?'

She went on shaking her head. Tears ran unchecked down her face. 'None of it's true! Not a word of it! It was never like that!'

'But you are, in fact, a good deal better off by Mrs Dalton's death.'

That brought her up sharp. She made a strong effort at control. She took out a handkerchief and dried her eyes. When she had achieved some degree of calm she said in a voice that still shook: 'That isn't the way I see it. I've lost the best friend I've ever had or am ever likely to have. I'm losing the only home I've ever known. I'll never have one even remotely like it again.' Her voice grew stronger. 'I've had time to think things over since Mrs Dalton died. I wish now I'd tried to do more of what she wanted me to do: study, take classes, go in for some proper training. I knew she was right but I kept putting it all off, I thought there'd be time for all that later on.'

She gave the Chief a direct look. 'I've made up my mind to do what she wanted, make something of myself, stand on my own feet. I'm not going to let her down, I'm going to be someone she could be proud of if she could be here to see how things turn out. I owe her that much, at least.'

It was late by the time the Chief finally got to bed on Thursday night, weary and dispirited. Tomorrow, Grace Dalton would be laid to rest and they were no nearer discovering the identity of her killer.

He sank almost at once into a restless sleep, assailed by the kind of dream that often troubled him in the middle of a difficult case. He was journeying by train, his luggage up on the rack. Opposite him sat a respectable looking old lady, busy knitting. The train reached a large station where there was a five-minute wait. He could see a bookstall a few yards away.

The old lady showed no sign of budging, so he asked if she would keep an eye on his luggage; she smiled assent. He left the train and went along to the bookstall, bought a magazine and turned back to the train, glancing in through the windows to locate his seat. Nowhere could he spot the old lady, or his luggage. He hurried on to the next coach, looking in; no luck there. Nor at the next coach or the one after that. He reached the front coach as the train was about to leave. He jumped in and began to work his way along the entire length of the train.

No sign of the old lady, no sign of his luggage, not a single passenger he recognized. They all sat reading, chatting, dozing. No one looked up at him with any sign of recognition; he felt himself passing by like a ghost. As he reached the rear of the train he was struck by a horrid thought: had he turned the wrong way when he left the bookstall? Turned to the wrong platform? Had he boarded the wrong train?

He woke up, sweating, as he always did at this point; his heart pounding, feeling totally lost, stranded and rootless. It took him some moments to orient himself in the darkness before he could reach out to switch on his bedside light. The clock showed two-thirty. He got out of bed, pulled on his dressing gown and slippers. He went along to the kitchen to heat some milk.

He paced about, sipping his milk, frowning down at the floor, yearning for some decisive action he might take, some path that might lead him out of the morass. After ten minutes he had come up with only one idea, and that seemed far from inspired.

He could ask everyone who had been at Elmhurst over the birthday week-end—including Dr Wheatley, Mrs Gosling's father and the two garden lads—to write out as detailed an account as possible of everything they remembered of the weekend: the sequence of events, their own movements, their observation of the movements and behaviour of others. With no discussion, no comparing of notes, no reading anyone else's account.

They would all surely be at the funeral. He would watch his moment to make discreet approaches, to an individual or a group, overlooking no one. He could allow the weekend for the task, that seemed reasonable. He could pick up all the accounts first thing on Monday morning.

The exercise might not amount to very much, or even to anything at all, but it would at least be a positive step, it might just conceivably yield some glimmer of light to point the way out of the morass.

He finished his milk and went back to bed. In no time at all he had fallen asleep again. This time he slept soundly until the trill of the alarm sounded and the new day began in earnest.

CHAPTER 22

The funeral of Grace Veronica Dalton was arranged for eleven o'clock on Friday morning. The previous vicar had declared himself more than willing to conduct the service for his old friend. She would be laid to rest under the yews of the village churchyard where her husband and his first wife awaited her, with other members of the Dalton family. There hadn't been a shred of jealousy or possessiveness in Grace's nature nor in the nature of Bernard's first wife; all three of them would lie peacefully together in the cradling earth.

The morning was brilliantly sunny; bright blue skies feathered with white cloud. The church was crowded with mourners; there was a vast array of floral tributes. The Chief took his stand, as always on such occasions, at the back and to one side, a position which allowed him a wide view of the congregation.

Esther Milroy was accompanied by James and their two sons, who had insisted on flying home for the funeral. There was to be no reception afterwards at Elmhurst. In that, at least, Esther had deferred to her stepmother's wishes. She had invited the old rector, together with Purvis and Dr Wheatley, to an early lunch after the funeral, at a quiet country hotel a few miles away, before the rector had to drive back home. Matthew and Nina would be there, as well as James and the two boys.

The Chief studied the Milroy family, the boys so like their father; they seemed to have an easy relationship with him. Their attitude towards their mother, though pleasant enough, seemed to carry a patronizing edge. Esther appeared something of an outsider in the group. She and James scarcely ever glanced at each other, never seemed to touch. Whenever the Chief encountered the pair of them together these days, he never received an impression of a united couple but rather a sense as of two ropes insecurely knotted together, being pulled in opposite directions, dragging inexorably apart.

During the service, the Chief saw many a tear shed for Grace's passing. Mrs Gosling, standing between her father and husband, dabbed ceaselessly at her eyes. Nearby stood the garden lads in their dark suits, heads bowed. Further along the pew Dorothy Nevett, in the same severe hat she had worn to the inquest, stared resolutely ahead. At her side, Jean Redfern struggled for composure between bouts of sneezing and blowing her nose.

Whenever the Chief's eyes wandered to the Milroy family he found James's head turned at a slight angle, permitting his gaze to rest discreetly on one of the occupants of the pew in front: Nina Dalton, elegant in black. Esther's eyes, the Chief observed, didn't fail to note the direction of her husband's gaze. Nina had known James for some months before she met Matthew, the Chief remembered Grace telling him once.

James would have been married some years by then, with much of his career still to make. Married with two sons on whom he doted, on whom he would never have turned his back. Both sons grown up now and independent.

As they came out into the sunlight, the air smelled fresh and sweet. Birds sang from the churchyard trees. At the moment of committal, Mrs Gosling wept openly. Nina leaned forward to cast a flower into the grave. Barry and Verity stood close together, Barry's face full of grief and loss, Verity's head bent, her dark fall of hair obscuring her features.

Afterwards, Matthew and Esther embarked together on a circuit of the mourners, pausing to speak to groups and individuals. The Chief managed, with some adroit dodging about, to get in all his requests for the drawing up of accounts of the birthday weekend; he encountered nothing but ready cooperation.

'Though I'm afraid I won't be here first thing on Monday morning, to let you have my account,' Dorothy Nevett told him. 'I'm going down to the caravan for the weekend. Alice will be there too. I'm leaving today, as soon as I get back to

Elmhurst to change. But I'll be sure to write out my account for you while I'm at the caravan. I can let you have it as soon as I get back—that should be around midday on Monday.' The Chief expressed himself satisfied with that.

Mrs Gosling also had some difficulty about Monday morning. 'I'll make sure I have my account finished for you by Sunday evening,' she promised the Chief, 'but I'll be out Monday morning—it's my turn to help with Shopaid.' This was a voluntary group that assisted the disabled and the frail elderly once a week with their shopping, at a time when the shops were least busy. 'I catch the early bus into Cannonbridge,' she said. 'I get back home about twenty past eleven.'

'That's all right,' the Chief assured her. 'I'll be leaving Elmhurst till the last in any case, because of Dorothy.'

When the crowd showed signs of dispersing, the Chief stationed himself in a quiet corner of the churchyard. Esther and Matthew positioned themselves by the lychgate, shaking hands with the mourners as they took their leave. On her way to join them, Nina was intercepted by a former member of the Elmhurst staff, a woman of forty-five or so, who had worked as a general domestic for the Daltons from the age of twenty until her marriage, five years ago. She began to chat to Nina with animation. It seemed her marriage hadn't prospered and she was now divorced, working in a hotel at a south coast resort. She was at present spending a holiday with her brother and his family in a town an hour's drive from Cannonbridge. She had read about Mrs Dalton's death in the county journal and had at once decided to attend the funeral, to pay her last respects. She had been given a lift by a neighbour driving over to Cannonbridge on business.

Nina took her over to the Elmhurst group and there was a fresh outpourings of greetings, questions, explanations, a swift summary of the last few years, a melancholy appraisal of the terrible end that had befallen Mrs Dalton, an assessment of the current situation with regard to Elmhurst.

'I'd ask you over to the house,' Dorothy said with apology, 'but I'm off to Dorset for a day or two, to the caravan.'

'I couldn't come just now in any case,' the woman told her, with a glance at her wristwatch. 'I have to be getting along to the village green, I'm getting a lift back to my brother's house.' A thought struck her. 'Your caravan isn't forty miles from the hotel where I work. We could meet down there some time.'

'We could indeed,' Dorothy agreed with pleasure. 'I'd better have your address.' She rummaged about in her bag and produced a jotter. She scrabbled about for something to write with, without success. 'I've got a pen,' Nina said with ready goodwill. She delved into her bag. 'Here you are.' She thrust the pen at Dorothy who gave her a nod of thanks and began to write at the woman's dictation.

As Nina turned her head, she caught sight of a fellow charity worker she wanted a word with. She excused herself and went rapidly off. A few minutes later, when she had said what she had to say, she looked across at the lychgate and saw Matthew standing with Esther, James and the two boys. The old rector was close by, with Purvis and Dr Wheatley. They were all looking her way, clearly waiting for her to join them, in order to set off for lunch for the hotel. She went quickly over and made her apologies.

When the last of the mourners had gone, the Chief crossed the churchyard to stand in the sunshine beside the grave. The air was full of the scent of flowers. He had a sudden sharp flash of vision: Grace smiling up at him from her sofa, that last time he had seen her. Come and see me again when you can, she had said. Better not leave it too long.

By two o'clock, Mrs Gosling had waved Dorothy Nevett off to Dorset, packed Jean Redfern, with all her snuffles and sneezes, off to bed, set a sustaining lunch before her husband and father—not forgetting to carry a tempting little tray across to Jean—and then cleared up after the meal and tidied her kitchen.

And still she couldn't settle down to relax, with her mind at ease; still she was plagued by restlessness, recurring waves of sadness that threatened to overwhelm her. She had a nagging thought that she ought to make a start on writing down her account for the Chief but she couldn't concentrate on that just yet.

Nothing for it, she decided in the end, but her old sovereign remedy for all ills of the spirit: a good, solid bout of cleaning.

She would have liked to set about Mrs Dalton's bedroom but that was still locked and out of bounds. But there was nothing to stop her giving Mrs Dalton's old bedroom, together with the adjoining dressing room and bathroom, a thorough going over. She would clean and polish every last inch, her own way of bidding farewell to Mrs Dalton and the days now gone for ever.

In the car on the way home from the hotel lunch, Matthew and Nina sat silent for most of the journey, lost in thought. Then Matthew roused himself to say: 'I won't be sorry to get back to work, take my mind off it all.'

Nina came out of her absorption. 'Will you be staying late?' she inquired.

'I did plan to,' Matthew said, 'but if you'd rather I didn't—'

'No, that's all right,' she assured him. 'Stay as long as you want. It's just that I thought if you were going to be working, I might go over to the cottage for a few hours, do a bit of gardening.'

'Good idea,' Matthew encouraged her. 'I've been thinking about the cottage. I know you'd hate to lose it. I can't see why I shouldn't take it as part of my share of the trust money.' Developers were showing keen interest in the Elmhurst land. The figures being mentioned were higher than he had ever hoped.

A radiant smile flashed across Nina's face. 'That would be wonderful!' she exclaimed.

'I thought you'd be pleased. It'll have to be properly valued, of course.' He pulled up to drop her at the house.

'I'll give you a ring around five-thirty,' Nina said. 'To see how much longer you're likely to be.' He gave her a tender kiss before driving off.

Nina stayed inside the house only long enough to change, then she was into her car and off to the cottage through the glittering afternoon, to the peace and beauty of the garden, a picture just now, with its glorious profusion of daffodils.

CHAPTER 23

Monday dawned bright and mild. It was no hardship for Kelsey or Lambert to get out of bed earlier than usual, in order to make a swift dash over to Brentworth.

They went first to the Milroy household. 'If you need to speak to me when you pick up my account,' James had warned them at the funeral, 'you'll have to be at the house before eight, I'm always off by then. I'd rather you didn't come to the office.'

The Chief intended staying at every call only long enough to cast an eye over each account, ask any questions that might immediately suggest themselves. A full scrutiny of the accounts would come later.

They found Esther and James alone; the boys had left on Sunday. The atmosphere in the house was brisk and businesslike. Both accounts were ready for them. James hadn't spent much time at Elmhurst over the birthday weekend and so he had covered very few pages in his neat, cramped writing. Esther had spent considerably more time at Elmhurst that weekend; she produced a much longer account, written in a sprawling schoolgirl hand.

The mood at their next call was a good deal more relaxed. Matthew was still at the breakfast table. Nina welcomed them with a smile and gave them coffee. Her account was moderately long, flawlessly typed. Matthew's was much shorter, written in a large, lively hand. 'I wasn't at Elmhurst very long that weekend,' he told them in his amiable way. 'I couldn't think of a lot to put in.'

Their next stop was at Verity's flat. Sergeant Lambert would have bet good money that Verity would keep them waiting before appearing, half asleep, in dressing gown and slippers, able to produce only a jumble of untidy notes and a string of excuses.

He would have lost his bet. She answered the door at once, fully awake, composed and at ease. She was dressed in outdoor clothes, ready to leave for the college. She handed over her account immediately—several pages, neatly typed. She uttered not one word beyond what was strictly necessary. They were in the flat only a very few minutes before going on to Barry's school.

Lessons had already begun. When Barry was summoned from class, he brought his account with him: several closely written pages.

Their last call—for the moment—was on Dr Wheatley. He was holding his morning surgery and saw them briefly between patients. He handed over a short account, clearly set out in an old-fashioned hand.

Then it was back to the police station, to read and digest. Shortly before eleven they went out to Elmhurst, calling first at the cottage, where Gosling had his account ready: a few pages, methodically set out. His father-in-law had couched his recollections in the form of a diary of the weekend, with staccato entries. Gosling called in on the two garden lads, who handed over their offerings: concise, workmanlike accounts.

Mrs Gosling turned up shortly before eleven-thirty. She produced a lengthy account, penned in a round, clear hand, in a new school exercise book. 'Jean should be awake by now,' she told the Chief as she took them over to the house. She hadn't seen her so far today; Jean had said she'd like a long lie-in this morning. As they approached the front door, she suddenly remembered the milk, still standing outside the back door, in the vitamin-destroying sunlight. She clicked her tongue at the thought. 'I'll just pop round and get it,' she said. 'I won't be a moment.' She darted off, returning with the bottles in a bird-proof container. 'I've been ordering extra these last few days,' she said as she set the container down, to take out her keys. 'Jean's drinking a lot of hot milk, with her cold. That, and eggs and soup, is about all she's been having.'

She unlocked the door and let them in. 'Doesn't Jean bolt the doors at night?' the Chief inquired.

'Yes, she always bolts them,' Mrs Gosling assured him. 'She's most particular about that. What she's been doing this last day or two, while she's been under the weather, she's been nipping down here first thing, when she wakes up, to unbolt this door so I can get in when I want to, then she pops back into bed.'

She left them in the hall while she took the milk along to the kitchen, then she came bustling back to take them up to Jean's bedroom.

She tapped lightly on the door. 'It's me,' she called. 'Are you awake?' There was no reply, no sound from within. She tapped again, more loudly. 'Are you awake?' she asked again. 'May I come in? I've got the chief inspector here. He's come for your account.'

Still no response, no sound. 'I expect she's in the bathroom,' Mrs Gosling said. 'She likes a good hot soak when she has

238

a cold. I'll just take a peep inside her room.'

She opened the door and glanced in. The bedside lamp was on, the curtains closed. Jean lay back against supporting pillows, her eyes closed, her hands lying slack outside the covers. Near the fingers of her right hand a prayer book lay open. She wore a nightgown and cardigan. In the subdued light she looked peacefully asleep.

'Jean?' Mrs Gosling said. There was no reply.

On a small table drawn up by the bed stood a tray, holding a whisky bottle, beaker, milk jug, two teaspoons on a saucer. And a small pill bottle, with its cap lying beside it.

Mrs Gosling gave a little gasp as she looked from Jean to the tray, back again to Jean, the open prayer book, the empty pill bottle. 'Oh, no!' she exclaimed in a voice of despair. She began to cry.

The Chief crossed to the bed and laid a hand on Jean's forehead. He raised an eyelid, felt for a pulse. 'She's dead, isn't she?' Mrs Gosling said in trembling tones.

The Chief straightened up with a long

sigh. 'I'm afraid so. She's been dead some time.' He looked down at the prayer book. A silk marker held the pages open at Prayers for the Dying.

He turned to the tray. The whisky bottle was one quarter full. The jug still held a little milk. A few drops of milk remained in the beaker. He bent down and sniffed at it. It smelled strongly of whisky. The pill bottle bore no label, though a surviving fragment of paper showed where the label had been.

'Why would she want to do away with herself?' Mrs Gosling asked brokenly. She gave way to a fresh bout of crying. 'I should never have gone out yesterday evening,' she said through her tears. 'If I'd stopped in, if I'd come over to see her, if she'd had someone to talk to, she'd never have done it.'

'You mustn't go blaming yourself,' Kelsey said.

'I should never have left her sleeping alone in the house, with Dorothy away,' she added in another burst of self-reproach. 'Full of a cold, as well, enough to make anybody feel down. I should have made her come over to the cottage. I did suggest it to her on Friday evening but she would

240

have it she'd be all right, she wasn't nervous on her own. She could have got to brooding about the way Mrs Dalton went, she could have got to feeling very low.'

'Did she strike you as depressed the last time you saw her?' Kelsey asked. 'When exactly was the last time?'

She dried her eyes. 'I brought her over a cup of tea and some cake at four o'clock yesterday afternoon. That was all she wanted. I can't say she struck me as depressed, but it's hard to tell when someone has a bad cold. She was certainly pleased she'd finished her account for you.'

'Her account!' Kelsey echoed. He glanced round the room. 'Do you know for certain that she did actually write it? And finish it?'

'I'm positive,' she declared. 'She didn't feel like starting it on Friday but on Saturday morning she decided to make a start on it. She put on her dressing gown and went along to her office next door, so she could use the typewriter. She mentioned the account to me two or three times after that. She said how it was coming along and I said how I was getting on with mine. I told her I'd bought an exercise book when I was out shopping on Saturday morning. She said she was using the good white paper from her office. When I took her the tea over, yesterday afternoon, she told me she'd finished the account.'

'Did you actually see the finished account?' Kelsey pressed her.

'Yes, I did. When she was talking about it, she pointed over to where she'd put it, ready for when you called.' She gestured at a chest of drawers with a Victorian toilet mirror on top. 'It was on that chest, beside the mirror, I definitely saw it there. It looked quite thick, several pages.' She sent a searching gaze round the room. 'I can't see it anywhere now.'

The two men made a rapid tour of the room. Lambert looked under the dressing gown draped over the back of an easy chair. He lifted the seat cushion, ran a hand inside the loose cover. He crouched down to look under the bed.

The Chief took a metal nail file and a folded tissue from his pocket. With their aid, and the lightest of touches, he eased open the drawers of chest and bureau, the doors of cupboards and wardrobe; he lowered the drop-front of the bureau.

Nowhere any trace of the account.

'She could have destroyed it,' Sergeant Lambert said. 'She may have changed her mind after she'd written it, got cold feet, maybe, decided she'd said more than she'd intended.'

An ornamental screen stood before the fireplace. There was no sign of ashes in the hearth—nor, as a quick look round the rest of the house revealed, in any other fireplace on the premises. The dustbins had been emptied three days ago and now held little waste; certainly not the account, or any part of it.

In Jean's office, Mrs Gosling showed them the heavy quality A4 paper Jean had used. They looked in every drawer and cupboard in the office, inspected the contents of the wastebasket, without success. The Chief took a sheet of the A4 paper along to the nearest bathroom, tore it into small pieces, dropped them into the pan and pulled the flush. After four flushes three pieces of paper still remained floating. A swift inspection of the other bathrooms and toilets revealed no such floaters anywhere.

As they were returning to Jean's bedroom, they heard a car drive up to the house. The

Chief went to a window and looked down. Dorothy Nevett was getting out of her car; Gosling was walking across to greet her. As they stood chatting, Gosling chanced to glance up and caught sight of the Chief—and the expression on the Chief's face. Dorothy followed his gaze and their conversation came to an abrupt end. They both turned at once towards the house.

The Chief left the window and went down into the hall to meet them. The sound of the front door opening and closing brought Mrs Gosling to the head of the stairs.

Neither Dorothy nor Gosling spoke as they entered. 'I'm afraid I've got bad news for you,' the Chief said heavily. 'Very bad news. I'm afraid Jean's dead.' They stood transfixed.

'She went and killed herself,' Mrs Gosling said shakily as she came down the stairs. 'We found an empty pill bottle.' She began to cry.

Gosling looked from her, back to the Chief. 'Did she leave a letter?' he asked.

'We haven't found one,' the Chief told him.

Dorothy roused herself to say: 'I can't say I'm altogether surprised.'

'Why is that?' the Chief asked sharply.

She drew a sighing breath. 'She seemed to have tendencies that way. She was very down a few years back, when she broke it off with Shaun Chapman. Mrs Gosling and I had to speak to her several times, make her see she'd got to snap out of it.'

'That's right,' Mrs Gosling confirmed. She dabbed at her eyes. 'She did talk very foolishly sometimes. But she was very young at the time, and she did seem to get over it. I never saw any sign of it in the last year or two.'

Back in Jean's bedroom a little later, as the Chief stood glancing about the room, it occurred to him there was one place they hadn't looked for the account and that was under Jean's pillows. He crossed to the bed where she still lay in her relaxed posture; he reached gently in under the lowest pillow.

His fingers encountered the hard edges of a book. Lambert stood watching as the Chief drew out his find: a diary, fairly large, two days to a page.

It opened at the last entry, where a pen had been slipped between the pages; a ballpoint pen, with the point exposed, the cap on the other end. The entry, several closely written lines, was for yesterday, Sunday, 22nd March.

He flicked back through the pages. Most days had similar closely-written entries. He turned again to the final entry. It broke off part way through a sentence, the last word only half completed. As if, he thought, Jean had been interrupted in her writing, had thrust the pen between the pages, not pausing long enough to cap the pen, and then pushed the diary under the pillows.

He scanned the final entry, glanced through the entries for the previous few days. Nothing in any way indicative of serious depression, nothing to suggest she was about to take her own life. He turned his head to look at the tray and its contents.

'I don't know about suicide,' he said to Lambert. 'We could be looking at murder.'

CHAPTER 24

In the middle of the afternoon, with Jean's body gone to the mortuary and the forensic team still at work in the house, the Chief left Elmhurst to call on Dr Wheatley, to acquaint him with what had happened. It was Wheatley who had brought Jean into the world, he had been her mother's doctor until she had left for the States, Jean's doctor until he retired.

The Chief caught him as he returned from visiting a patient. He told Wheatley what had happened, without deductions or surmises; Wheatley listened with shock and sorrow. 'The postmortem's at six-thirty,' Kelsey added. It would be held at the Cannonbridge General Hospital. 'We're on our way now to Brentworth, to break the news to Matthew Dalton.'

The Chief asked if Jean had consulted Wheatley recently but the doctor shook his head.

Had he ever considered Jean a suicide risk?

Wheatley looked thoughtful. 'I can't say there was ever a time when I felt that was a definite possibility,' he replied after some moments, 'but, looking back on it now, her temperament was always liable to depression. There were a lot of negative feelings there, a lot of unresolved anger and resentment towards her mother. She did her best to keep it all buried away but it popped out from time to time. The Daltons were very good to her but she always had this feeling of never having been wanted, having no real family, being absolutely on her own, an outsider at Elmhurst. If she came under any additional stress, I believe she would have found it very difficult to cope.' He paused. 'Taking all that into account, I suppose I must say now—with the benefit of hindsight—that she could have been considered a suicide risk.'

It was Matthew Dalton's secretary who dealt with the two policemen when they arrived. Matthew was in conference; he would be there for some time. 'I'm afraid we must ask you to disturb him,' the Chief informed her. 'We must speak to him and we can't wait. We won't keep him more than a minute or two.' She went off without further protest. Matthew came along almost at once and took them to his office.

It was clear from his look and manner that the Chief's unannounced visit had prepared him for unpleasant tidings of some sort. When Kelsey gave him the bald facts he dropped his head into his hands and sat in silence for several moments, then he raised his head and looked across at the Chief, his face wretched. 'Where will it end?' he asked. His eyes searched the Chief's face. 'What do you make of it? Her dying like that?' Kelsey made no reply. 'She was barely twenty,' Matthew said in anguished tones. 'She had her whole life before her.'

The Goslings were in their cottage when the Chief got back to Elmhurst. Mrs Gosling was in the sitting room, resting with her feet up, trying to restore herself. At the sound of the car, Gosling came out to meet him. 'We would like to talk to you both,' the Chief said. 'Particularly your wife. We'll keep it as short as possible.' Gosling went off to see if his wife felt up to it, coming back a minute or two later to assure them it would be all right. They followed him inside.

Mrs Gosling was sitting up, tidying her hair. Her face was flushed; she looked heavy-eyed and weary. The Chief began by asking if either of them had seen or heard anything of a car yesterday afternoon or evening.

'We were all out yesterday evening,' Gosling told him. 'The old man, as well.' They had left the cottage at five-thirty. All three of them went every Sunday to evening service, in whichever parish church it was being held. They always went for supper afterwards to one or other of their many relatives scattered over the neighbouring countryside, returning home by ten.

'I've spoken to the garden lads,' Gosling added. 'Neither of them came near Elmhurst yesterday. They were both at a clay pigeon shoot in the afternoon, they went out afterwards with some of their mates.'

The Chief asked Mrs Gosling if there had been any visitors for Jean over the weekend. Had she received any phone calls? No, there had been neither visitors nor phone calls—or none Mrs Gosling knew of. 'I wasn't over there all the time,' she pointed out. 'I was there all Friday afternoon and she had no callers then.' She made a little grimace. 'I spent the afternoon cleaning Mrs Dalton's old rooms, I made a thorough job of them—I was upset after the funeral, I couldn't rest.' She moved her head. 'I daresay some would think there wasn't much point to it, but I do know it made me feel a lot better.'

The Chief asked if any member of the Dalton family had been over to the house since Grace's funeral. Again he was told no, not to Mrs Gosling's knowledge.

Had she come across any pills or tablets when she was turning out Grace's old bathroom? She shook her head. 'The cabinet's empty. It was cleared out when Mrs Dalton moved downstairs.'

Had Jean's prayer book been in evidence when Mrs Gosling last saw Jean, yesterday afternoon? She thought back but couldn't recall seeing it. In the ordinary way it would be kept on a bookshelf near the bed.

She could explain the presence on the tray of the two spoons, which showed a milky residue in their bowls. It seemed

Jean had never been able to swallow any sort of tablet; she would crush it between two spoons before stirring it into whatever liquid she was using to wash it down.

Did she know of any tablets Jean had?

She pondered. 'She usually had some aspirin and paracetamol. And she had some painkillers from the doctor after she pulled a muscle, playing tennis last summer with some of her old schoolfriends.' She didn't know of any other pills or tablets.

As they talked she began to exhibit fresh signs of distress, finally bursting out: 'You don't think she could possibly—?' She broke off, answering herself an instant later: 'No, of course she couldn't. She could never have done such a thing.'

'What could she never have done?' Kelsey wanted to know.

She was silent for a moment and then blurted out: 'You don't think she could have killed Mrs Dalton? And then thought it was bound to come out, with everyone writing down what they remembered. And that was why she killed herself.'

'I'm not at all sure Jean did kill herself,' Kelsey responded.

She stared up at him. 'But it couldn't

have been an accident, surely?' Her eyes searched his face.

'No, it couldn't have been an accident.' He paused. 'But it could have been murder.'

She gave an appalled gasp. 'You mean she could have been murdered by the same person who killed Mrs Dalton?'

'Yes,' Kelsey said flatly. 'That's precisely what I do mean.'

Dorothy Nevett was upstairs in her room when they went back into the house. The Chief went up to see her. She was sitting in an armchair, her hands idle; she looked tired and dejected.

He apologized for disturbing her. He would like to take a look in her bathroom cabinet; he was making a round of all the bathrooms and any other rooms likely to hold a medicine cabinet; he would like her to accompany him. Dorothy heard him out in listless silence, then with an effort she rose to her feet. They went first to her own bathroom nearby, small and plainly furnished.

The cabinet held branded makes of indigestion tablets and throat lozenges, aspirin and paracetamol. Two bottles, dating back some time, were almost empty; one held a few painkillers, the other sleeping pills. Dorothy couldn't say if any tablets had recently been removed from any of the bottles.

She went down with them to the next floor where there were three bathrooms, apart from the one en suite with Mrs Dalton's old bedroom, unused these days. Two of the bathrooms were large and well appointed, in the vicinity of bedrooms used by guests. In one of these the cabinet held a bottle of aspirin, half full. Again, Dorothy had no idea if any aspirin had recently been removed.

The third bathroom was small and simply furnished, along the corridor from Jean's bedroom and used only by her in recent times. The only bottle in the cabinet contained five paracetamol tablets.

The bedroom in which Grace Dalton had died, and the bathroom leading off it, were still kept locked. The Chief went down there now. The contents of the bathroom cabinet looked much as he remembered when he had given a routine look inside after Grace's death. Dorothy agreed that nothing seemed to have been disturbed; the level of contents of the various containers appeared unaltered as far as she could tell.

She told the Chief there were no other medicine cabinets in the house, nor, as far as she knew, any other tablets. As they left Grace's room, Dorothy suddenly exclaimed: 'I never gave you the account I wrote out for you! It took me a lot longer than I expected but I finished it yesterday evening. It went clean out of my head, with all that's happened. I'll get it for you now, it's up in my room.'

The postmortem of Jean Margaret Redfern was carried out by the same pathologist who had performed the autopsy on Grace Dalton two weeks earlier. Dr Wheatley was able to get along in time to observe the final stages. He joined the Chief and the pathologist in the corridor afterwards, as they discussed the results. The Chief didn't intend going over to Brentworth again tonight to pass on the findings to Matthew Dalton. He would give them over the phone, and call over to see Matthew in the morning.

There could be no doubt about the cause of Jean Redfern's death: she had ingested a quantity of alcohol, together

255

with an assortment of medications. She had swallowed the lethal mixture during the late afternoon or early evening of Sunday. Death had followed between midnight and four in the morning. Accident could be ruled out, but the pathologist could make no choice between suicide and murder.

He told the Chief the medications Jean had swallowed were such as were either freely available over the counter, or commonly prescribed, likely to be found in any dwelling.

Or—in answer to the Chief's question—in any hospice.

CHAPTER 25

After a briefing and press conference on Tuesday morning, it was turned ten by the time Kelsey was able to leave for Brentworth. As Sergeant Lambert negotiated the traffic, Kelsey leaned back in his seat with his eyes closed. He had got to his desk early, to give himself time to read through Jean Redfern's diary, study its contents and implications. Now, as the miles slipped by, he sat mulling it over.

Nowhere had he been able to find any suggestion of a suicidal frame of mind, nowhere any suggestion that Jean had been in any way involved in the death of Grace Dalton—though, if she had been involved, she would hardly have been likely to commit damning evidence to paper, even the private pages of her diary. She appeared to have been genuinely shocked at Grace's death, genuinely grieving, sincere in her wish to make something of her life. He had come upon nothing to indicate that she had any desire in recent times to marry Shaun Chapman. She made mention of phone calls between the two of them over the last few days, merely noting the fact of a call, saying nothing of what the call was about.

In her final entry, on Sunday, the whole tone was positive and cheerful. She felt she was over the worst of her cold. She referred to having finished typing her account for the Chief. She mentioned Mrs Gosling bringing over a tray of tea, and a phone call she had received soon after Mrs Gosling had left again, after she had finished her tea. The call was from a girlfriend she referred to as Kay. It seemed she hadn't been in touch with Kay for some time and was pleased to hear from her. She hoped to be able to meet her again shortly, when her cold was better.

She referred also to a radio programme she had enjoyed, listening to it till it finished. The Chief had checked the time and discovered the programme had ended at six o'clock. It would seem from her entry that she had begun writing in the diary immediately after the programme ended.

She was writing in full flow when she broke off—at a sound, the Chief conjectured. The sound of either the phone ringing in her office next door, or the front doorbell. Every outside door had been dutifully locked and bolted, with the exception of the front door, where the bolts had been drawn back, strongly reinforcing in the Chief's mind the notion that it had been a ring at the front door that had put an abrupt end to the diary writing. If it had been the telephone, why thrust the diary away out of sight? The doorbell might announce the arrival of someone she might be expected to admit, someone who might come back upstairs with her, into her room. It would be a natural enough reaction—especially on the part of a secretive person like Jean—to slip the diary under her pillows before going down to open the door. And the fact that the Chief had found the front door unbolted on Monday morning strongly suggested to him that when the caller left—if caller there had been—Jean was in no condition to go downstairs to bolt the door again but was lying helpless in her bed, sinking into her last long sleep.

Nothing in the way of fingerprints suggested that anyone but Jean had gone downstairs to fix the tray and carry it back to her bedroom. The pattern of palm and fingerprints on the beaker clearly recalled the way the Chief had seen Jean clasping a hot drink. Mrs Gosling's prints, as well as Jean's, were discernible on the whisky bottle, as was to be expected.

The fatal cocktail of medicaments had been mixed only into the contents of the beaker; neither the milk in the jug nor the whisky in the bottle had been tampered with. Again, that squared with suicide, as did the presence of the prayer book, open at Prayers for the Dying.

But to set against all that, the Chief reflected, we have the strong probability of a ring at the doorbell; we have the diary thrust under the pillows and never taken out again; we have the final entry never completed.

Sunlight broke through the clouds as they reached the outskirts of Brentworth. The gardens were bright with colour. Forsythia and Japanese cherry flowered along the avenues. Their first call was at the Milroy house in Oakfield Gardens. Lambert had rung to make sure Esther would be in; James was to come along shortly from his office.

Esther's manner was subdued but composed. 'I phoned Verity and Barry yesterday, after Matthew rang to tell me what had happened,' she said. 'I didn't want either of them to hear the dreadful news on the local radio. That would have been an appalling shock.' Matthew had rung her again last night to tell her the postmortem findings but she hadn't passed that information on to Verity or Barry. 'I don't know what you make of Jean's death,' she went on, 'but it seems very much like suicide to me.' She gave the Chief a direct glance. 'Do you think it's possible Jean killed Grace? And then killed herself?'

The Chief didn't answer that. He asked when she had last been in touch with Jean.

At Grace's funeral, she told him. She had neither phoned nor been over to Elmhurst since.

How had she spent last Sunday?

She had no difficulty in recalling. Both the boys had left on Sunday, the elder in the middle of the morning, the younger at around three in the afternoon. After driving his younger son to the airport, James had gone on to his chess club. Later in the afternoon, Esther had decided to go along to the hospice, to visit a female patient she had befriended. She had walked to the hospice, arriving at about a quarter to five; she had stayed a little over an hour.

'I found it all rather upsetting,' she told the Chief. 'The patient's younger than me. She doesn't seem to have any friends, any family—or none she'll admit to. I don't believe she's given us her real name.' She drew a long sigh. 'You can tell she came from good beginnings. She was picked up sleeping rough. She had a bad drink problem, on top of everything else.' Esther had spent part of her Sunday visit in an

261

attempt to persuade the woman to tell them of someone they could get in touch with, but she had stubbornly maintained there was no one at all.

When Esther got home, she took a long, hot bath, to soothe herself, put on a housecoat and tried to watch television. But she found her thoughts straying relentlessly back to the patient. At about nine-thirty, she decided to take a sleeping pill and go to bed. She had no idea what time James had come in, she hadn't heard him. 'We have separate rooms,' she added, in answer to the Chief's inquiring look. 'We've had them for years.'

The Chief cast his mind back. 'Didn't you share a room at Elmhurst over the birthday weekend?'

She smiled slightly. 'We always do, at Elmhurst.' She paused, correcting herself. 'I should say: We always did. We won't be visiting Elmhurst together again, to stay the night.' She fell briefly silent before continuing. 'We'd always been put in together at Elmhurst, from the time we were first married, it was simpler to leave it like that, and we were never there together for more than a night or two.'

'And if I remember aright, you took

a sleeping pill that Saturday night at Elmhurst?'

'Yes, I did,' she replied without hesitation.

There was the sound of the front door opening and closing and James came briskly in. He greeted the Chief, nodded at his wife, glanced at his watch. 'I hope this won't take long,' he said as he sat down.

'We won't waste any time,' the Chief assured him. 'We'd like an account of your movements on Sunday. We're asking everyone.'

'You don't think Jean's death was suicide then?' James responded instantly. 'I'm inclined to agree with you. I would never have thought her a suicidal type, she struck me as a born survivor. I couldn't see her lying down to die at the age of twenty.'

'Could you see her killing Grace, being overcome by guilt or fear of being found out, and then deciding to kill herself?'

'Good God, no!' James exclaimed. 'She was devoted to Grace. She would never have dreamed of harming her.'

He had got to his chess club around four-thirty on Sunday. He had arranged to meet Matthew Dalton there for a game but Matthew had phoned shortly before lunch to say he wouldn't be able to make it, he had to go into his office. When James got to his club, he found there weren't many members in. He had spent the evening with a retired engineer, a bachelor by the name of Riordan, who had recently joined the club. They had played chess, had dinner together. He had left the club earlier than usual. 'Riordan was off to Holland next day, on a trip to the bulbfields,' he explained. 'He had to be at the airport for six. I left the club when he did, around ten.' He had gone straight home, had watched TV for half an hour or so, before going to bed.

Kelsey asked for Riordan's address and James supplied it. 'But he won't be back from his trip till late on Saturday night,' he pointed out.

CHAPTER 26

From Oakfield Gardens, the Chief went on to Matthew Dalton's house, where Nina was expecting them; they would be going on to Matthew's office after speaking to Nina. Unlike his brother-in-law, Matthew offered no objection to the police calling at his business premises and had willingly rearranged his schedule to fit them in.

Nina spoke with sorrow of Jean's death. Although the news had come as a great shock, she couldn't truthfully say, on reflection, that she was altogether surprised. She knew the postmortem results hadn't been able to decide between suicide and murder but she seemed to take it for granted the death was suicide. It didn't appear to cross her mind that Jean might have killed herself because of some involvement in Grace's death; she put the suicide down to quite another cause: the fact that for the first time in her life Jean was going to have to stand on her own feet, go out alone into the world. 'I think she felt overwhelmed by everything,' she said. 'Her grief at Grace's death, all the changes she had to face. She must have been at a low ebb after the funeral, and a heavy cold couldn't have helped.' She had had no contact with Jean after Grace's funeral. She blamed herself for that now, she should have realized the state she was in. She looked across at the Chief. 'You know her mother and stepfather are living in America?'

Yes, the Chief did know. 'We have their address,' he told her. 'We'll be in touch with them shortly. They won't be out of bed yet, over there.'

He asked how Matthew had spent last Sunday.

Playing golf in the morning, she told him. After lunch he had gone along to his office.

The Chief asked if she knew Matthew had had an arrangement to play chess with James Milroy on Sunday afternoon.

Yes, she had known that. 'Matthew rang James before lunch to say he couldn't make it, he had work to do at the office. He knew James wouldn't mind, he could get a game of chess with someone else.'

'Couldn't Matthew have gone into the office on Sunday morning instead of playing golf?' Kelsey asked. 'Then he could have kept to his arrangement with James.'

'He wasn't playing golf just for pleasure,' she replied at once. 'It was more in the nature of a business date.' He had played with a prospective client; the date had been made a week before.

She had gone over to the cottage after lunch on Sunday, returning home around seven-thirty. Matthew had come in some fifteen minutes later. They had supper, watched TV, went to bed around eleven.

Had she spoken to anyone while she was at the cottage?

'I spoke to Mrs Ayliffe,' she told him. 'And to her husband. They live in the next cottage along the lane. Mrs Ayliffe is a very sensible, reliable woman. Her children are grown up and she does various little jobs—she keeps an eye on the cottage for us, gives a hand if it's needed. Her husband works in a DIY store in the town. He's very obliging, the sort of man who can turn his hand to anything. He does a bit of maintenance for us at the cottage.'

They were kept waiting only a very few minutes before being shown into Matthew's office. He appeared now to share his wife's view of Jean's death. 'It's a tragedy that should never have happened,' he said heavily. 'We were all too wrapped up in our own affairs to appreciate what the poor girl must have been feeling.' He hadn't seen Jean since Grace's funeral, he hadn't been over to Elmhurst.

During his stint at the office on Sunday he had not only attended to business matters, he had also finished writing his account for the Chief. He had left the office at seven-thirty, arriving home at a quarter to eight.

They had arranged to meet Verity at her flat during the college lunch hour. She was clearing up after a snack meal when they arrived.

She didn't ask what the postmortem findings had been. She appeared to have at once concluded that Jean's death was a suicide, though she offered no theory to explain it. Although she strove for calm, she was plainly still deeply upset; her manner was tense and agitated. She didn't sit down all the time the two policemen were in the flat but stayed on the move, pacing about, picking things up and putting them down.

The Chief asked her how she had spent Sunday afternoon and evening.

'I was here in the flat on my own, on Sunday afternoon,' she told him. She had made a start on writing her account for the Chief. In the evening she had gone to the theatre with Barry. The play was one of a series, of an avant-garde, non-commercial nature, put on from time to time on Sunday evenings at the Brentworth repertory theatre by a local amateur group, each play being performed for one evening only. Barry and Verity had gone together to all these Sunday evening plays.

They had arranged to meet in the foyer at twenty minutes to six; the curtain rose at six. When the play ended, shortly before nine, Barry went straight back to school and she went home to her flat, to finish writing her account.

Sergeant Lambert gave her a considering look as they were leaving. Her restlessness showed no sign of abating. Did she have the temperament for murder? he asked himself. The patience to plan, the capacity to put her plan into action, the strength of nerve not to go to pieces afterwards?

CHAPTER 27

The afternoon session had begun by the time they reached Barry's school. Barry had been shocked and grieved to learn of Jean's death. Like Verity, he made no inquiry about the postmortem results; like her, he appeared to believe the death was unquestionably suicide; like her, he offered no theory about motive. But he displayed none of Verity's unrest, although he was clearly upset by what had happened.

He had spent Sunday afternoon at school, in the study he shared with two other boys. Tea was at four-thirty. He had left school at around five-fifteen to cycle to the theatre, to meet Verity. They took it in turns to book and pay for tickets; it was his turn on Sunday.

There was always coffee and discussion after the plays. Sometimes they stayed on, sometimes not. This Sunday they didn't stay on, as Verity had the rest of her account to do and Barry had to finish an essay. Verity drove off to her flat and he cycled back to school.

After Esther had phoned him on Monday evening to break the news of Jean's death, he had immediately gone over to see Verity, knowing how distressed she would be. She had been very upset and had cried a good deal. He could stay only an hour, he had to get back to school. To his relief, she had calmed down considerably by the time he left.

Among the messages awaiting the Chief when they got back to Cannonbridge was one from a woman solicitor in a local firm specializing in legal assistance to the less well off sections of the community. She had rung the police station at two-thirty to say she thought she might have information of interest, concerning Jean Redfern.

Kelsey at once put through a call and was able to speak to her. It seemed her secretary had got back from lunch to say she had heard mention on the local radio of a second death at Elmhurst, the postmortem yesterday evening, and this morning's press conference. The secretary had heard with shock the name of the dead person: Jean Redfern—the young woman who only a week earlier had signed the will she had asked the solicitor to draw up.

The solicitor could see the Chief if he came round right away. On the way over, he gave thought to what assets Jean might have had to leave—apart from the legacy under Grace Dalton's will. He had found among her things a bank book showing modest savings and a trinket box containing a few pieces of old jewellery, attractive enough, but of no great value. According to Mrs Gosling, these had all been presents from Mrs Dalton at various Christmases and birthdays in recent years.

The solicitor was a middle-aged woman with a pleasant manner and a penetrating gaze; the Chief had occasionally come across her in the law courts. She told him Jean Redfern had phoned on the afternoon of Wednesday, 11th March, asking for an early appointment to make a will; she was given a time for the following morning.

She had been frank about her circumstances, making no secret of the fact that the bulk of what she had to leave would be the legacy from Mrs Dalton. The solicitor hadn't known Mrs Dalton personally but had known of her; she was also aware of the circumstances of Mrs Dalton's death. 'I could hardly avoid knowing,' she observed.

'She had died only a few days before. The town was buzzing with it.'

The solicitor had asked Jean if she had any particular reason for haste in making her will. She was told no, other than that Mrs Dalton's death had come as a great shock to her, a great blow. It had brought home to her what a precarious business life was, made her realize the importance of making her own will.

The solicitor immediately asked if Jean knew of any survivor clause attached to the legacy. Jean didn't understand the term and the solicitor explained that in these days of car crashes and aeroplane disasters, where more than one member of a family might die or be gravely injured in the same accident, it was common practice to specify that a legatee should survive the testator—or, in this case, the testatrix—for a stated length of time: thirty or sixty days, or any other chosen period.

Jean told her she knew nothing of any such clause attached to her legacy but she would check with the Dalton solicitor; in the meantime, she wished to go ahead with drawing up the will. She asked what would happen to her legacy if indeed there was such a clause and she failed to survive the necessary period. 'I told her the legacy would then form part of the residue of Mrs Dalton's estate,' the solicitor said. 'The residue would be distributed according to the terms of Mrs Dalton's will.'

Jean had rung later that same morning to say she had checked with Purvis and had been assured there was no survivor clause attached to her legacy.

A draft of the will was sent off to Jean. She came in with it on the following Monday morning, to say it was all in order but she would like to add one more small bequest; this was duly done. The will was engrossed the same day and Jean came in the following afternoon, Tuesday, 17th March, to sign it. A copy had been posted to Jean at Elmhurst yesterday afternoon, together with the solicitor's bill.

'I have the will here,' the solicitor told the Chief. 'It's a simple, straightforward document. I asked Jean if she had any dependants, any parents or close relatives. She said she had no dependants. She did have a mother she hadn't seen for years. The solicitor grimaced. 'What she actually said was: "If you can call her a mother—she didn't even want me to be born. I'm only here at all because the Daltons managed to talk her out of having an abortion." She said her mother had married some years ago and was now living in the United States. Jean had had very little to do with her since the marriage. It seems there are some children of the marriage but Jean had never seen any of them. She had no intention of leaving a single penny in that quarter; she was quite vehement about it. I assured her she was under no obligation to leave anything to any of them. Then I asked her about her father. She told me she was an illegitimate child, born when her mother was single; Redfern was her mother's maiden name. She had never laid eyes on her father. From what little she did know, she gathered he had been some commercial traveller her mother had known very briefly.

'I asked if she had any trusted friend or relative she would like to name as executor but she said she wanted the firm to act as executor.'

The solicitor picked up the will and glanced through it. 'She was very clear about what she wanted, she'd thought it out.' She had left a thousand pounds each to Mr and Mrs Chapman, in recognition of their kindness. A specified item of jewellery had gone to Dorothy Nevett and to each of three girlfriends. The Christian name of one of the girls, the Chief noted, was Kay, the name of the girl Jean had mentioned in her diary, as phoning her on Sunday afternoon. He made a note of the addresses of all three girls.

Jean had left the rest of her jewellery to Mrs Gosling, together with her books and the wristwatch given to her by Mrs Dalton on her eighteenth birthday—it was the wristwatch she had remembered when checking the draft of her will and made the subject of the extra bequest. Her other personal possessions went to Mrs Chapman.

The remainder of her estate she left to Shaun Gerald Chapman.

'Jean didn't go into explanations,' the solicitor said. 'I gathered Shaun Chapman was or had been a boyfriend.'

'Do you know if she intended telling Shaun she was making a will?' Kelsey asked.

'She didn't exactly say so,' the solicitor replied, 'but I got the impression she intended telling him. When she told me she wanted the remainder of her estate to go to him, I remember her saying: "He'll be pleased about that. He'll realize he still means a lot to me." I took that to mean she intended telling him.'

'You don't think she could have meant: "After I'm dead and he learns about the will, he'll be pleased to discover what I've left him, how much I thought of him"?'

The solicitor was silent for some moments, then she said, 'I suppose she could have meant that, though it didn't strike me that way at the time.'

'How would you describe her frame of mind? Did she seem depressed?'

She shook her head with energy. 'No, not in the least. She seemed calm and controlled, very purposeful.' She gave the Chief a level look. 'I see what you're getting at, the question of suicide. All I can say is that in my opinion, the determined, concentrated way she set about making her will by no means rules out the possibility that she could have been thinking of taking her own life.' She paused and then added reflectively: 'She did seem to harbour strong feelings of resentment against her mother. It's not unheard of for people who feel rejected to take their own lives as a way of punishing those they believe have rejected them.'

As they left the office and walked back to the car, Sergeant Lambert observed: 'So the legacy Mrs Dalton intended to give Jean a start in life ends up in Shaun Chapman's hands. I wonder what Mrs Dalton would have made of that.'

The Chief made no response. Shaun might squander every penny; the money might merely serve to propel him along the path of idleness and folly.

Or it might be the making of him. Grace would surely have savoured the irony of that.

After a moment, Lambert continued: 'That open prayer book on Jean's bed. I don't think I can see Shaun knowing his way round a prayer book.'

'Maybe not,' Kelsey said. 'But I'll tell you what I *can* see. I can see him sitting by Jean's bed, waiting for her to sink into a coma. I can see him passing the time by picking up her prayer book from the shelf, flicking through it to see if he could come across something suitable. And feeling mighty pleased with himself when he found it.'

CHAPTER 28

They went along at once to see if they could get a word with Purvis and were shown into his office after a brief wait.

'I intended calling in at the station on my way home,' Purvis said before the Chief had a chance to say what he'd come about. 'I only heard of Jean Redfern's death this afternoon, when Matthew Dalton rang to tell me. He tried to ring me at home yesterday evening but I was out. And he tried to get me here this morning but I was in court. He told me what the postmortem found. I thought you'd want to know that Jean came to see me the week before last. It was on the Thursday morning, March the twelfth—I've checked the date. She asked if there was any survivor clause attached to her legacy from Mrs Dalton; she wanted to know as she was making a will. I told her there was no such clause.'

'That's why we've come to see you,' Kelsey said. 'We've just left her solicitor.'

'Did Jean go ahead and make the will?' Purvis asked.

'She did indeed. The bulk of what she left—which means, in effect, Mrs Dalton's legacy—goes to Shaun Chapman.'

Purvis acknowledged the information with a wry glance.

'Did you see Jean again after that Thursday morning?' Kelsey asked.

Purvis shook his head.

'What did you make of her state of mind that morning? Anything in her manner that might indicate suicide?'

'I've been thinking about that,' Purvis answered. 'She seemed calm, detached, not in the least nervous or strung up.' After a pause for further reflection, he added: 'I think I'd put it this way: her manner was not incompatible with the notion of suicide.'

On leaving Purvis, they went straight over to Elmhurst. Mrs Gosling took them along to the kitchen where Dorothy Nevett was at work. Both women had learned of the postmortem findings from Nina Dalton; she had phoned that morning to give them the information.

As Mrs Gosling put on the kettle, she

remembered something. 'A letter came for Jean this morning. I put it to one side.' She bustled off and came back with the letter: a long, legal-looking envelope of stout manila, the address expertly typed, a Cannonbridge postmark. From Jean's solicitor, no doubt, containing the copy of her will and the solicitor's bill. Kelsey didn't open it. Nor did he say anything to the two women about the will Jean had made.

He told them he intended putting through a call to Jean's mother in America, to tell her what had happened. He would like either Dorothy or Mrs Gosling to speak to her first, break the news gently; it would probably come to her as marginally less of a shock. They both agreed that this would be the best course. They agreed also that the person to do it was Dorothy, as Mrs Gosling was almost certain to break down in tears halfway through. Dorothy told the Chief she had written to Jean's mother by airmail a week ago, to tell her of Mrs Dalton's death, but she hadn't yet received a reply; there had scarcely been time.

The call was put through and was answered by Jean's mother. As soon as she realized it was Dorothy on the line she began to talk about the letter she had received from her, pouring out a stream of comments, questions about Mrs Dalton's death. She had been about to reply to Dorothy's letter; she was also attempting to compose a letter of sympathy to Esther and Matthew. Her daughter's name never once crossed her lips.

The Chief and Mrs Gosling, standing close by, had no difficulty in hearing every word. When Dorothy at last managed to interrupt the flow long enough to break the news of Jean's death, she was met at first by a stunned silence, followed by a fresh outpouring of questions, and finally a storm of tears which took some time to abate. By the time Dorothy handed the receiver over to the Chief, she was looking more than a little strained.

The Chief revealed the results of the postmortem and Jean's mother asked to be kept informed of the progress of the investigation and the date of the funeral. She wouldn't be able to attend, she had her family to look after, but she would want to send flowers. She burst into tears again. She hadn't heard from her daughter in a long while, hadn't received so much as a card from her last Christmas, though she had remembered to send one herself. When the Chief finally rang off, all three of them stood in silence for some moments. 'She doesn't change much,' Mrs Gosling said at last, with a slow shake of her head.

Kelsey told the two women he had the names of three of Jean's girlfriends. Did either of them know of any other girls Jean had been close to? But they couldn't help him, they hadn't even known the names of the three girls he had mentioned.

Dorothy walked with Kelsey to the door when he left. 'I've been turning it all over in my mind,' she told him. 'It's my firm belief now that Jean was mixed up in Mrs Dalton's death, one way or another. I'm certain Shaun Chapman was in it somewhere, too. I don't know exactly how it was done or which of them did what, but I'll take my oath they were in it together.' She looked up at him. 'I believe Jean killed herself because she was afraid you were getting on to the truth.'

'There's no proof that Jean's death was suicide,' the Chief reminded her.

'That makes no difference to what I think,' she retorted. 'If it wasn't suicide, then it was murder. And if it was murder, it was Shaun Chapman that murdered her. Afraid she'd lose her nerve and give the game away.' She stared grimly up at him. 'That young man is no good and never has been any good.'

It was the Chief's intention, when they got back to the police station, to leave again very shortly, to make sure of reaching Shaun Chapman's lodgings before he got in from work. But they hadn't been in the station many minutes before a young woman turned up, asking to speak to the Chief.

It was Jean's girlfriend, Kay. This was her afternoon off from the day nursery where she worked. She had just rung Elmhurst to speak to Jean, to find out if her cold was better, if they could fix a time to meet. Mrs Gosling had answered the phone and had broken the news to her of Jean's death. Kay had at first been unable to take it in.

As soon as Mrs Gosling learned that Kay had spoken to Jean over the phone on Sunday afternoon, she told her the police would want to know about that, she must go along at once to speak to Chief Inspector Kelsey.

Kay was still plainly in a state of shock. The Chief sat her down and sent for tea; he waited till she was ready to go on.

It was some time since she'd seen Jean. Her own mother had been in poor health since the beginning of the year and most of Kay's free time had been spent in looking after her and coping with the household chores. Her mother had recently begun to improve and Kay found herself able to get out more. She had rung Jean on Sunday at around five o'clock, to suggest a meeting. Jean was delighted to hear from her. She said she was in bed with one of her bad colds but the worst of it was over.

She told Kay she was now coming to terms with Mrs Dalton's death. She would have to leave Elmhurst before long as the place would be sold. She had come to terms with that as well and was determined to take a very positive attitude about it. She intended to make a good new life for herself and was anxious to take some proper training.

It was agreed that Kay would ring Jean again on Tuesday afternoon.

The Chief asked if Jean had made any mention of Shaun Chapman and was told no.

Had Jean said anything about being left a legacy by Mrs Dalton? Or about making a will herself? No, she hadn't mentioned either.

Had Jean appeared in any way depressed?

Far from it, Kay responded at once; she had sounded cheerful, in spite of her cold. 'She was a lot more confident than I remembered her, I was quite struck by that. I would have expected her to be nervous about starting out on her own but she didn't sound at all nervous. She really seemed to be looking forward to making a new life for herself, being independent.' Tears glittered in her eyes. 'I can't believe she was thinking of killing herself. It just doesn't add up.'

CHAPTER 29

They had little chance now of reaching Shaun Chapman's lodgings in time to sit in the car to await his arrival. Sergeant Lambert made what speed he could, but early evening traffic was building up and they were subject to delays more than once.

The Chief glanced about as they got out of the car and walked up the front path. There was a shed to the left of the house, set back a little, its door open; inside he could see a man's bicycle.

The landlady answered the door to them. On their previous visit, the Chief hadn't identified himself but he did so now. He asked if Shaun had got in from work and was told yes, he had come in a few minutes ago and was now on the phone. His mother had rung earlier and left a message for him to call her the moment he got in.

Kelsey asked if they might step inside; there were one or two questions he would like to ask her. 'I hope nothing's wrong,' she said with an anxious frown as she admitted them. 'Shaun's a decent lad. I wouldn't like to think he's in any trouble.'

The Chief assured her she had no need to worry. Shaun happened to know someone in a case they were working on, he might be able to give them some information.

Through a partly open door leading into an inner hall, the Chief could hear Shaun talking on the phone but he couldn't make out what he was saying. He stayed in the vestibule to put his questions to the landlady. He began by asking if Shaun had received any other phone calls during the last few days.

The landlady thought back. 'Yes, he had a call on Thursday evening. I know it was Thursday because that's when my lodgers pay me. Shaun had just settled up when the phone rang and it was for him. A young lady, it was. I remember she sounded upset. She had a bad cold, she had a fit of sneezing while she was talking to me.'

Had there been any other calls from the young lady? She shook her head in reply.

Did she know if Shaun had left the house at all on Sunday?

'He was out in the afternoon,' she recalled. She couldn't say what time he had come in. 'I know he was here for supper, that's at eight o'clock on Sundays. I remember he ate hardly anything, most unlike him. I said to him: "You're not very hungry" and he said he'd had something while he was out.'

Had she noticed if Shaun had burnt any papers after coming in on Sunday? She looked surprised at the question but shook her head at once. 'He couldn't burn anything here, we've got no grates. All the fireplaces were closed up years ago, when the central heating was put in.'

The Chief asked when her dustbins were last emptied. 'Yesterday,' she told him. 'The dustmen always come Monday morning.'

There was the sound of the receiver being replaced in the inner hall. 'May we go through?' Kelsey asked.

'Yes, of course.' She led the way. Shaun was standing by the phone. He looked stunned; he scarcely seemed to notice their approach.

'Was it bad news?' the landlady asked with ready concern.

He became aware of her, he gazed at her blankly. She repeated her question. 'I'm afraid so,' he answered. He took in the presence of the two policemen.

'We need to talk to you,' the Chief told him. Shaun nodded slowly in reply. He remained where he was.

'I'll make you a pot of tea,' the landlady said. She looked up at the Chief. 'You won't keep him long? He's had nothing to eat.'

'We'll be as quick as we can,' Kelsey promised.

'You can use my sitting room.' She gestured along the passage. 'First on the left. You won't be disturbed.' She hurried off to the kitchen.

Shaun went docilely with them into the sitting room. 'I gather that was your mother on the phone,' the Chief said as they sat down.

Shaun nodded. He drew a deep sigh. 'She told me about Jean. She'd read about it in the evening paper.' He looked down at the floor. 'She was very upset. She was fond of Jean.' He put both hands up to his face and sat silent for a minute or two, then he dropped his hands and looked across at the Chief. 'How exactly did she die? Mum only knew what she read in the paper.' He listened intently as the Chief gave him the details, the postmortem findings. 'Could it have been some sort of accident?' he asked when the Chief had finished.

Kelsey shook his head. 'It was either suicide or murder. We can't rule out either at present.'

The landlady came in with a tray of tea. 'I've made it good and strong,' she said as she dispensed it. The door had scarcely closed behind her again when Shaun broke into rapid speech. 'It was never suicide, I'll never believe that. Jean had no reason to kill herself. We talked on the phone three or four times over the previous week. She wasn't feeling too bright because of her cold, but she never once sounded suicidal, or anywhere near it.'

'When was the last time you spoke to her?' Kelsey asked.

'On Sunday afternoon,' Shaun replied promptly. 'About three o'clock. I rang from a call box when I went out after lunch.'

'What did you talk about?'

'I wasn't on the phone long, it was really only to see how she was. We'd had a longer talk the day before, on Saturday afternoon.'

'If it wasn't suicide, then it must have been murder. Who do you think would want to murder her?'

Shaun was silent for some moments, then he said: 'She could have found out who killed Mrs Dalton. That person knew she'd found out and killed her.'

'Do you think it's possible she killed Mrs Dalton herself?'

Shaun jerked up in his seat. 'Jean? Kill Mrs Dalton? Never in a million years! Jean couldn't kill a fly! She thought the world of Mrs Dalton! She was heartbroken when she died.'

'Maybe she'd got around to sharing your view—that Mrs Dalton had had her three score years and ten, it was time her money passed to other people.'

He shook his head fiercely. 'Not Jean. She never thought like that.'

'You wouldn't have thought any the less of her if she had killed Mrs Dalton, would you? You set no value on the lives of old ladies?'

Shaun made no reply to that. The muscles tightened along his jaw.

'When you had your talk with Jean on Saturday afternoon, did she mention an account she was writing of the birthday weekend?'

He nodded. 'She said it was taking longer than she'd expected, with having to put in every little thing.'

'Did she say anything about making a will?'

He shook his head.

'Had she ever mentioned making a will?'

Again he shook his head. 'She didn't have much to leave.'

292

'You know Mrs Dalton left her a legacy?'

He nodded.

'What do you suppose happens to that legacy now?'

He pondered before replying. 'I should imagine it goes to whoever gets what's left of Mrs Dalton's estate after all the other legacies are paid out.'

'That's not the case,' Kelsey informed him. 'Jean did in fact make a will. She made it a few days before she died. It was properly drawn up by a solicitor. She left most of what she had to you—and that includes her legacy from Mrs Dalton. That legacy still stands.'

Shaun regarded him in silence, his face wiped clear of expression.

'I don't know if you're aware of the size of the legacy Mrs Dalton left her,' Kelsey said. 'It's a tidy sum.'

Shaun made no response. His eyes grew bright with unshed tears.

The Chief made an abrupt switch. 'I believe you have a car.'

Shaun blinked away his tears. 'I did have,' he answered, 'but I haven't got it now. I sold it a few days ago. A man in the pub offered me a good price for it.'

'How much was this good price?'

Shaun gave him a figure.

'Exactly when did this deal take place?'

'Last Thursday evening. He paid me in cash at the pub next evening, Friday, and I handed over the car.'

'Can you give us the name and address of this man?'

'Yes, I can.' He produced a used envelope from his breast pocket and handed it to the Chief. 'That's his name and address on the envelope.'

How was Shaun currently getting to and from work? No problem, the Chief was told. A mate from the same construction gang was in digs up the road; he gave Shaun a lift, both ways.

How had Shaun spent Sunday afternoon and evening?

He had gone out for a bike ride, he told the Chief. 'There's a bike here the landlady lets us borrow. It's old but it's OK. I gave it a good going over before I went out on it.' He rode over to a well-known beauty spot several miles away. He had a snack, got back around seven-thirty, had supper, watched TV, went to bed around ten-thirty.

'Did you go over to Elmhurst at all on Sunday?' Kelsey asked.

He shook his head. 'I was nowhere near Elmhurst.' The beauty spot lay in a precisely opposite direction.

'When you talked to Jean on Saturday afternoon, didn't she suggest you might come over, some time during the weekend?'

Again he shook his head. 'Neither of us suggested it. She wasn't feeling much like visitors.'

Kelsey sat regarding him. There were none of Shaun's prints in Jean's room, any more than there had been in Grace's bedroom.

As Kelsey stood up to leave, Shaun inquired about the inquest and the funeral. 'The inquest's set down for tomorrow afternoon,' Kelsey told him. 'Three o'clock at the Cannonbridge court house.' It would be merely opened and adjourned. As for the funeral, impossible to say, at this juncture. 'The coroner has to release the body first. He may do that tomorrow or he may not. My guess is that he will release it.' He would imagine that Esther Milroy would be taking charge of the funeral arrangements but he couldn't see her welcoming phone calls from Shaun Chapman. 'You could give Gosling a ring in the next day or two,' he suggested.

'He should be able to tell you what the situation is about the funeral.'

Shaun looked the Chief in the eye. 'I hope you get the bastard that killed Jean,' he said between gritted teeth. He didn't offer to see them out but stayed where he was, in the middle of the room. Even now, Sergeant Lambert thought, he can't bring himself to make the customary avowal: If there's anything I can do to assist the police, I'm only too willing to help.

The attitudes of twenty-two years were not, it seemed, to be so easily altered.

Lights showed from a downstairs window when they reached the Chapmans' council semi, shortly after eight. When Lambert set his finger on the doorbell the front room curtain was at once pushed aside. The Chief caught a glimpse of the lively face of a lad of about ten, before the curtain dropped back into place. There was a swift interchange of voices, hushed but excited, the sound of flying footsteps as the lad came racing into the hall to fling wide the door.

'You're coppers!' he cried triumphantly before the Chief could utter a word. The lad craned forward, peering past them to the gate. 'Can I have a look inside your car?'

'You'll do nothing of the sort,' his father called out as he emerged into the hall, followed by his wife and a gaggle of children. Last of all came the sixteen-year-old girl, in the bloom of her advancing pregnancy. 'Take them all upstairs,' Mrs Chapman commanded her. 'Keep them quiet. And don't wake the baby.' In the course of shepherding the protesting band towards the stairs, the girl slid several interested glances at Lambert.

A measure of peace descended and Mrs Chapman steered the callers into the living room. 'We read about Jean's death,' Chapman said heavily. 'We could hardly believe it.'

'We didn't know what to make of it,' his wife said. 'Can you tell us any more than what was in the paper?'

The Chief gave them such facts as could be made public.

'Sounds like suicide to me,' Chapman said.

'But what could make her do such a thing?' his wife asked. 'She had all her life before her.'

Chapman asked about the funeral and

again the Chief launched into explanations, again he suggested ringing Gosling towards the end of the week. Without any change in tone, he went on smoothly to ask: 'Did Shaun have his car when he was over here on Sunday?'

Before Chapman could reply, his wife answered with a frown: 'Shaun wasn't here on Sunday. He hasn't been here since he left, more than two weeks ago.'

'Has Shaun still got his car?' Kelsey asked Chapman.

Again Mrs Chapman stuck her oar in. 'We haven't the faintest idea. Shaun's the one you should ask.'

Undeterred, the Chief addressed his next question to Chapman. 'Did Shaun come over here on a bicycle on Sunday?'

'I keep telling you,' Mrs Chapman said loudly. 'Shaun never came over here at all on Sunday.'

The Chief was still pitching his questions at Chapman. 'Did you have any kind of contact with Shaun over this last weekend?'

And Mrs Chapman was still slamming back the answers. 'We had no contract with him over the weekend,' she responded fiercely. 'No contact of any kind.'

Uproar suddenly broke out in the upper

regions. The baby began to howl.

The Chief sometimes felt in his bleakest moments that his time in the force had taught him little. But one thing at least the long, slogging years had indubitably taught him: to recognize a situation where he hadn't a cat in hell's chance of getting anywhere.

'Right, then,' he said abruptly. 'That's about it. We'll clear out and leave you to it.'

CHAPTER 30

The inquest proceedings were as brief and formal as the Chief had foreseen; the body was released for burial. In the early evening the Chief called on the two girls Jean had named in her will. He found them both at home. Neither had been in touch with Jean in the last few weeks; neither could tell him anything of significance.

'Tomorrow afternoon,' he said to Lambert as they drove back to the station, 'we'll see if we can nip down to Dorset.' To the farm where Dorothy and Alice kept their caravan. To find out, if at all possible, exactly how Dorothy had spent last Sunday afternoon and evening.

And luck was with them next day. After a snatched lunch they were able to set off for the Dorset coast.

The farm was easy enough to find, a quarter of a mile inland. The farmer was out at market but his wife was able to spare them ten minutes from her busy day. She didn't ask why a senior police officer should travel so far to inquire into the movements of two patently respectable spinsters, but accepted at once the Chief's assertion that it had some bearing on a case he was working on.

The caravan was the only one on the farm. It wasn't visible from the house, being specially sited for privacy and shelter behind a belt of trees. She took them across a field and pointed out the caravan to them, some little distance away.

'Miss Nevett brought some cases and boxes with her when she came last weekend,' she told them as they walked back to the house. 'I'm storing them till they move into the cottage.'

It was usual for the first of the two ladies to arrive to look in at the farmhouse to say hello. One of them would also look in at the end of their stay. On this last visit, Miss Upjohn had arrived first. She had put her head in around noon on Thursday. Miss Nevett had turned up at the farmhouse early on Friday afternoon, to unload her boxes before going on down to the caravan. She had seen nothing of the two ladies over the next two days; this was quite usual. Miss Nevett had looked in at the house in the middle of Monday morning, to say goodbye.

Sergeant Lambert didn't follow the same road back to Cannonbridge but swung round in a detour that would take in the town where Alice Upjohn lived. Alice had got in from work shortly before they reached her flat. She didn't appear surprised to see them. She took them along to the kitchen where she set about preparing tea and sandwiches for them.

She had been horrified to learn of Jean's death. Dorothy had rung on Monday evening to give her the dreadful news, and had rung again yesterday evening to tell her about the inquest. Alice had never met Jean but had heard of her over the years and knew her history; it had felt like losing someone she knew. 'I couldn't stay alone in Elmhurst overnight, the way Dorothy's doing now,' she declared with a shudder. 'Not after all that's happened there. I asked her if she wasn't terribly nervous, I know I would be. But she said she wasn't in the least nervous. Mr Gosling had offered to get the garden boys to take it in turns to sleep in the house, but Dorothy wouldn't hear of it.'

The Chief steered her towards their stay in the caravan over the weekend. 'I got to the caravan before Dorothy,' Alice told him. She had arrived on Thursday, around noon. 'I had a couple of days' leave still due to me,' she explained. 'I wanted to use it up before the end of the month, when I finish for good, so I decided to take the Thursday and Friday off—I couldn't put the two days on to the other side of the weekend as I had to leave on Sunday, to get back here.'

The Chief sat up. 'You left the caravan on Sunday?'

She nodded. 'I set off before lunch. Dorothy was staying over till Monday morning. She didn't mind me going off, she'd known all along I had to be back here by Sunday afternoon.' The chapel Alice attended was celebrating its centenary. There was a special service early on Sunday evening, followed by a reception. Alice had promised weeks before that she would be on hand to help with preparations for the reception. 'I had quite a good drive back,' she added. 'Not too much traffic.' She smiled. 'I'll never be as good a driver as Dorothy, I've always been on the nervous side. Nothing Dorothy likes better than driving, and she's very good at it, always has been.'

CHAPTER 31

A detective constable from the investigation team came along to the Chief's office first thing on Friday morning. He had called the previous evening at the address Shaun Chapman had produced, the address of the man he claimed had bought his car.

The constable had found the man at home. He confirmed everything Shaun had told them about the sale of the car.

A little later, Sergeant Lambert drove the

Chief out to Elmhurst. Over a cup of tea in the kitchen, the Chief asked Dorothy exactly how she had spent last Sunday, from lunch-time onwards. She'll know we talked to Alice yesterday evening, Sergeant Lambert thought. Alice would have rung her after they left.

'I was on my own,' she told them. 'Alice left before lunch, she had to get back, for some do at her chapel.'

In the early afternoon she had gone for a drive along the coast road, stopping at various little bays she was particularly fond of. At some places she went down to the beach for a stroll. At one stop, around tea-time, she had a snack at a stall. She had got back to the caravan around six.

How had she spent the evening?

'I wrote out my account for you,' she said. 'That took most of the evening. I had some supper and listened to the radio. I went to bed around eleven.'

Had she seen or spoken to anyone after Alice left—apart from when she bought her snack at the stall?

'I spoke to the farmer's wife just before I left on Monday morning,' she said. 'To tell her I was off.'

'What about Sunday?' Kelsey persisted.

'Did you speak to anyone at the farm after Alice left?'

She shook her head. 'I had no occasion to.'

So what it boils down to, he thought, is that there is nothing to say how you spent the time between midday on Sunday and the middle of Monday morning. You could have been anywhere.

But he didn't voice the thought aloud.

A good slice of the rest of the morning was taken up by attempts to verify what various folk had told them about the way they had spent last Sunday. They went first to the Brentworth hospice.

Yes, Esther Milroy was a regular visitor at the hospice. Her visits had increased over the last two or three weeks as one of her special patients was now in the last phase of her illness.

The patient occupied a small single room, somewhat out of the way. Visitors were in and out of the hospice all the time. No one the Chief spoke to could say with certainty exactly when Esther had visited the hospice over the weekend.

It wasn't possible for the Chief to speak to the patient herself; she had lapsed into a

305

coma two days ago. He would be informed if she recovered consciousness and was judged in a fit state to be questioned. Matron made it plain that she considered such a possibility very remote indeed.

Their next call was at the Brentworth repertory theatre where they were given the address of the woman who had looked after the box office on Sunday evening.

They went along to the address but found no one at home. A neighbour told them the woman was out at work; she was usually home around six.

On next to the club James Milroy said he had visited. The Chief's discreet inquiries revealed that James had indeed been in the club on Sunday. He had arrived during the afternoon and had stayed till around ten. He had spent the time in the company of a member named Riordan.

Straight on to Riordan's flat, where their ringing produced no response. The woman in the flat below told them Riordan was away, he had gone to Holland for a short holiday, he was expected back late on Saturday.

Shortly after six, they made a second call at the home of the woman who had managed

306

the box office on Sunday. This time they found her in.

The names Barry Fielding and Verity Thorburn struck no chord with her but when the Chief described Barry she did recall a lad answering that description hanging about the foyer on Sunday evening, waiting for someone. When the play was about to begin, he had approached the box office to say he was expecting a girl to join him but she hadn't turned up. 'He wrote down her name and his own name on a bit of paper,' she added. 'He gave it to me, along with her ticket, in case she came along later, but she never showed up.' The lad returned to the box office during both intervals to see if there had been any message from the girl, but there had been none. The woman had kept neither the ticket nor the piece of paper with the names.

The Chief looked at his watch as they went back to the car. Time they were getting back to Cannonbridge. But it was tempting to try for a word with Verity first.

They might have spared themselves the effort. They found Verity's flat in darkness; their rings went unanswered. 'We'll be back first thing in the morning,' Kelsey told Lambert as they turned from the door. 'We'll catch her before she has a chance to go anywhere.'

The curtains were closed when they reached the flat next morning, there was no sign of life. Lambert planted himself on the doorstep and pressed the bell every few seconds. At last there were stirrings from within and Verity appeared in a dressing gown, tousled and unwashed, her great dark eyes full of sulky resentment.

She was by no means disposed to admit them but the Chief brushed aside her protests. 'We have good reason to believe you were not at the theatre with Barry on Sunday,' he said brusquely. 'Where were you? We're not leaving till you tell us.'

She offered no further resistance but admitted them in sullen silence. In the living room she flung herself down without a word into an easy chair. The two men took their seats unasked, close by.

'What were you doing on Sunday afternoon and evening?' Kelsey demanded.

She gazed back at him. Her ill-humoured expression had evaporated, she looked sharply alert. 'I spent the first part of the afternoon writing my account for you,' she replied at last, civilly enough. 'That part of what I told you was true, except that I finished the account around four o'clock—I told you I finished it after I got back from the theatre.'

'What were you doing after four o'clock?'

'I was busy making a fool of myself,' she responded coolly. 'Not for the first time and I daresay not for the last.'

He asked what form the folly had taken.

She gave a wry smile. 'The usual form. I decided to go round to see Ned Hooper.'

'Did you get to see him?'

She shook her head. 'I hung about, hoping he might come out, on his own, but he never came out at all. The doorman saw me and told me to get lost. I made out I was going but I just went round the corner and stayed out of sight. I kept sneaking looks but it was no good, I never saw Ned. I gave up after a while. I didn't come back here, I was too fed up.' She drew a long sigh. 'I'd got myself into a pretty low state, crying on and off.' She moved her shoulders. 'I forgot all about meeting Barry at the theatre, it went clean out of my head. I walked about till I was tired out, I've no idea where I got to. Then I came back here and fell into bed. I cried myself to sleep.'

'What time did you come back here?'

'Somewhere around ten, at a guess. I didn't look at any clocks. I know I was absolutely knackered. I slept like a log till morning.'

'Why didn't you tell us this before?'

'And lay myself open to all sorts of suspicion?' she threw smartly back at him. 'Esther rang me on Monday evening to tell me about Jean. I was terrified out of my wits, I was sure you'd think I had something to do with it. Barry came over as soon as he heard about Jean. He asked me where I'd been on Sunday evening. I told him the truth, as I've just told you. I said I couldn't tell the police that if they asked, it would look very bad, it was no sort of alibi. I could say I'd been to the theatre with him if he'd go along with that. He thought about it and then he said OK.' She fell silent for a moment, then she added in a steady voice, looking the Chief in the eye: 'I had nothing whatever to do with Jean's death. Or with Aunt Grace's death.'

As they stood up to leave a few minutes later, Sergeant Lambert gave her a long, assessing glance, as he had done at the end of their previous visit, four days ago. He had asked himself then, watching Verity move restlessly about the room, if she had the temperament for murder. Four days ago he would have leaned towards the answer no; today he came unhesitatingly down on the side of a yes.

CHAPTER 32

Ned Hooper and Mrs Bradshaw had just finished a leisurely breakfast when the two policemen called. They knew nothing of Jean Redfern's death; her name didn't mean anything to them. Nor did they know of any attempt on Verity's part to speak to Ned on Sunday afternoon. They had been out together from mid-morning onwards, they hadn't got back to the flat till after nine. The doorman had made no mention of Verity.

But when the Chief spoke to the doorman on the way out, the man was positive in his recollection. He had indeed seen Verity hanging round the place on

Sunday afternoon. He had spotted her around four-thirty, he had called out to her to clear off. As far as he knew she had done so, he certainly hadn't noticed her again. He had said nothing about it to Mrs Bradshaw or Mr Hooper; he hadn't seen the need.

Barry's headmaster was as courteous as before but he made it plain all the same that the Chief hadn't chosen the most convenient moment to ask to speak to Barry. He would appreciate it if the Chief would keep the boy as short a time as possible. A ceremony was due to take place in the main hall at eleven; the money raised by the school for the new Cannonbridge hospice was to be handed over in the presence of parents who had helped with the fund-raising, various local dignitaries, and other friends of the hospice movement. 'Mrs Dalton—Mrs Matthew Dalton—has promised to accept the cheque on behalf of the hospice,' the headmaster added. 'It was Barry who suggested asking her.' He smiled. 'It never hurts to have a good-looking woman perform these duties. It guarantees a good picture in the paper.'

The Chief promised to be as quick as possible and the headmaster sent for Barry. The Chief was able to speak to him privately in a small adjoining office. He lost no time in coming to the point. 'We spoke to Verity earlier this morning. She has now given us a very different account of the way in which she spent Sunday evening. She tells us she persuaded you to go along with her story about being at the theatre with you.'

Barry looked vastly relieved. 'I'm very sorry about the lies, I'm glad she's decided to tell you the truth. I didn't want to mislead you but I felt my first duty was to protect Verity.'

Kelsey pounced on that. 'Why should she need protecting? What had she done wrong?'

Barry's gaze didn't waver. 'Nothing, I'm sure of that. But that doesn't mean she can't be suspected of being mixed up in Jean's death—and Aunt Grace's death. Innocent people do get suspected of crimes and some of them get convicted. You can't deny that.' He looked earnestly across at the Chief. 'Verity can't cope with too much strain. I couldn't stand by and watch her go to pieces, being suspected of

313

something she hadn't done.'

The Chief wanted to know exactly what his contacts had been with Verity over last Sunday and Monday. 'And we'll have the truth this time,' he added.

Barry gave a nod. He had cycled over to the theatre on Sunday evening, as arranged. When Verity failed to show up by six he left her ticket at the box office and went inside. A boy he knew, a sixth-former from the Brentworth Grammar School, had a seat nearby; Barry spoke to him during the intervals and after the performance was over. He gave the Chief the boy's name but he didn't know his address. When he left the theatre, he cycled over to Verity's flat, to find out why she hadn't come to the theatre. He rang and knocked but could get no reply. No lights showed; she was clearly out. He left and cycled back to school.

He intended ringing Verity after school next evening, but before he could do so he was called to the phone to speak to Esther Milroy, who told him of Jean's death and that she had just broken the news to Verity. He went over at once to see Verity.

He found her in tears, distraught at

Jean's death. And terrified she might be suspected of having a hand in it. She poured out the story of her miserable Sunday evening, how she had gone round to see Ned Hooper, had failed to see him and had wandered about till she was tired out.

'If you discovered that Verity did have something to do with either of those deaths,' Kelsey said, 'would you cover up for her?'

Barry looked down at the floor. 'That's a hard one,' he said at last. He raised his head and met the Chief's eye. 'I honestly can't say how I would react. I have no idea.'

A little after seven in the evening a call came through to the Cannonbridge police station from the Brentworth hospice. The patient Esther Milroy had befriended had died half an hour earlier, without regaining consciousness.

It was over to Brentworth yet again for the Chief on Sunday morning. As they turned into Oakfield Gardens shortly after ten they saw a car halting in front of the Milroy house. Matthew Dalton got out.

He looked round as Sergeant Lambert pulled up.

'I'm just off to the office for an hour or two,' he told them. 'I want a word first with Esther. It won't take long, then I'll be off, out of your way.' He rang the bell and Esther came to the door. She was alone. James had gone off to golf. She seemed surprised to see the three of them standing before her; she looking inquiringly from one to the other.

'We haven't come together,' Matthew said lightly. 'We met outside the gate. I just wanted a quick word with you about Jean's funeral.' It was to be held at three o'clock on Monday afternoon. Esther had hurried things along, to have it out of the way before the foundation stone ceremony for the new hospice, long arranged for Tuesday morning.

'Nina and I have been talking it over,' Matthew said as they followed Esther into the sitting room. 'We feel it only right the funeral should be paid for by the family. I'm sure it's what Grace would have wished.'

'I quite agree,' Esther responded warmly. 'I woke up this morning thinking the same thing myself. I thought you and I might share the cost between us.'

'That's settled then,' Matthew said with energy.

'By the way,' Esther said, 'I had an airmail letter yesterday from Jean's mother. She must have sat down to write it the instant she heard Jean was dead.' She crossed to her bureau and produced the letter. 'She's very much the bereaved mother now,' she added on a note of distaste. 'I don't recollect her being all that loving when Jean was alive.'

Matthew began to read the letter and Esther turned to the Chief. 'What was it you wanted to see me about?' she inquired.

He asked if she knew that the patient she had befriended had died yesterday evening.

Her face took on a look of sadness. Yes, she did know.

'We were never able to talk to her,' the Chief went on. 'In fact, we haven't been able to establish with any certainty that you actually were at the hospice last Sunday, at the time you said you were.' He raised a hand as Esther opened her mouth. 'I'm not for one moment suggesting you weren't there, only that we have no proof you were there. I'm sure you can appreciate our difficulty.'

'I can indeed,' Esther returned wryly. 'And I hope you can appreciate mine. But I've remembered something that might help. When I came out of the hospice on Sunday evening, I didn't fancy going straight home to an empty house. I thought I'd look to see if Matthew was in his office. If he was, I could pop up for five minutes for a chat, take my mind off the patient.'

Matthew reached the end of the letter. He had been half listening to the conversation and he looked up now to give his full attention to what his sister was saying.

'I saw the light on in his office,' she continued, 'so I went in. It would be a few minutes after six.'

'You're mistaken,' Matthew said pleasantly. 'You didn't call in last Sunday evening. You're confusing it with some other time.' He looked at the Chief. 'She does sometimes call in when she's passing and she knows I'm there on my own, but she didn't call in last Sunday.'

He's a trifle slow on the uptake, Sergeant Lambert thought. Can't he see she's asking him for an alibi? And supplying him with one for himself at the same time.

Esther seemed not at all put out. 'If I might explain,' she said easily. 'I did and I didn't call in last Sunday. I'm certainly not confusing it with any other time. I did go in, I got as far as the entrance hall. There was no one there but I could hear voices round the back somewhere.' She looked at the Chief. 'It was Matthew and the caretaker, they were having a bit of an argument. I decided it wasn't the best time to call, so I turned round and went out again. I went off home.'

'That explains it then,' Matthew said. He handed her back the letter.

'What did you think of it?' Esther asked.

He grimaced. 'Very much what I'd expect from that lady.'

Esther asked the Chief if he'd like to see the letter. He took it and ran his eye over it. Sympathy for the death of Mrs Dalton, sorrow over Jean. All laid on with a trowel. He handed it back without comment.

Matthew got to his feet. 'I must be off,' he said, 'or I'll get nothing done.'

'We must be off ourselves,' Kelsey said. 'We've got another call to make.'

The call the Chief had in mind was at

Riordan's flat, to see if he was back from his trip to Holland. As Lambert halted the car, the Chief spotted the woman from the flat below Riordan's standing on the front doorstep, chatting to a caller. She broke off at the sight of the two policemen. 'Mr Riordan's not back yet,' she said as they came up. 'He rang from Holland yesterday to say he's decided to stay on over the weekend. He won't be back now till late Monday evening.'

As they went back to the car a thought struck Lambert. Maybe Matthew Dalton hadn't been so obtuse after all. Maybe that little exchange between brother and sister was actually a nifty bit of work, designed to prove very neatly that the pair of them couldn't conceivably be in cahoots.

He said as much to the Chief, but Kelsey's mind was on other things and he only half heard what Lambert was saying.

It was several hours later, as the Chief was thinking of calling it a day, that the Sergeant's words came back to him. He sat pondering and then glanced at his watch. It wouldn't hurt to have another word with Matthew Dalton. Might be a good time now to catch him at home.

And Matthew was at home. He and Nina were ensconced in the sitting room, enjoying a glass of sherry before supper. A delicious savoury smell wafted along from the kitchen, sharply reminding the Chief of just how hungry he was and that ahead of him in his flat lay the prospect of a very scratch supper.

The Daltons waved aside the Chief's apology for disturbing them; they were happy to help in any way they could. They proffered sherry which the Chief was obliged to decline. He addressed himself to Matthew. 'You say you were at your office on Sunday evening?'

Matthew nodded. 'I went there after lunch. I was there till around seven-thirty.'

'Was any member of your staff there during that time?'

He shook his head. 'I always work alone at the weekend or in the evenings.'

'Any callers?' Again Matthew shook his head.

'Any phone calls?'

Another headshake. 'Folk don't ring, they don't know I'm there.' He moved his head. 'Except Nina, of course. She always rings to ask what time I'll be home.'

'Did she ring last Sunday evening?'

'Yes, she always does, to know what to do about supper.'

As Kelsey turned towards Nina, a sudden overpowering wave of tiredness washed over him, he felt hollow with hunger. 'Do you confirm that you rang your husband at his office on Sunday evening?' he asked her.

'I do,' she replied with energy. 'I rang from the cottage—and I can tell you exactly what time I rang. I looked at my watch when Matthew said he'd be working till seven-thirty. It was six-twenty by my watch. I remember thinking: That gives me time to clear up here and get off by a quarter to seven, home by seven-thirty.'

'That didn't allow you much time to prepare supper before your husband got in,' Kelsey observed.

She smiled. 'It was a cold supper, already prepared. All I had to do was heat up the soup, put the coffee on and lay the table.'

So that would seem to be that, Kelsey thought, as they left the house. If Matthew was in his office at six-twenty, there was no way he could get over to Elmhurst, deal with Jean, drive back again to Brentworth in time to walk in through his own front door at a quarter to eight. It simply could not be done. Quite apart from the fact that the killer—if killer there was—had in all probability been ringing the Elmhurst doorbell at around six-fifteen, if Jean's diary was anything to go on. And the fact that Esther Milroy maintained she had stood in the entrance hall of the Brentworth office building at a few minutes after six and heard Matthew arguing with the caretaker.

CHAPTER 33

A chill breeze sprang up at dawn on Monday. The sky grew steadily more overcast as the day advanced. In the middle of the morning, the Chief made time to go over to Brentworth, to make two calls. The first was at the grammar school, where he was able to speak in private to the sixth form boy whose name Barry Fielding had given them.

Yes, he had attended the theatre on

the evening of Sunday, 22nd March. And yes, he had found himself sitting near Barry Fielding, whom he knew fairly well. Barry was alone; he said he had bought two tickets, the other being for some girl who never showed up. They had chatted during the intervals and after the performance.

The Chief had one further question to put: had Barry been in touch with him since that Sunday? The lad shook his head. He had had no contact of any kind with Barry since they said good night outside the theatre.

Kelsey's second call was at the building housing Matthew Dalton's offices, where he sought out the caretaker, a dour-looking individual who eyed him without enthusiasm.

Yes, Mr Dalton had come into his office that Sunday; he had arrived some time in the early afternoon. No, he couldn't say what time Mr Dalton had left for home. Nor if Mr Dalton had at any time during the afternoon or early evening left the building and returned.

Could he recall if he had been talking to Mr Dalton around six o'clock that Sunday evening? Talking somewhere round the back, out of sight of the entrance hall but within earshot of it? Having some sort of argument, maybe?

He didn't bother to cast his mind back but replied at once that he had no idea if he had spoken to Mr Dalton that evening. He had more to do than record every little conversation and exactly where it took place. And now, if the chief inspector would excuse him, he must get back to what he was doing, he wasn't paid to stand around gossiping.

By three o'clock, the weather had turned showery but it would have taken more than a drop of rain to interfere with the media coverage of Jean Redfern's funeral. Shaun Chapman took time off work to attend. He sat with his parents, all three grim-faced and uncommunicative. Neither Barry nor Verity put in an appearance.

Among the floral tributes two stood out: a beautiful cross of white flowers from Shaun Chapman, and a vast, showy offering from Jean's mother.

Jean was laid to rest in a secluded corner of the churchyard, at some distance from the Dalton graves. At the committal, Kelsey looked across to where Esther and

Nina stood side by side. His gaze lingered on Nina. Had she in fact rung her husband at six-twenty that Sunday evening? It was certainly convenient for Matthew suddenly to remember the call; he'd said nothing about it earlier.

Not that the Chief could see Nina contemplating for a moment that Matthew could have had any actual hand in the two deaths. But if she thought he might be unjustly suspected, she would probably see it as no less than her plain duty to throw him a lifeline, even if it meant advancing or retarding the time here or there.

He chewed his lip. He could do worse than have a word with the Ayliffes, in the cottage along the lane from the Dalton cottage. Not very likely that either of them would know at exactly what time Nina had rung her husband that Sunday evening, or at what time she had left the cottage, but there was always an outside chance.

Fatigue again threatened the Chief as he left the station shortly after six, in the hope of catching the Ayliffes at home.

And they were both in, they had just

finished eating. They seemed a cheerful, friendly couple. The Chief introduced himself and apologized for disturbing them; he would try to keep his visit as short as possible.

They had been horrified to learn of the way Mrs Dalton had died. They hadn't known Jean Redfern. Yes, they understood the routine necessary to check every statement.

'Mrs Nina Dalton tells us she was over here, at the cottage, a week ago yesterday,' Kelsey said. 'Sunday, March the twenty-second. Can you confirm that?'

'Yes, she was definitely here,' Mrs Ayliffe replied without hesitation. 'She looked in to say hello, and have a little chat, the way she always does. It was about three o'clock when she came.'

'That's right,' her husband agreed. He had been working in his garden at the time, he had gone across and spoken to Nina when she got out of the car.

'Do you know what time she left the cottage?' Kelsey asked.

'She told me she intended staying till around six or half-past,' Mrs Ayliffe answered. 'It would depend on what time her husband would be home, she'd be ringing him later to find out.'

'Do you know if she did actually ring him?'

She shook her head. 'I couldn't know that.' She hadn't set foot in the cottage that Sunday.

'Do you know what time she actually left?'

Again she shook her head. 'I didn't see her again that day. I went off to work just after four-thirty.'

'You work on a Sunday?' Kelsey asked.

She nodded. 'I work seven days a week at present—it's only part-time, of course. I work for a woman who has a baby a few months old, and two other young children, as well. Her husband's a salesman, he's away a lot, travelling. I go in two hours, morning and evening, to give a hand. I go a bit later over the weekend, not being school days. They live a mile or two out the other side of the village, but I've got my scooter, so it's no trouble getting there.'

'And you left here shortly after four-thirty?'

'That's right. I'm supposed to be there by five but I always like to be on the early side. I finish at seven, I'm usually home by twenty-past, but I was later that Sunday. There'd been a spill on the road I usually take so I had to go round another way, it was a good ten minutes later than usual when I got home. I remember looking at the clock when I got in, when I was telling my husband why I was late—it was turned half past seven.' She had glanced over at the Dalton cottage both times as she went by, going and coming. 'Force of habit,' she said. 'I always look as I go by, to see everything's in order.' Nina's car had been there as she went past on her way to work; it was no longer there when she returned.

Kelsey turned to Ayliffe. Could he say what time Nina had left?

He shook his head. 'I didn't go near the cottage that Sunday.' He had been busy with indoor jobs after his wife had gone off to work. 'Nina does sometimes drive up here again when she's leaving for home. If she's come across something at the cottage that needs seeing to by either one of us, she'll look in to have a word about it.' He was positive she hadn't looked in again that Sunday.

CHAPTER 34

The Chief had managed to get to bed early for once. After a sound night's sleep he woke refreshed and energetic. Over to Elmhurst at the first possible moment, he decided as he threw back the covers. With every day that passed he became more convinced that Jean's death was no suicide but a cold-blooded murder, carefully planned and skilfully executed. He had an overpowering urge to make another tour of the rooms, see what the house had to say to him now.

It came to him as he pulled on his dressing gown that Riordan should be back from Holland by now; he must remember to get a word with him, some time today.

An hour later, after a substantial breakfast, he let himself out of his flat. Barely an hour after that, he left the station and set off with Sergeant Lambert for Elmhurst.

Mrs Gosling admitted them. She wasn't in her usual working gear but smartly dressed, her hair professionally coiffed. She smiled as she registered the Chief's expression. 'Today's the great day,' she said. 'I've made a special effort. All done but the finishing touches. Dorothy's still getting ready, she's just had her bath.' They were all going over to Brentworth to an exhibition of amateur arts and crafts, got up in aid of the new hospice. The exhibition was being housed in a gallery attached to the public library; it was due to open in the afternoon. An entrance fee would be charged and on Friday evening all the exhibits would be auctioned off. 'It should raise a pretty good sum, all told,' Mrs Gosling prophesied. They were taking the articles they'd made over to the gallery this morning. There would be time for a look round at what other folk had brought before they had to set off back to Cannonbridge for the laying of the hospice foundation stone.

'We've all made something,' she told the Chief with pride. 'We're all meeting up at the gallery.' Verity was giving one of her watercolours, Barry a pair of carved bookends he'd made at school. 'My father's made some wooden toys and jigsaw puzzles,' she added. 'But he won't be coming along to the exhibition, or to the hospice ceremony. Too long a day for him, too much standing about.' She gave a long sigh. 'If only Mrs Dalton could have been here to see this day.' Tears threatened but she made a resolute effort to avert melancholy. 'Shaun Chapman's coming too,' she said.

'Shaun?' the Chief echoed in surprise.

'Yes, he specially asked to come, in Jean's place. He hasn't made anything himself, he's taking the sweater Jean knitted. She made a lovely job of it and I've given it a good pressing. Shaun went back home with his parents yesterday, after the funeral. He caught the bus out here first thing this morning, he's over in the cottage now. He's coming with us to the hospice ceremony as well. He made a collection among his workmates and in the pubs, he's going to hand the money over for the hospice, in Jean's name.' She gazed earnestly up at the Chief. 'Shaun's not such a bad lad. My husband thinks he might make something of himself yet.' She suddenly bethought herself. 'What was it you came over for? I hope it's not going to take too long.'

'It's nothing you need concern yourself with,' Kelsey assured her. 'You go ahead with whatever you've got to do. Don't mind us. I just want to take another look round.'

'Right you are,' she said. 'I'll pop up and let Dorothy know you're here.'

As soon as she had gone, the Chief opened the front door. 'You stay where you are,' he instructed Sergeant Lambert. 'I won't need you for the present.' Lambert asked no questions.

Kelsey stepped back outside, then turned to face the door. Now he was standing in the shoes of the killer, poised to ring the bell, shortly after six, that Sunday evening. I hear Jean come to the door, he said to himself. She speaks through it, asks who it is. 'It's me,' I tell her. 'I've come to see how you are.' She knows my voice, she doesn't hesitate to admit me, she draws back the bolts. I step inside, she closes the door behind me.

I follow her upstairs and into her room, Kelsey told himself, suiting his actions to his thoughts. She tells me how she is, what she has been doing, tells me she has finished her account, indicates where she has set it down. I tell her she must get back into bed. She does so. I offer to make her some hot milk and whisky.

333

'Oh yes, please,' she says. 'I'd like that.' 'And you'd better have a couple of aspirins or paracetamol,' I say. 'They'll help your cold.' 'Is it all right to take them with whisky?' she asks. 'I always take them with whisky myself, for a cold,' I tell her, smiling. 'They've never done me any harm.' 'Then you'll have to bring me up a couple of spoons,' she says. 'I'll have to crush the tablets.' 'Right you are,' I tell her. 'I won't be long.'

I go from the room. No need to worry about leaving fingerprints on the doorknob, there would be a blur of existing prints on all the doorknobs. I go down the back stairs to the kitchen. I must be careful to leave no prints on the tray or any article on the tray, so I pick up the rubber gloves draped over the sink and put them on before doing anything. I heat the milk, set out the tray. I have brought with me the pharmacy bottle with a couple of tablets for Jean to take—and the prepared mix of medicines I intend to add to the beaker. The whisky bottle is already to hand; Mrs Gosling had taken a full bottle from the drinks cupboard on Friday afternoon and kept it in the kitchen.

When I'm ready for the journey back

to Jean's room I take a clean teatowel from a drawer, open it out and place the laden tray on top of it, the edges of the cloth coming up over the edges of the tray. I manoeuvre the tray on to my left arm, ease off my rubber gloves and leave them in the kitchen. I set off for the back stairs. I steady my load with my right hand, grasping the tray only through the cloth.

I reach Jean's room. As I approach the bed, chatting pleasantly, I move the little table forward towards the bed with my foot or my knee; it glides easily on its castors. I stoop by the bed, holding out the tray. Jean takes the tray and sets it down on the table. I retain the teatowel.

It is Jean who handles everything. She crushes the tablets, stirs them into the beaker, starts to drink. She has little sense of taste or smell, thanks to her cold. 'I didn't put in much whisky,' I say. 'Put in more if you want to. And there's more hot milk in the jug. Drink plenty, it'll do you good.' She happily helps herself to more. Her prints are on everything; there are none of mine. I go on chatting. She is relaxed and drowsy, her eyes begin to close.

Using the teatowel, I pick up her prayer

book and look through it. Jean is now asleep. I lay the open prayer book by her hands. I cross the room and pick up her account. I leave the bedside light on, close the door and go down to the kitchen to replace the teatowel. Now all I have to do is let myself out through the front door and go quietly off to where I left my car. Or my bicycle.

Kelsey paused by the front door. Is there anything else I would have done before leaving? he asked himself, but could think of nothing. Now he embarked on a room by room tour of the house, reaching in due course Grace Dalton's old bedroom. He opened the door and glanced in. It was beautifully orderly, glitteringly clean.

His gaze lighted on a telephone on a table by the bed. At the sound of footsteps along the corridor, he turned his head and saw Dorothy Nevett coming towards him, groomed and dressed, ready for the sortie to Brentworth. She stopped to exchange a few words. He glanced back into the room. 'That phone in there,' he said. 'Have you used it since you got back from Dorset?'

She looked surprised, shocked, even. 'No, of course not. No one ever uses that phone now.'

He asked if she knew where Mrs Gosling was.

'She's in the kitchen,' Dorothy said. 'I'm going down there now. Do you want me to send her up?'

'If you would.'

When Mrs Gosling came along, he asked if she had used this phone lately. Like Dorothy, she looked shocked at the idea. Certainly not, she wouldn't dream of using it. Did she know if anyone else had used it recently? No, she couldn't think of anyone. 'I'm sure it's never been used since Mrs Dalton moved out of this room,' she declared positively. The three phones in the house were on three separate lines, with separate numbers. Mrs Dalton had disliked extensions, with their potential for misuse.

'I'd like you to think carefully before you answer my next question,' Kelsey said. 'I want you to be absolutely sure about what you say. If you're not sure, say so.' She looked greatly intrigued. 'When you gave this room a thorough cleaning on the Friday afternoon after Mrs Dalton's funeral, did you clean the telephone?'

She closed her eyes in thought. 'I'm absolutely certain,' she replied after some moments. 'I did clean it.' She looked earnestly up at him. 'I cleaned it very carefully. Every bit of it.'

'Were you wearing rubber gloves? Or household gloves of any kind?'

'I was wearing cotton house gloves,' she replied at once. 'I always wear them when I'm giving a room a good turn-out.' She looked down at her hands, spread her fingers. 'It's to keep the skin smooth, for my quilting. If you let your hands get rough you can snag the material, especially silk.'

'I may need to make some phone calls when I've finished up here,' Kelsey said. 'All right if I use the phone down in the hall?'

'Yes, of course.' She went off and the Chief went swiftly across the bedroom to the phone. From his pocket he took his bank card and metal nail file. With their aid he manoeuvred the receiver from its rest, careful not to touch any part of the instrument with his fingers. He laid the receiver on its back, on the table. With the tip of the file he briefly depressed the memory-recall button. He stooped low with his ear over the receiver, listening to the ringing. A voice spoke. He made no reply but touched the phone rest with the edge of his card, severing the connection. With the card and file he manoeuvred the receiver back into position.

A minute or two later he went downstairs to make his phone calls. When he had finished he sought out Dorothy. He found her with Mrs Gosling in the staff sitting room, packing their craftwork contributions into cardboard boxes. 'We have to get back to the station now,' he told Dorothy. 'But another officer will be here very shortly, in a matter of minutes. He'll need to go into Mrs Dalton's old bedroom. I've locked the door.' He laid the key on the table. 'I don't want anyone going near that room before he gets here.'

Dorothy frowned. 'How long will this officer need to be in the house? We'll be here to let him in but we must be off ourselves in ten minutes, fifteen at the outside.'

'That's all right,' Mrs Gosling put in. 'I can get my father to come over. He can stay here till the officer's finished, he can lock up after him.'

At the police station the Chief spoke to a constable on his team, a man who could be relied on to carry out instructions to the letter. He gave him details of a number of phone calls he expected to come in before long, supplying information he had requested. The constable was to note down all the information, ready to retail it accurately if the Chief should phone him for it later in the morning.

The Chief then left the station with Sergeant Lambert and set off for Brentworth. When they reached the Milroy house the door was answered by a cleaning woman. Kelsey asked if he might speak to Mrs Milroy.

'She's not here,' the woman informed him. 'She left about three-quarters of an hour ago. She won't be back here till this afternoon. She went over to her sister-in-law's—Mrs Dalton.'

They went over there at once. As they approached the front door it opened, revealing Nina, elegantly clad, carrying a cardboard box. 'You've only just caught me,' she greeted them.

'It's Mrs Milroy we want to talk to,' Kelsey explained. 'We understood she was here.'

'She was here,' Nina confirmed, 'but only for a few minutes. She looked in to see if I was ready to go to the craft exhibition.' She smiled. 'But I was far from ready, so she went ahead without me. That's where I'm off to now.' She looked down at the box. 'I've made some soft toys. They always go well.'

The Chief stood pondering. He wasn't very taken with the notion of seeking Esther out in a public gallery.

'Is your husband going to the exhibition?' he asked.

'He is, but not today,' Nina answered. 'He'll be going to the auction with James, on Friday evening. But they're both coming to the hospice ceremony this morning. And they're stopping on afterwards for the buffet lunch.'

'Where's your husband now?' Kelsey asked.

'He's at his office. We're picking him up on the way from the gallery.' She gave him a quick glance. 'Why do you ask?'

'We'd like another word with him.'

'You're going along there now?'

He nodded.

'Then I'm coming with you,' she announced with swift decision. 'I won't take my car, I'll ride with you. I'll give the gallery a miss for now, I can take the toys along this afternoon.' She turned to go back inside. 'If you hang on a moment, I'll give Esther a ring at the gallery, to explain. They can all come along to Matthew's office and pick us both up there.' She stepped back into the hall and picked up the phone.

When they got into the car a few minutes later, she took her seat in the rear, beside the Chief. She tackled him at once. 'You can't seriously believe Matthew had any sort of hand in either of those deaths.'

Kelsey made no response.

'He wasn't even there when Grace died,' she continued with energy. 'He'd left Elmhurst and gone back to Brentworth before Grace went to bed.' Her tone grew more intense. 'And he was nowhere near Elmhurst the Sunday Jean died. All his time that Sunday is accounted for. I don't know why you can't accept that.'

She'll stand by her husband, come hell or high water, Sergeant Lambert thought. He couldn't tell if she thought Matthew innocent or if she thought him guilty—alone, or in cahoots with Esther. He believed it made no difference to her stand. She would do anything in her power to help him, innocent or guilty. She would put loyalty to her husband ahead of all other considerations.

'Matthew could never have harmed either Grace or Jean,' Nina persisted, in the face of the Chief's continuing silence. 'He was fond of them both. He could never harm anyone, it's not in his nature.' She fell silent as they reached Matthew's office.

None of the three spoke as they walked across the car park and in through the front door.

CHAPTER 35

Matthew wasn't in his office. According to his secretary he was out visiting an elderly, housebound client in her home; he was expected back shortly. She showed the callers into a waiting room. Nina made no further attempt to take issue with the Chief but picked up a magazine and settled herself to read it. Twenty minutes crawled by before Matthew came hurrying into the room, full of apologies for keeping them waiting.

Explanations were till going forward

when there was a stir outside in the corridor and the door opened to admit Esther and James. Esther glanced round the group. 'Have you finished?' she inquired. 'Can we get off to Cannonbridge?'

'I'm afraid we haven't even begun,' the Chief informed her.

'I've just got in,' Matthew added.

Esther wasn't best pleased, though James didn't appear put out, he seemed in good spirits. 'We can't be long,' Esther declared. 'The others will be here any minute.'

'The rest of you can go ahead without me,' Matthew suggested. 'I can follow later.'

'I'd prefer you all to stay, now you're here,' the Chief put in, in a tone that brooked no argument.

'Then the sooner we get started, the sooner we'll be finished,' Matthew said briskly. He took them along the corridor to a large room furnished with a long mahogany table surrounded by a dozen chairs.

As they entered, James said to the Chief: 'Riordan's back from Holland. I rang him this morning. He'll confirm we were together at the club that Sunday evening. He'll be looking in at the police station some time this afternoon.'

When they were all seated, the Chief addressed himself to Matthew. 'We keep coming back to the fact that we have only your unsupported word for where you were during the afternoon and evening of Sunday, March the twenty-second.'

'His word's not unsupported,' Nina struck in at once. 'There's my phone call to this office. You can't ignore that.'

'With all due respect,' the Chief returned blandly, 'the word of a devoted wife isn't usually regarded as proof positive.'

'That doesn't alter the fact that it happens to be the truth,' Matthew said courteously.

Esther turned to Matthew. 'I've been racking my brains to see if I could remember anything else about that Sunday evening. I did remember something—not much, but it might help. It came back to me what it was you and the caretaker were arguing about. It was something to do with water-hammer.'

Matthew's face broke into a relieved smile. 'Water-hammer! Of course!' He turned to the Chief. 'We did have a set-to about the water-hammer but I'd forgotten exactly what it was. The pipes had started playing up whenever anyone drew water. The caretaker got a man in but it was no better. I told him to get someone in who knew what he was doing and look sharp about it. He said he'd see to it first thing next morning.' He jerked his head. 'And he did. We've had no trouble since.'

All that came a trifle trippingly off the tongue, Sergeant Lambert thought. Matthew and Esther could have fixed up that little exchange after we spoke to the pair of them last Sunday morning.

He found himself a moment later being despatched by the Chief to seek out and bring up the caretaker. He ran his quarry to earth but made no mention of the water-hammer, merely telling the caretaker he was wanted by Mr Dalton. Upstairs again, the sergeant resumed his seat at the table while the caretaker remained in the doorway, surveying the occupants of the room with morose curiosity.

Yes, he remembered a bit of a barney about the water-hammer. He had had the pipes seen to the very next morning. 'I can prove it,' he declared truculently, apparently under the impression it was his competence in his job that was being questioned. 'I can show you where it's written down in my work-book. And I've got the receipted bill.' Off he went, returning shortly with both bill and work-book. The Chief cast his eye over them. There could be little doubt: the work would seem to have been carried out on Monday, 23rd March.

But on the matter of the precise time the water-hammer argument had taken place—which was, after all, the point at issue—the caretaker stood on ground a good deal less firm. Some time during the afternoon or evening of that Sunday was as near as he was prepared to estimate.

The caretaker had scarcely taken himself off again when there was a knock at the door and the secretary put her head in to say a Mr Gosling had called. Matthew gave the Chief a questioning look. 'Ask Mr Gosling to come in,' the Chief instructed.

When Gosling came along a moment later, he halted on the threshold, looking uncertainly from Matthew to Nina. 'The others are down in the car park,' he said apologetically. 'We waited five minutes and then I thought I'd better come up and see what's keeping you.'

'Who have you got with you?' the Chief inquired.

'There's my wife and Dorothy Nevett,' Gosling replied. 'And Shaun Chapman. Verity followed us over in her car, she's got Barry with her.' He consulted his watch. 'Time's getting on. There'll be some heavy traffic between here and Cannonbridge.'

'Would you ask them all to come up?' the Chief said.

Gosling hesitated, but as no one else said anything he turned and went off downstairs. There was silence in the room till he returned with the others, who didn't appear too pleased at the prospect of further delay, though the only voice to utter a complaint was Shaun Chapman's. He was hardly inside the door before he fixed the Chief with his eye. 'I hope this isn't going to take long,' he began pugnaciously. He wore the dark suit, white shirt and black tie he had worn yesterday to Jean's funeral. 'I can't be late for the ceremony. I have money to hand over in Jean's name. I've been given time off specially.'

Gosling laid a hand on his arm. 'Don't fret, lad,' he said quietly. 'We'll see the money's properly handed over, one way or another.'

The Chief waved them all down into

seats; every chair was now occupied. 'It's just as well you're all here,' he commented. 'It simplifies matters.' He looked at his watch. 'I have to ring the station,' he told Matthew.

'You can use the phone in my office,' Matthew said. 'You'll be private in there.' He took the Chief across, returning a moment later. While the Chief was gone, Dorothy Nevett closed her eyes and leaned back in her chair. The movement tipped her hat—a festive hat today, lighter in colour and material but otherwise little different from the one she wore on sombre occasions—slightly forward over her eyes, giving her a faintly tipsy look. Shaun Chapman glanced restlessly about, drumming his fingers on the table. Esther murmured to Matthew, Verity whispered to Barry.

All heads turned when the Chief came back. He swept a look round the table as he sat down; his gaze came to rest on Nina.

'Would you tell us once again,' he began briskly, 'about the phone call you say you made to your husband that Sunday evening, March the twenty-second.'

She drew a little breath of resignation.

'I rang Matthew from the cottage at six-twenty.'

'When did you last set foot in Elmhurst?'

'I haven't been over there since we all left, on the Monday after Grace died.'

The Chief took out his notebook and looked down at a page. 'I have just been informed,' he said, 'that British Telecom have no record of any call being made from the Dalton cottage on Sunday, March the twenty-second.'

Nina gave another small sigh. 'British Telecom aren't infallible.'

The Chief consulted his notes again. 'But they do have a record of a call made to this office at six-nineteen on Sunday, March the twenty-second, from the phone in Grace Dalton's old bedroom at Elmhurst—the first call recorded from that number for some considerable time.'

'That call has nothing to do with me,' Nina declared with energy. 'Whoever made it, it certainly wasn't me. I was nowhere near Elmhurst that Sunday.'

'There are clear fingerprints on the phone in Grace Dalton's old bedroom.' The Chief looked directly at her. 'I have just received information that those prints belong to you.'

'Then they're obviously old prints,' she returned at once. 'At least two years old. They must go back to some call Grace asked me to make for her when she was still using that bedroom. I haven't set foot in that bedroom since Grace moved downstairs, I've never had occasion to.'

'The prints can't be two years old,' the Chief pointed out. 'Mrs Gosling gave that bedroom a thorough cleaning on the afternoon of Mrs Dalton's funeral. The prints must have been made since that Friday.'

Nina drew another small sigh. 'You're assuming Mrs Gosling remembered to clean the phone. She must have overlooked it. That's easily done.'

Mrs Gosling's face grew pink. 'I'm positive I cleaned the phone,' she asserted. Nina gave her a little smiling glance of understanding.

'What time did you leave the cottage that Sunday?' Kelsey asked Nina.

'I left at a quarter to seven and drove straight home,' she answered.

'Did you encounter any hold-ups or diversions on your journey home?'

She shook her head. 'No, I did not. I had a good run.'

'What road did you take?'

'The one I always take. Straight out through the village, right at the first crossroads, half a mile out of the village.'

'You couldn't have taken the road through the village,' the Chief countered. 'Not if you left the cottage at a quarter to seven.' Again he consulted his notes. 'I have just been informed that that road was closed to traffic because of a spillage that Sunday evening. It was closed from ten minutes to six until eight-fifteen.'

'You're quite right,' Nina acknowledged with a movement of her head. 'The road was closed, I'd forgotten. I've been over to the cottage quite a few times lately. I was over there that Friday and Saturday, as well as on the Sunday. I'm afraid I got the days mixed up. But I've got it straight in my mind now. I did have to turn off before I got to the village.'

'Exactly where did you turn off?'

She reached back and picked up her handbag from the side table where she had set it down earlier. 'I'd better draw you a little map,' she told the Chief. She dipped into her bag and took out a pen and jotter. She began to sketch with swift, sure strokes.

Across the table, Mrs Gosling uttered a sudden sharp sound. 'That pen,' she said. 'Where did you get it?'

Nina glanced up. 'You know where I got it. It's the pen that was presented to me. You've seen it before.' She resumed her sketching.

'That pen was in Jean's bedroom.' Mrs Gosling wrinkled her brow, trying to work it out. 'She was keeping it for you. It was there on the Sunday afternoon, I saw it when I took the tray of tea over at four o'clock. The pen was on top of her bureau.' She turned to the Chief. 'Nina lent Dorothy the pen at Mrs Dalton's funeral, so she could write down an address. When we were in the car, going back to Elmhurst after the funeral, Dorothy suddenly remembered she hadn't given the pen back to Nina.'

'That's right,' Dorothy put in. 'I opened my bag to get a handkerchief and I saw the pen; I'd slipped it into my bag without thinking. I was going off to Dorset right away, so Jean said she'd take the pen and keep it safe till she could hand it over to Nina or someone else in the family. She wouldn't put it in the post to Nina in case it went astray.'

353

Mrs Gosling still frowned, thinking back to that day. 'Jean went off to bed when we got back from the funeral. I told her I'd phone Nina later on, to let her know we'd got the pen safe—I couldn't phone her right away because she'd gone to lunch with the vicar and the others. I did try to ring her during the afternoon but there was no reply. Then I forgot about the pen till I saw it on Jean's bureau on the Sunday afternoon. I didn't like to tell Jean I still hadn't phoned Nina. I had another try at it on our own phone, on the Sunday afternoon, after I took the tea tray back over, but I still didn't get any reply. Then, with all that happened next day, the pen went clean out of my head.'

'It went out of my head too,' Nina told the Chief. 'I didn't miss the pen for a day or two, then I remembered lending it to Dorothy. I didn't worry about it, I thought she'd taken it with her to Dorset, she'd give it to me when she got back. But with all that happened the day she got back, I never gave the pen another thought.' She looked down at it. 'I don't know how it could have got back into my bag.' She sent a ranging glance round the table. 'I can only suppose one of you must have picked the pen up from Jean's room and then slipped it into my bag some time this morning. I'm positive it wasn't in my bag before today, I'd definitely have noticed if it was.'

Barry leaned forward, his face pale and distressed. 'You did have that pen before today,' he said. 'You used it at my school last Saturday afternoon. I was standing next to you on the platform. You had that same bag with you, you took the pen out of it. You used it to write out the receipt for the money we'd raised. The headmaster noticed the inscription and you gave him the pen so he could read it.'

In the deathly silence that followed, Nina raised her shoulders. 'Ah, well,' she said in a tone that was almost flippant, 'one can't think of everything.'

CHAPTER 36

Kelsey faced Nina. 'You picked up the pen that Sunday evening, in Jean's bedroom.'

Nina made no reply. She sat erect and composed.

'You didn't leave the cottage at a quarter to seven,' he went on. 'You left earlier, before the spillage. And when you reached the crossroads you didn't take the road home to Brentworth, you took the road to Elmhurst. You got there around six-fifteen.'

She made no response.

'You did ring your husband that Sunday evening,' he continued. 'But not from the cottage. You rang him from Elmhurst at six-nineteen, soon after you got there. You had to ring him to find out how much time you had for what you planned to do—before he took it into his head to ring you at the cottage and discover you were no longer there. If he then tried to ring you at home he'd discover you weren't there, either. You used the phone in Mrs Dalton's old bedroom, to be sure Jean wouldn't hear you. Once you'd got the call out of the way you could go ahead, go down to the kitchen, set about preparing the tray for Jean.'

Matthew swung round in his seat to face the Chief. His face was haggard. 'It's all some horrible mistake,' he said in shaking tones. 'It must be.' He swung back to look at Nina. 'Tell them,' he urged. 'Tell

356

them it isn't true, you didn't do any of it. You never killed Grace. You couldn't have. Why would you do such a terrible thing?'

'She was an old woman,' Nina said. 'She'd had her time.' He gave a horror-stricken gasp. Along the table, James sagged in his seat. He looked like a man who has been struck a mortal blow. Beside him, Verity wept in anguish. Barry put an arm round her shoulders.

Matthew stared at Nina in agonized disbelief. 'An old, helpless woman, asleep in her bed. You went in there and killed her in cold blood? What had she ever done to you?'

Her composure began to crumble. 'I did it for you!' she cried. 'You must see that! I knew the mess you were in, however much you tried to hide it. You had to have the money. I couldn't see you ruined. She could have lived another two or three years.'

His face was contorted. 'She trusted you! She looked on you as a daughter! She was fonder of you than of anyone!'

'It wasn't her money,' she threw back at him. 'It was family money, yours by right.'

He collapsed into stricken silence, he dropped his head into his hands.

'What about Jean?' Shaun Chapman flung at her with savage ferocity. 'Was Jean an old woman? Had she had her time?'

She didn't look at him. 'I had no choice,' she said flatly. 'She'd seen me. I was going back into my bedroom. I hadn't put the light on, I was using a torch. She opened her door and came out, to go along to the bathroom.' She stared back into that paralysing moment. 'I was carrying a book I'd picked up in the playroom, in case I met anyone, to look as if I hadn't been able to sleep, I'd just gone down for a book. I held up the book and smiled at her. She gave me a little nod and smiled back, she went along to the bathroom. She never said a word about it afterwards. I was sure she'd thought nothing of it, she wouldn't mention it.' She drew a long breath. 'But then we all had to write our accounts. I knew she would do what she was asked, she'd put down every little thing she could remember, she'd mention the torch, and the time—two o'clock in the morning. When I went over to Elmhurst that Sunday evening and she was chatting away to me, I could see she still hadn't the slightest suspicion, she still hadn't put two and two together.' She looked at the Chief.

'But I knew you would, as soon as you read her account.'

Shaun half rose from his seat. 'She was twenty years old. She had her whole life before her.'

'It was her or me.' She flicked him a dismissive glance. 'What was she, after all? A servant's by-blow.' He reeled back into his chair.

A dark flush rose in Gosling's cheeks. 'May God forgive you,' he said with fierce revulsion. 'I never can.'

Esther suddenly spoke up, addressing Nina in a voice of steel. 'You didn't do it for Matthew, you did it for yourself. All you were concerned about was how it would affect you if Matthew went down. You never really cared tuppence for Matthew, only for what you could get out of being married to him. You couldn't have James, so you took Matthew.'

Nina scarcely glanced at her. 'James got no encouragement from me, after I married,' she said brusquely.

'I can believe that,' Esther threw back

at her. 'You'd never waste your favours for no return. But I don't imagine it was for want of trying on James's part.' She levelled at her husband a coldly judicial gaze. 'You wanted it to be Matthew who'd done the killings, you hoped Nina might come your way at last.' He sat in stricken silence, staring down at the table. 'It wasn't easy, curing myself of you,' she told him. 'It took me a long, long time, even after I realized you'd only married me so you could be part of the Dalton family. Then I saw your car over at the cottage a few weeks back, her car was there too. I went away again. I knew then that things would never be any different between us; however hard I tried, it would never be me, it would always be Nina. It was easier after that. I was finally able to make up my mind to leave you. I intend to do as I please with the rest of my life.'

Silence descended on the room. The Chief spoke abruptly into it. 'Jean's account,' he said to Nina. 'What did you do with it?' She made no response. He sat contemplating her. He saw her leaving Jean's bedroom, the account in her hand. She had to get out of the house at once, in case of a chance caller. She had to be

360

back home, tranquil and smiling, supper ready, when Matthew walked in.

He saw her slipping out through the front door of Elmhurst, along the drive, out through the gates. What to do with the account? She daren't take it home to destroy at leisure, she couldn't risk having it in her possession if for any reason Jean was found early. She had known before she left home after lunch that she had to lay hands on Jean's account, she would have decided then how to dispose of it, she wasn't a woman to leave anything to chance.

Along the table, Gosling's brain was pursuing the same line of thought. He had got Nina as far as the gates, clutching the account. She lets herself out through the wicket gate, he thought. She's about to set off for the quiet spot where she's left her car.

He stuck his hands together, seeing the stretch of stone wall on either side of the gates, the scarlet post box let into the wall. 'You posted the account!' he exclaimed. 'You brought the envelope with you, addressed and stamped. You dropped it in the box by the gates.'

And saw by the jerk of her head, the

look she flashed him, that he was right.

'What address did you put on the envelope?' Kelsey demanded but he got no reply. He furrowed his brow. She would have put her own name, but not her own address, she couldn't have it turning up in her home so soon. 'You sent it to some place where it could lie unnoticed till you got round to picking it up in your own good time. You could destroy it then, after the first commotion over Jean's death had died down.' He chewed his lip. 'Some place where there was no risk of anyone else opening it. Where it could still be waiting now.'

'Friends of the Third Age!' Esther cried in triumph. Nina moved sharply in her chair. 'She goes there once a fortnight,' Esther told the Chief. 'They let her use a desk for the governess charity she deals with. Her mail's always put on one side for her, no one else ever opens it. She's due there again on Friday morning.'

Nina offered no resistance when the Chief made his formal request for her to accompany them to the Cannonbridge police station. As she rose to her feet the

362

chimes of a nearby church clock struck the half-hour.

The ceremony, Sergeant Lambert suddenly remembered. At this moment, over in Cannonbridge, they would all now be assembled. The TV entertainer would be on the point of laying the foundation stone of the new hospice.

If the same thought crossed Nina's mind, she gave no sign of it.

CHAPTER 37

Shortly after nine next morning, the Chief left the station to drive over alone to Elmhurst. He was making the call as a private citizen, not as a police officer. It was a glorious morning, full of the surging vitality of spring.

Nina had been formally charged with both murders yesterday evening. She would be making a brief appearance before the magistrates later this morning.

When the Chief called into the charity offices on the way back to Cannonbridge yesterday, Jean's account had indeed come to light among the mail laid aside for Nina. It was enclosed in a large, stout envelope addressed in bold block capitals to Mrs Nina Dalton, marked in the top left-hand corner: PRIVATE AND CONFIDENTIAL. Underneath that, the words: ATTENTION MRS NINA DALTON ONLY. The postmark confirmed Gosling's guess about the time and place of posting. Nina's fingerprints were among those on the envelope; they appeared also on the account inside.

Jean had composed her account with scrupulous care. She had faithfully recorded every detail of the little encounter with Nina in the early hours of that Sunday morning, attaching no importance to it, including it merely as one of the many trivial happenings to be meticulously set down.

The Chief reached Elmhurst and turned in through the gates. Dorothy Nevett's car, baggage lashed to the roof-rack, was drawn up by Gosling's cottage. Dorothy, ready for the road, was talking to the Goslings. Mrs Gosling's father and the two garden lads stood nearby.

Dorothy's face broke into a smile of pleasure when she caught sight of the

Chief's car. 'I'd given you up,' she said as he stepped out into the sunshine. 'I was just about to go. I thought something had cropped up and you couldn't get away to say goodbye.'

'It would have taken a great deal to stop me,' Kelsey said. He crossed to her car and opened the door for her. More luggage was stacked inside. 'And there's still more in the boot,' she told him with a smile. 'I've put out no end of stuff for Oxfam. It's amazing what you accumulate over forty years.' A tear shone in her eye. She looked up at him. 'Any time you feel like a breath of Dorset air, you know you'll always be more than welcome.' He stooped to kiss her cheek, for the first time in his life. It was soft and cool.

When she had gone and the others had departed about their duties, Kelsey walked over to his car with Gosling. 'Not long now before everything will be changed round here,' Gosling said, looking about with a melancholy eye. The air seemed full of ghosts, echoes of the past.

Part way along the drive Kelsey halted his car and got out. Gosling had disappeared into the gardens. Birds sang in the glittering air, the trees were laden with blossom. New

365

life everywhere, fresh beginnings. I can't afford sadness, Grace had said that last morning; it's a debilitating emotion.

He gave one last look back, at the house and lawns, the beds and borders, spinneys and shrubberies, then he got into his car again and drove on and out, heading back to Cannonbridge and the engulfing business of the day.

The publishers hope that this book has given you enjoyable reading. Large Print Books are especially designed to be as easy to see and hold as possible. If you wish a complete list of our books, please ask at your local library or write directly to: Magna Large Print Books, Long Preston, North Yorkshire, BD23 4ND, England.

This Large Print Book for the Partially sighted, who cannot read normal print, is published under the auspices of

THE ULVERSCROFT FOUNDATION

THE ULVERSCROFT FOUNDATION

. . . we hope that you have enjoyed this Large Print Book. Please think for a moment about those people who have worse eyesight problems than you . . . and are unable to even read or enjoy Large Print, without great difficulty.

You can help them by sending a donation, large or small to:

**The Ulverscroft Foundation,
1, The Green, Bradgate Road,
Anstey, Leicestershire, LE7 7FU,
England.**
or request a copy of our brochure for more details.

The Foundation will use all your help to assist those people who are handicapped by various sight problems and need special attention.

Thank you very much for your help.